D0595650

MURDER
Takes to the Hills

Jessica Thomas

Bella
BOOKS

2010

Copyright © 2010 by Jessica Thomas

Bella Books, Inc.
P.O. Box 10543
Tallahassee, FL 32302

All rights reserved. No part of this book may be reproduced or transmitted in any form or by any means, electronic or mechanical, including photocopying, without permission in writing from the publisher.

Printed in the United States of America on acid-free paper
First Edition

Editor: Katherine V. Forrest
Cover Designer: Stephanie Solomon-Lopez

ISBN 10: 1-59493-178-X
ISBN 13:978-1-59493-178-9

Acknowledgments

For John and Carol with the hope your neighbors forgive my peopling your scenic town with a bunch of kooks and crooks.

And to my editor Katherine V. Forrest for catching the bad spots and complimenting the good ones. See, Katherine, no unnecessary commas!

CHAPTER ONE

It may not have been the worst of times, but it sure as hell wasn't the best of times, either!

For a couple of years I had known that the roof on my house was working itself into replacement mode. Strong winds would bring down a shingle or two, and heavy rains or sleet left little streaks of grit at the bottom of the downspouts. At that time, I had checked with the bank about getting a loan. The VP and CEO, Choate Ellis, was ever so gracious: they'd be happy to lend me the money...and if I wanted any other improvements or repairs they'd be happy to lend me that money, too. They should be happy. Fisherman's Bank has held mortgages on every piece of property my family has owned for the last one hundred and fifty years.

I was living alone at the time and decided to take Choate up on his offer and add a second bedroom and splurge on a bathroom especially for me. And I would spring for one of those walk-in showers that fired water at you from every direction at any heat and any strength that pleased you…from drizzle to fire hose. It included everything but the compliant blonde to scrub your back. Oh, yeah. Dream on.

About that time, Cindy Hart came to town to head up the bank's new Personal Investments Department. She rented a small cottage from my Aunt Mae, and of course, we met. We fell in love and discovered—*voila!*—that we also liked each other. Finally, Cindy moved in with me.

But she also kept the cottage. It was our safety net, she said, for times when one of us wanted to be alone for a day or so; it was also our get-away when we both wanted to be unavailable to the world. It was a bit strange to have a get-away only about a mile from our main residence, but we found great peace on the little deck overlooking a small pond and the pine woods stretching beyond it. Wells, our lovely, petite black-and-white cat, enjoyed hunting in the reeds, and Fargo, our black Labrador retriever, took delight in leaping off the old dock to scatter invading ducks and geese. And we loved watching them.

Somewhere along the way, I sort of lost track of the roof.

Last month a whopping nor'easter brought a steady drip into the pantry, and I called Orrick Construction. My brother Sonny had recommended them, reminding me they, too, had been around for a century or so. And I'd gone to school with Bobby Orrick, who was now the main honcho of the company, so I felt at ease with him. He proved *extremely* helpful.

The Master Suite, as he referred to my idea for another bedroom and bath, would present no problems. He suggested we also run an enclosed walkway from the back door of the house to the side door of the garage, thus providing not only shelter between the two, but also storage space so we could fit both cars into the garage.

While I was trying to guess what this would cost, Cindy pointed out that this walkway would make a small U-shaped alcove when attached to the garage and the house. It would give that part of the yard protection from the wind on three sides, so why didn't we put a deck outside the Master Suite (apparently she liked that phrase, too)—which would be completely private, so that we could enjoy it in our pajamas or whatever.

Bobby agreed it was a genius idea. He added that since that area would get the afternoon sun, we might want to consider a small rock garden with a little fountain. This could be our own miniature Eden—I never knew him to be such a poetic type in school—and when we had guests we could use the larger, more open backyard.

By now I had visions of a feature appearing in *Better Homes and Gardens*...about three days after we became bankrupt and homeless.

"Look," I finally managed to squeak. "We can't afford all this! My God, you two are planning the Taj Mahal!"

Cindy patted my hand and laughed. "Darling, you forget— the house is also in my name now and, as I am an employee of the bank, we will have a *much* better deal than they offered you last year, not to mention that lovely rebate the government is handing out on income taxes. Relax. Enjoy."

I did neither. But I gave in, as we all knew I would.

Orrick's began work two days later. From eight in the morning to five in the evening, except for the lunch hour, we were treated to hammers, drills, saws, a small backhoe, trucks and men with loud voices...doubtless compensating for hearing damage from the hammers and drills. At night the house was covered with a large blue plastic tarp, which protected us from moisture and small critters and flapped all night in the slightest of breezes. And Orrick's worked a six-day week in order, we learned, to get Bobby's crew to the next victim on schedule.

The animals suffered most. Wells took up residence under the bed, where she hissed and slapped at any attempt to get her out before five fifteen p.m. Fargo barked himself hoarse every day by nine a.m. He had to be taken out on lead, even when the men had left for the day, because he had stolen several small tools and probably buried them somewhere, dug an artistic addition to a trench that was ready to have a foundation poured and chewed through an extension cord, which was thankfully unplugged.

I was pretty well undone most mornings by ten. And I was trying to get my work set up for summer, which could be hectic. My work? Well, I'm a private investigator and my name is Alexandra Peres...but please, *please*, call me Alex. My work varies greatly, from checking out potential employees to checking up on spouses who are thought by their mates to have forgotten that famous little clause, "forsaking all others."

I also investigate employees who are thought to be cheating on their employers in some way. I occasionally look for teenage runaways, although I duck those painful jobs if I can.

And—the biggest part of my job: I investigate visitors to Provincetown who are filing personal injury claims against a B&B or motel, restaurant, store, etc. Several insurance companies retain me to handle their Provincetown customers, and it keeps me busy during tourist season...which seems to get longer every year.

It also keeps me entertained. Some people are nothing if not clever in their efforts to have a profitable vacation, and some are incredibly dumb. Last summer, for example, after his wife was startled by a bird and stumbled backward into a large rose bush, the husband sued the B&B where the two of them were staying. Not for her injuries themselves, which were briefly painful but medically minor, but because he was denied his conjugal rights for over two weeks. Assuming the fellow would be thought mad, the insurance company let the case go to court. They lost.

In another instance, a rather athletic woman staged a spectacular fall down a flight of stairs, due, she said, to a tear in the carpeting. Unfortunately, the scissors she had used to make the tear fell out of her handbag on the way down, and were immediately visible to an honest witness who happened to be standing at the foot of the stairs.

Anyway, I was busy updating the list of clients that *my* clients represented. I was making sure I had the seemingly hundreds of various new forms I needed and tossing out the old ones.

And I was also busy at my second job—one which I hoped would someday replace my first one. A few years back I had gotten into nature photography as a hobby. I had become good enough to be doing it professionally, with several well-respected art galleries in Ptown and a couple of adjacent towns handling my photographs. It meant not only taking photos, which took Fargo and me on hikes that we loved, but also numbering and matting them and placing them in simple wood frames. I then took them to the galleries to see which new ones they wanted to show, and how many older ones they wanted to re-order. And, how many copies they wanted of each.

Sudden loud noises did not help me in any of the above endeavors.

Cindy had the best of it, missing all but an hour of the activity in the morning and another hour in the evening, plus Saturdays. Of course, the water might be abruptly cut off for unknown reasons at any hour, or strange men might go up a ladder outside our bedroom as she dressed, or a sudden hammering might begin just as she applied mascara. None of us was having it easy.

We spent as much time as possible at the cottage. The quiet, the rejuvenated pets, the ability to say and do what we wished when we wished without benefit of a sudden audience restored us to some form of sanity. But even the cottage began to show its imperfections as we spent more time there. Closets were tiny, the bed was a double, not a queen, and Fargo and Wells seemed to take up more than their share of space in it. The kitchen was not built for two and there was no dishwasher. There *was* a clothes washer and dryer slightly younger than I am and slightly less noisy than the Orrick crew.

But the main problem seemed to be around Cindy's clothes for the office. She had ninety percent of both closets—my usual daily attire this time of year consisted of jeans, shirt, sweatshirt or light jacket, crew socks and loafers or sneakers...all of which could be stored most anywhere. Somehow, though, her clothes problem seemed in her mind to be my fault.

This morning, for example, I was out on the deck enjoying my coffee in the unusually warm April sun and watching Wells and Fargo on their morning patrols.

The screen door slammed, and, startled, I stood up and turned around. Cindy stood before me, mouth a straight line, hands clenched at her sides, her almost-Roman nose wrinkled in displeasure. This was unusual. Most mornings Cindy met the world with her gamin smile and her gray eyes on bright to see what the day held in store.

"Would you just *look* at this mess!" She shook her head in disgust, undoing most of her efforts to control her wonderful dark curls.

I looked more closely...and fought down a laugh. She had on a pale green skirt, a rather brilliant lavender blouse, a burnt orange blazer and blue pumps. I understood the shoes. She had worn a blue dress to work yesterday, and they were probably the only dress shoes she had here. The rest of it was a mystery to me. Usually, when Cindy was dressed, she was ready for a photo in the fashion pages of the *New York Times Magazine*.

"It's very interesting," I said neutrally, and then the laugh got away from me.

"It's not funny!" she snapped. "Now I'll have to go by the house with those thugs peering through the window while I change. I'll be late to work. How could you do this to me?"

"Me? How do you figure it's my fault?"

"You picked up the cleaning yesterday."

"I nearly always pick up the cleaning," I answered reasonably. "I do not pick out what you wear to work."

"You could have called me and told me everything you picked up clashed."

"Darling, I never even look at what I redeem from that bunch of thieves. I just pay their ransom and bring the stuff home. If I phoned you in the middle of a workday to tell you what portions of your wardrobe I had in the car, you'd think I had lost my mind."

"Well," she answered weakly, "now is different, with all this

6

shit going on!"

My eyebrows went up. Cindy rarely swore, and almost never scatologically. I still tried to be reasonable...I thought. "Look, I've got a clean white shirt in the bureau, and your light blue jeans are here—that should do it. It's dress-down Friday."

"It's not *that* dress-down, and anyway, I'm not going in there wearing a too-big shirt, probably with a frayed collar. Alex, you're just impossible!"

"No." At this point I was a little snappy myself. "*I* am not impossible, I'm just trying to be helpful. Anyway, where are all your clothes that were here the other day? Isn't there something you could wear?" I didn't mention that this mindless discussion was making her ever later for work: that would dawn on her soon enough.

"I took them home. The closets were getting so crowded."

"Couldn't you have left just one or two outfits and some shoes? That way I wouldn't need to be your personal dresser and try to figure out what you'd like to wear every time I get *your* cleaning."

"You don't have to get snotty and..."

"Girls, girls! For heaven's sake, I heard you all the way in my house." My Aunt Mae came up the stairs onto the deck, looking like a troubled pouter pigeon wearing glasses slightly awry. Her still-pretty round face belied her late fifties age...even if she *had* put on a pound or ten. Always soft-spoken, this morning her voice had a bit of a low-pitched edge to it. Had she really heard us all the way up the hill?

"Now," she said quietly, "I know workmen around a house are noisy and inconvenient, but you are both behaving like children. Here, Cindy, this light tan blouse of mine should fit you pretty well, and go with your blazer and skirt, and these tan shoes should get you through the day. Run inside and change before you're good and late. You two would still be at it at lunchtime." She shoved the clothing into Cindy's arms and pushed her gently toward the door. Cindy went.

"Goodness, I hate to hear you two quarrel." Raised voices

7

were not in Aunt Mae's repertoire. "You're both strung out with all this repair and remodeling, but you shouldn't take it out on each other. I hope you don't do this often."

"You're right Aunt Mae." I was embarrassed that she had heard us all the way up the hill. "We rarely quarrel, honestly. I guess we are just feeling put upon or put out or some damn thing. Even Wells and Fargo are grumpy."

"Well, they have some excuse…they don't understand what's going on. You two…"

"…have no excuse whatsoever," Cindy completed for her. She came out looking reasonably well put together if not quite her perfect self. "I should probably move under the bed with Wells and we could hiss and scratch together. I am sorry for my operatic performance." She kissed us both on the cheek and started off the deck to her car.

"You know what?" Aunt Mae called after her. "You both need a vacation. Leave the carpentry to the carpenters and go away somewhere. I'm serious."

"And probably right," I agreed.

"Ah, Paris in the spring!" Cindy sighed.

"Chestnuts in blossom," Aunt Mae added.

"Do you think the Louvre would like some of my photos?" I asked.

Neither of them answered.

CHAPTER TWO

I had returned to the house and was just wrapping up the spring cleaning activities in my office when the phone rang. Fortunately, the Orrick boys were working on the other side of the house, and I could actually hear my caller.

"Alex? Ralph Ryder here." Ralph and Becky Ryder ran a B&B down in the East end, and their insurance company was one that kept me on retainer to check out personal injury claims. They ran a tight ship, one might say, and I didn't recall ever dealing with a claim against them. In fact I hardly knew them.

"Ah, yes, Ralph, what can I do for you?"

"Well, we've got a spot of trouble here, and I thought I should ring you up."

Then I remembered: Ralph had moved here from England when he was about three, but held doggedly to his accent, tweedy clothes, pipe and, probably outmoded, British slang.

"Could you take a run over for a recce?" he asked.

"Could you tell me what the problem is? I hate to walk in blind."

"One of our guests came barefoot out of his bathroom and whacked his middle toe against a leg of the chest of drawers. You know those things hurt like the deuce. And he's limping badly. Since hiking 'round the pine woods and the beech woods are his main reasons for coming, he's not got much reason to stay, what?"

"Probably not," I answered, "but you didn't push him into the furniture, either, did you?"

"No. Of course not. I wouldn't dream of doing that!" He sounded shocked, and I remembered that a sense of humor was not his main characteristic. "But that furniture leg was sticking out a bit," he added. "Probably pulled away from the wall by one of the maids in cleaning, and not pushed back where it belonged."

"That changes the picture, Ralph. I guess I'd better stop by…how's now?"

"Perfect. Couldn't be better! Ta-ta."

"You bet."

I went to my safe and took two brand-new hundred-dollar bills from a small stack of ten, which I kept for situations like this. Over time I had discovered that sometimes a crisp bill or two would eliminate lawyers and a plethora of forms—or *vice versa*—so I usually took some with me, just in case. Next I traded the sweatshirt for a blouse and blazer, considered myself properly dressed—with no histrionics, I might add—and left, with Fargo hard at my heels.

As we drove down Bradford Street, I saw that Ptown was aware spring was coming. Many of the B&Bs showed new or cleaned awnings and glistening windows and neatly trimmed shrubs. Even Evans' Market had a man out painting the yellow lines in the parking area.

We found the Ryders in the living room…along with the injured guest, whom they introduced as Mr. Williams. He looked like a grandfather direct from Central Casting: wispy white hair, pale blue eyes, a slight paunch and a sweet smile. The only sour note was his left foot: wrapped in a large towel, which I assumed contained some crushed ice.

He seemed embarrassed by all the attention, and insisted he was not badly injured. I agreed that he probably wasn't seriously damaged, but that it probably hurt like hell. I had experienced that type of injury a couple of times, I mentioned, and had felt as if amputation were quite possible.

Williams gave me a smile and admitted to some pain, although he figured all anyone could do was to tape the damaged toe to the next unhurt one and try to stay off it as much as possible.

It was the "staying off it" that bothered him most. "You see," he explained. "I come up every spring to watch the returning birds pairing off and starting their nests, and that requires considerable walking." He sounded so sad, Fargo had walked over to comfort him, earning himself a friendly scratch behind the ears.

I now had my answer to the problem. "I understand, sir, and I have a suggestion.

"There will, of course, be no charge for your stay so far, and the Ryders will happily treat you to a stay in June. And if you don't mind, my dog Fargo and I will join you on one of your hikes—we're bird lovers, too. And by June we should get a good laugh at the fledglings making fools of themselves learning to fly."

The Ryders didn't look terribly happy, probably because by June they could be renting his room at full summer rates. But Mr. Williams, I was sure from his pleased and relieved expression, would not be filing any lawsuits, and a long free weekend seemed the least he deserved. The Ryder B&B was clean and comfortable, and served an adequate breakfast, but it was a no-frills operation. Williams probably would be staying elsewhere if his wallet were heavy.

He gave the Ryders that sweet smile, and they both broke down and smiled back, although Mrs. Ryder's was doubly strained. She kept looking at Fargo as if he were likely to bite her, urinate and dig a hole in the carpet at any moment.

"Now," I concluded, "Mr. Ryder will run you over to the clinic to get that toe taped, courtesy Pilgrim Insurance. Pilgrim is also aware of the current gasoline price of about a dollar per teaspoon, and we wouldn't want you to be out anything for making the extra trip from home and back, so-oo..." I handed him one of the two crisp hundred dollar bills.

"Oh, no, I can't accept that!" He handed the bill back to me.

"Sure you can. Otherwise, you and I could not sign this terribly official insurance form in triplicate—you know how insurance companies are."

He signed it. I gave him his copy and firmly handed him the money, gave the Ryders their copy and stood up. "My work is finished here. Here's my card. Call me in June, sir, and we have a date."

He blushed as if I'd asked him to the prom and shook my hand about six times. I gave the Ryders a brisk nod and left, feeling righteous.

I was also feeling thirsty and hungry, and since it was noon-ish, my thoughts turned naturally to the Wharf Rat Bar. Fargo and I would treat ourselves to lunch as reward for a job well and neatly done.

I lucked into a parking space right up the alley from the Rat. Even in early April there was considerable traffic on Commercial Street. It was a good thing the sand dunes were part of the National Seashore, with very limited access, or I guessed people would be skiing down them in January.

Fargo hunkered down beside the big old anchor half-buried in front of the Rat, and I arranged his leash to give him a choice of shade or sun. "Luncheon will be served shortly," I reassured him, and went in.

The Wharf Rat Bar never changed regardless of season. Tables and chairs were unmatched, walls were hung with lobster pots and old wooden buoys, fishnets and oars. In one dim corner stood a ship's telegraph taken from a ferry long gone to some phantom crossing in the sky, the indicator frozen on dead slow astern…I thought it a fitting motto for the Rat. Taking a seat at the bar, I greeted Joe, the owner/bartender and added, "Thanks, Joe," for the cold Bud he placed in front of me. "His Nibs is out front and would like a super-rare hamburger, plain, and some water. What would I like? What is Billie's triumph du jour?"

"A lobster salad that's going fast. I better put your order in." He turned for the kitchen. I didn't argue. Anything Billie made was always good. It was talking with her that was sometimes a problem. Her conversation could be a little hard to follow.

After serving the carefully cut-up hamburger on a plastic saucer and a bowl of water with an ice cube afloat in it, I returned inside to find my own luncheon sitting on the bar and Joe's wife, Billie standing behind it. "This seems to be selling good and I think the tourists like it, too. I wanted your opinion on it, whether or not I put in on the regular menu. Not that they would know it. You and your Mama know good food…though she ain't here today. How is she? It's what they call labor intensive."

I took a sample bite, using the time to sort out Billie's comments. "Mom's fine, and this is delicious! It's also beautifully served. I'll have to send her by to try it. Will you have it on the menu tomorrow?"

"For Jeanne I will. Not for the *hoy old boy*."

I thought for a minute; then I got it. Mom would be glad she was not considered one of the hoi polloi." I smiled. Billie smiled and returned to her kitchen, a tall, spare, rather colorless woman whose food needed no makeup and no lessons in syntax.

As I ate the salad—large chunks of tender lobster mixed with chopped black olives, celery hearts, a caper here and there, a bit of cilantro and very little mayonnaise—all put back in the shell and served with two miniature biscuits and corn muffins, I found myself relaxing after the rather hectic morning.

Idly, I watched Joe mixing drinks, pouring beer, as he served other customers. He and Billie were a strange couple. Joe was shorter than she and muscular, as if he might have been a boxer in his youth. And he wore a little mustache across his upper lip as so many short men do. He liked the ladies, and rumor said some liked him back. But I always wondered how he escaped the eagle in the kitchen.

Soon, I recognized a familiar greeting.

An aroma of fried fish, onions and beer announced the arrival of Harmon, winner by an easy length of the title Town Character. He had been lunching at the large round table in the front of the Rat, sharing it with a group of part-time fishermen whom Joe had dubbed The Blues Brothers, because of their continuous chorus bewailing the quotas on fish, the paucity of fish, the incursions on their fishing grounds by foreigners and even swordfish-hunting Floridians and the outrageous cost of fuel it took to go after the fish in the first place.

Harmon was a Blues Brother in good standing but, even more than he despised poachers, he hated drug dealers. And he saw them on every street corner every hour of the day. According to Harmon, Provincetown dealt more dope than Colombia could supply. In Harmon's program, local fishing boats took heavy loads off mother ships far out in the Atlantic. By other accounts, private aircraft landed it boldly at our airport, and seaplanes splashed down in our harbor, with wives and children acting as covers for their true cargo. Tour buses delivered dealers by the dozen and private pleasure boats didn't bear examination.

It would have been a harmless obsession had Harmon merely kept these tales for his front-table confreres. Unfortunately, he insisted on reporting every new discovery to my brother, Detective Lieutenant Edward J. (Sonny) Peres of Provincetown's finest. Sonny, although fond of Harmon, had developed many ways to dodge him, which meant that Harmon sent many of his messages to Sonny through me. I wasn't good at dodging, and—anyway—I wouldn't have hurt his feelings for the world. He was honest, kind, gentle and a marvelous handyman. In Ptown nowadays, one does not knowingly estrange a good handyman.

"Hello, there, Harmon, how's life treating you?"

"Not bad, Alex, not bad, but I need to get hold of Sonny, and at the police station they don't seem to know where he is. I wondered if you did."

I shook my head. "No idea." I moved my hand in a circling motion, and Joe set a beer in front of each of us. I nodded my thanks and pushed some money across the bar to cover the beers and my lunch. "Can I help you with anything?" I knew he'd ask me anyway.

"Come to think of it," Harmon replied, "I'm sure you can. Cassie's a friend of yours, and I'm afraid she may be in serious danger."

I suddenly lost interest in the plate before me and turned rapt attention toward Harmon. Cassie Deane had been my close friend for years. She owned Outer Cape Charter Aviation—which had a fleet of one lovely, sleek twin engine Beechcraft. Cassie was CEO, pilot, mechanic, receptionist, skycap and business manager of the firm.

The thought of Cassie in danger had me ready to go get my Belgian Browning .32 automatic out of my safe and dash to the airport.

"Tell me, Harmon. Who's after Cassie, and why?"

"Druggies. Three of 'em."

"Oh, come on, Harmon, Cassie isn't into drugs, never has been."

"I know that. It's her plane they want, and if she won't rent it to them, they'll hire her to fly it and then kill her when they get there."

"Start at the top," I snapped. "You're not making sense."

"Okay." He frowned, and I could almost see his mind working back to where he should start his latest drama.

"Okay," he repeated. "Yesterday I was at Ms. Lynn's place, paintin' her picket fence out in front of the house…and you know there ain't nothing gives you more time to think about somethin' else than painting a picket fence!"

I laughed. I had one myself and so did my mother, and Harmon was dead right.

He grinned at me and continued. "Well, there was three fellas come along and sat down on one of them benches the town has put up along the sidewalks here and there for the tourists to take

15

a rest from spendin' money on stuff they don't need. They started talking, and I kind of half painted and half listened to what they had to say. Now, Alex, it's going to be one of the biggest drug trades Provincetown ever seen...I kid you not!"

I should have guessed. "Well, how about that!" I shook my head. "And just how is Cassie involved?" My worries about my friend's safety were waning fast.

"It seems like these big dealers ain't satisfied with shipping drugs down to Connecticut and New York no more—these men were talking about a shipment to some little town way out near Pittsburgh! I tell you, we'll be supplying the whole country soon. They want to rent Cassie's plane in early May and fly themselves and what they called their 'cargo' out to this little town...one of the men apparently has a pilot's license. But Cassie, she wasn't buying. She told them she goes where the plane goes."

"Yes," I agreed. "She doesn't trust a soul but herself with that plane. You can't blame her, it's her livelihood. And anyway, she loves it."

"I know, Alex, I know. Anyway, this one guy, he says he don't want to get involved with no woman pilot: if she don't crash them, she'll set 'em down somewhere in Alaska. The other guy says he hears she's a super-good pilot and shouldn't have no trouble with a night landing in a unlit field, but if she does the flying, what do they do with her once they get there?"

That sounded strange to me. If the charter were legitimate and Cassie had no return passengers, they'd have to get her some motel room overnight and, of course, pay for gas and time on her trip home. And what was this about an unlit field? I took a sip of my beer, lunch now pushed aside, and lit a cigarette. It was my third of the day. If I exceeded five, I'd give my wrist a good hard slap.

Harmon drained his bottle of beer, wiped his mouth daintily on his sleeve and went on. "The fat guy says you can always just fill up her handbag with the cargo and send her home; that ought to make her happy. They all laughed at that, but the hard-to-please guy says, 'You got to do more than that, and you know it.

You can't leave that plane in the middle of your pasture, Frank, half the town would be climbing all over it. And what about her. She's bound to tumble to what's up, and lots of people don't exactly love people like us. Then we'd have to take care of her some way.' That's exactly what he said, Alex. And that don't sound good to me."

It didn't sound good to me either. Apparently one man was fat. One was called Frank. And that was all we knew except they were taking "cargo" to a pasture somewhere near Pittsburgh and would have to do something with the pilot after they landed. It would be virtually impossible to track them down here in town—and they might not even be staying in Ptown. Well, they had to be in contact with Cassie. Sonny could put a cop on her and find out what this *cargo* was.

"Harmon, it sounds downright bad to me. I'll chase Sonny down and have him contact you. You may remember something else they said and what they looked like or maybe the name of the town. I don't want Cassie kidnapped or something worse. Thanks a million for being bored with your fence!"

"Tell Sonny I'll be at Ms. Lynn's…painting the *back* fence. Thanks for the beer."

He patted my shoulder and left.

I went back to my lunch, but I finished the salad, more to keep from hurting Billie's feelings than from any great appetite.

17

CHAPTER THREE

I knew exactly where my cell phone was...for a change.
Usually my phone calls were not crises and could wait until I
got home or to a pay phone without causing a problem. Sonny
insisted that someday a bear would be coming through the front
door, and I'd be asking myself where I might have left the cell
phone. I told him I would simply exit through the back door and
leave the bear with the house, the bowl of porridge, the just-right
bed and the cell phone if he could find it.

Actually, I knew Sonny was right and once again promised
myself to keep the damned thing in my pocket or purse, if I were
carrying one, which was rare. I was pretty sure the phone was
on my bedside table, and I hated to go home. It was only two
o'clock. And the Orrick crew would be at full afternoon volume.
I decided to see if my mom were home and start my Sonny search
from there.

Theoretically, Sonny lived with Mom...for the third time since childhood. He was now twice divorced, with only one ex-wife remarried and two kids approaching the expensive teen and then college years. So he was on a tight budget, and Mom's midget rent included many meals. She drew the line at laundry, however. If he could drive a car, she opined, he could run a washer and dryer.

His current girlfriend, Trish, was a smart and successful young lawyer here in town—too kind, I thought, for her own good. Fortunately, neither she nor Sonny seemed to have marriage on the mind. For which our family—and doubtless hers—gave frequent thanks. Sonny did, however, spend numerous nights at her apartment.

Anyway, Mom might know his schedule for the day. At least I could use her phone to have Nacho at police headquarters track him down.

As I turned into her driveway, I noticed Mom's car in the garage, so probably she was home. And it was still home to me, too, in a way. I guess the house you were raised in is always home, no matter where you spend your adult years.

The house today looked much as it had when I was a kid. Like most old Cape homes, it was set close to the street, with a small front lawn and the de rigueur white picket fence.

The house itself was a cheerful yellow with maroon shutters—if it had ever been painted anything else, it was before my time. The backyard was sizeable by Provincetown standards, with several flower beds and a very small vegetable garden that grew an amazing crop. Mom said her success was due to placing the plants so close to each other, there was no room for weeds. I've never figured out if she were serious about that or not, but it seemed to work.

The lady of the house was in residence, busily washing down the outdoor furniture, which had spent the winter in the basement.

"Hello, darling!" She turned the hose away and presented a damp cheek for a kiss. "I don't know how I always seem to get more water on me than on the tables and chairs," she grumbled.

"It's because you have a secret wish to return to childhood and play in the water," I replied.

"And just how do you know that, Dr. Freud?"

"Becauss, I do ze same thing myself, you zilly voman." I laughed and gave her a hug, water and all.

At that moment Fargo felt neglected and jumped against Mom with muddy paws, and began to slurp a drink from the hose she held. "My, God," she squealed. "It's endemic! Get down, you beast!"

She turned to me. "Well, dear, did you just stop by to raise havoc, or is there some other reason for this very welcome visit?"

"Actually, I'm looking for Sonny."

She shook her head. "You won't find him this afternoon unless it's truly a matter of life and death. He and Mitch are checking auto repair garages all the way down Cape, trying to come up with the car that played hit-and-run with old Mr. Alves yesterday. It cost him a leg, you know, and all sorts of lesser injuries."

I shook my head. "I hadn't even heard about it. And I was just at the Wharf Rat. What's happening to our jungle drums? Is he going to be okay…I mean as much okay as possible?"

"I don't know. Last night he was critical, but stable, whatever that means. Come on in, I could use a coffee break, not to mention some dry clothes."

We went inside. While Mom changed clothes, I wiped Fargo down with a clean, dry rag which rapidly became no longer clean or dry. He then sat down and stared up at the canister where Mom kept his treats. I fished one out. "You don't deserve this, but it's easier than watching you melt away from starvation." He accepted it graciously.

I remembered to say thank you for the coffee, after Mom returned and we sat at the kitchen table. And I accepted the chocolate chip cookie graciously. After a sip or two of coffee and a bite or two of the cookie, I told my mother essentially what Harmon had told me.

She held her cup in front of her and frowned at it as if it were withholding valuable information.

"You know," she said, "the problem is that it's Harmon who overheard the conversation. If it had been anyone else, we'd be sitting at the hangar door holding shotguns until the police force could arrive. But with Harmon, you tend to think their 'cargo' will end up being a bunch of fishing nets, lobster pots and buckets of sand to decorate the town swimming pool."

"I know," I agreed. "But then I remember how he has accidentally been right about some things. I mean, think of that State contractor. Harmon thought he was into drugs…and it was graft…but it was still a crime, and the guy is in jail for it."

Mom sighed. "Yes, I recall. And if I live to be a hundred, I'll never forget that alligator. No one ever proved that Harmon was actually *wrong*."

Last summer a sizeable alligator appeared on the loose in Ptown. The first anyone knew of his presence was the night he chased a naked lady up a mimosa tree. His other antics were considerably less humorous. Harmon was convinced a drug distributor had brought the thing to town to teach an errant dealer to toe the line, and something had gone awry with his plan.

Most of us thought that was pretty far out—but, then, every explanation we could come up with was pretty far out, too.

I had to laugh. "Well, Mom, maybe these guys are just *saying* they want Cassie to fly them to Pittsburgh. Once they're airborne, they'll tell her to fly to Florida, pick up an alligator and bring it back to finish the job."

Mom gave me a wide smile. "I would not wish to be the person who told Cassie Deane she had to put a swampy gator in that spotless plane of hers. But, seriously, I don't particularly like the sound of this. Of course, it may turn out to be perfectly harmless, but I think we should let Sonny decide that." She pushed the kitchen phone down the table toward me, and I made the call to headquarters. Nacho assured me she'd have him call or stop by as soon as he surfaced.

I was in no mood to go home and listen to the Orrick version of *The Anvil Chorus*, so my mother got two unscheduled helpers with her furniture cleaning. One of us was paid off in cookies; the other received a chicken gizzard saved from dinner the night before. We both found the remuneration quite satisfactory.

My timing was good. Just as I pulled in my own driveway, Orrick's crew was packing up for the day. I checked the yard for loose tools and wires within Fargo's reach and found none, so I let him go. He grinned at his freedom and inspected every inch of yard to check where those Huns had been, whuffling with disapproval from time to time. I know the vet says that cheek-puffing noise I call whuffling is simply the animal's way of processing a strange smell, but to me, it always sounds censorious.

I confirmed Orrick's progress for the day and thought there just might be the palest of lights at the end of the tunnel. I figured Orrick would eventually finish. My question was: would Cindy and I survive until he did.

My musings must have been out loud, for a voice answered, "You'll survive better if you just go away and let him have at it. Contractors, workmen and owners don't mix well."

It was Sonny. "I hear you are looking for me? I hope it isn't to move furniture, I'm beat. And all for no results. And I hate to tell that to Mrs. Alves."

"That's too bad. I hope you get the guy—I assume it was a guy. Weren't there any witnesses?"

"Oh, yes, plenty. And three-to-two of them make it a man driving. Four say there were two people in the front seat, one holds out for just one person, and one insists there was a child in the backseat. The color of the car was dark green, navy or gray, and the make may have been anything from Kia to Acura. Actually, we're just looking for anything with front-end damage, and there *will* be some damage. They really walloped the old guy."

"How is he?"

"Conscious but looney tunes, possibly for good."

"Oh, dear," I sighed. "Well, fortunately the sun is over the yardarm. Come on in."

Sonny folded into a chair at the kitchen table.

"Do you have a beer? I'm afraid anything stronger will have me asleep before you tell me *your* tale of mortal danger for good old Cassie. Mom made it sound like we should ask for the National Guard."

"She may be right." I fished a bottle of beer out of the fridge and set it in front of him with a glass, which he ignored. He did not, however, ignore the pack of cigarettes and lighter I had tossed onto the table earlier. "Dammit, Sonny, don't you ever buy your own?"

I made myself a light bourbon and water and sat down.

He shook his head. "Not when someone is about to tell me a Harmon story. I deserve all the perks I can get."

I told him the Harmon story, and his reaction was much like Mom's.

"If only it hadn't come from Harmon. It just doesn't make sense that three men planning some sort of crime, possibly ending in murder, would casually discuss it on a park bench with a guy painting a fence right behind them."

He had brought forth one of my own early thoughts. "I know, but maybe they didn't know he was there. If he was down toward the corner of the fence, I think there are a couple of shrubs that would pretty well conceal him, and he wouldn't be making much noise…especially if there was any traffic to override it. And doubly so if Harmon was concentrating on them, not the paintbrush."

"I guess it could be," he agreed. "But it seems a god-awful complicated way to bring dope to a Pittsburgh suburb! You'd at least have to have some merchant vessel meeting a smaller fishing boat or pleasure craft at sea and bringing the dope into Ptown. Then a private charter plane from here to a non-airport where it would cause all sorts of interest, landing in the middle of the night. And, finally, as they said: what do they do with an uncooperative pilot?"

He tapped his cigarette thoughtfully into the ashtray. "I think I'd just pick up the 'cargo' somewhere in Texas or Florida, toss it in a pickup with a camper modification and toodle up the highway. Two men could be in the front and one catching some sleep in the camper part. They could drive straight through, and if they obey the speed limit and don't have an accident, there's no reason to stop them. Harmon has them doing this the hard way, and those guys are rarely fools. Hell, Alex, they probably want to charter her plane to ferry—you should pardon the pun—four or five of our sweet boys for rent, to entertain at the church supper."

"That's not nice."

"It makes more sense than bringing in drugs via every place but the Oval Office."

"You could send Harmon down to Washington to investigate. That should make the six o'clock news."

Sonny laughed and reached for another cigarette. Was he this heavy a smoker when they were his?

"Well," he placed the lighter back on the table. "What we can do is this: I'll talk to Cassie. If she doesn't have a whole different tale to tell, we'll put Hatcher into some greasy coveralls and send him out to play Cassie's mechanic for a day or so and see what we come up with. She can kind of play along with them and see if they furnish anything factual. If they even show up again."

"Sounds good to me," I agreed.

"I'm beginning to feel human," Sonny said and got up to get another beer. "Freshen your drink?"

"No thanks, I'm okay for now."

Just as he turned back to the table, Cindy came in the door.

She was wearing a navy blue linen suit and white blouse with a deep V-neck. She had on navy and white shoes with her signature three-inch heels. And she had had her hair done at some point during the day. She looked lovely but somehow stressed.

Sonny put his free hand on her shoulder and leaned down for a peck on her cheek. "I'll be damned, honey, you look good enough to have for dinner!"

Cindy looked up at him, said, "...Let's say... Oh, God!!" And burst into tears.

Sonny dropped his hand like he'd been shot and took a giant step backward into the refrigerator door. "Cindy! I'm so sorry. I didn't mean anything wrong! It's just...you looked so pretty...I must have just said it wrong...please don't cry."

I knew he hadn't meant anything out of line—and, more to the point, so did Cindy. There was considerable affection between the two, and she would never have taken offense at what he just did and said. And if she *had* thought he was out of line, a swift verbal one-two punch would have been a much more likely reaction than tears. What on earth was wrong with her?

Before I could phrase the question, Cindy abruptly sat down at the table and fished a tissue from her jacket pocket. Dabbing at her eyes, she looked up at Sonny.

"It's not you. I'm the one who's sorry. You didn't do anything." She blinked back a fresh round of tears and got control of her voice.

"I think I'm being stalked."

CHAPTER FOUR

Nobody said another word. Sonny and I just stared at her as if she'd placed a smoking bomb on the kitchen table.

Fargo was the first to get his act together, scrambling to his feet and going to her and putting his head in her lap. That seemed to unlock Sonny and me. And we were full of questions.

"Darling, how awful for you! When did this start?"

Before she could answer, Sonny asked, "Is it a male or a female?"

"Is it someone you know or recognize?" I queried.

"Have you been harmed or threatened in any way?" Sonny was looking fierce.

Waving her hands as if she were shooing away flies, Cindy spoke jerkily between short breaths. "Wait! Just *wait!* You're both picking on me. I can't answer you both at once. I just can't!"

It finally dawned on me that she was understandably near

hysteria, and firing questions at her would not help the situation. Count on Fargo—he'd handled it correctly right from the get-go. I lowered my voice—both in pitch and volume.

"Absolutely right, angel. Take your time. Sonny, would you make Cindy a drink and freshen mine, as you so kindly offered earlier." He headed for the dining room, where the liquor lived.

"Sure. And just remember, Cindy, you're perfectly safe now… and we'll make certain you stay that way. Try to tell us about it as you feel up to it."

Sonny soon handed out the drinks. Taking a sip, Cindy began to speak. "You know how you somehow become aware someone is staring at you? They don't have to wave or say anything; you just feel it. Most of the time it's okay…someone you know wanting your attention, or some woman wearing the same dress you are, or a tourist about to ask directions. You know…nothing."

We nodded agreement and she continued. "But the last week or so I've had the feeling someone was watching me a lot. Then when I looked up or looked around, I felt as if they had quickly looked the other way, or stepped behind another person, or were suddenly reading the newspaper."

Sonny asked gently. "Has this been a specific person or just a kind of general feeling?"

"Just a general feeling. Why?" she asked defensively. "You think I'm paranoid?"

"Far from it," he smiled. "Knowing you, if you could tell who it was, you'd have long since confronted them. Right?"

She returned his smile, and I felt better. Obviously, so did she. "You bet!" she said. "And at this point I would confront them with a baseball bat."

I put my oar in the water. "Where have you been when you had these feelings?"

"Most often at work. Usually downstairs in the main banking area. Or in the parking lot at work…mostly at the end of the day. And also on my lunch hour, walking to a restaurant, doing an errand, just getting some fresh air."

"No phone calls?" Sonny was making notes on a pad he had

27

commandeered from its little cage on the wall next to the kitchen phone.

"No."

"Has anybody said anything strange to you? Or touched you unnecessarily, even though it seemed innocuous at the time?" Sonny scribbled on.

"No."

Whoever this was, was beginning to seem like a real phantom.

Digging into her purse on the table, she sighed heavily. "Today I found this under my windshield wiper. I almost tossed it; it makes no sense. I still think maybe somebody got the wrong car."

She pulled out a note and handed it to me. I took it gingerly by a corner, hoping there might be fingerprints. It was fairly neatly printed on what was probably a page torn from a pocket calendar and read: *Don't worry about anybody giving you a hard time. I will be there for you. Love, your lifegard.*

Sonny leaned over my shoulder and read it aloud. "Whoever it is, seems fairly well educated…it's grammatical and neat."

"Lifeguard is misspelled," I noted.

"Yeah," Sonny nodded. "Maybe it's one of those words you just don't seem able to spell right…like I always tend to put an extra *a* in apart*a*ment."

"Maybe." I laid the note carefully on the kitchen counter. "I'll get an envelope for this in a minute. You know, Cindy is right; this thing makes no sense. It sounds as if he's saying he'll protect you against himself."

"I know," Sonny answered. "Unless the stalker has a stalker."

"Oh, my God," Cindy groaned. "Two of them are all I need!"

"Well, they might as well get used to a crowd, because I'm going to be stalker number three, right behind you every inch of the way." I lit a cigarette and blew a cloud of smoke forcefully toward the ceiling.

"The hell you are," Sonny snapped. "Having you as a

bodyguard would make about as much sense as my tailing her in full uniform, blowing a tuba. Whoever knows Cindy, probably knows you two are a pair. In fact, I've been trying to think whom I could use to trail her from a distance. I've decided everybody on the force would probably stand out like a cat at the dog show to anybody local. There's no point in having someone follow her if the stalker connects the two of them. He'd just quit until we took the tail off. Or he might switch to someone we won't know about. Or he might get nasty."

"Well, somebody has to be near her. I can always wear a disguise."

Sonny roared, and even Cindy had to smother a giggle.

"I could think of something," I insisted. "But if you don't like my idea, what's yours?"

"Very simple," he smirked, and I wanted to slap him. "There's a cop down in Eastham who retired last year. He told me recently he's bored to death and has nothing to do but argue with his wife. He'll jump at this, I know. I'll make Edgar a temporary deputy tomorrow morning. He and I will be having lunch at noon at the Hot Diggity Dog. You come in, Cindy, and say hello to me but keep going, place your order and go outside to eat. We'll stop on our way out and chat for a moment. Simple way for you to know who he is. After tomorrow, he'll be somewhere near you from the time you leave the house in the morning till you get home in the evening. Even if you don't see him—and you often won't—he'll be there."

Cindy nodded silently, and I told Sonny it sounded very good. "Guess I won't have to dream up an effective disguise, after all."

Giving me a sour grin, Sonny said, "Yeah. Like a couple of Halloweens ago you got all decked out in my old army camouflage uniform plus a mask…and everyone in town told me the next day how good you looked in my uniform."

Cindy tittered, "I didn't know that."

"You weren't here," I muttered. "Anyhow, Mr. Big Mouth, how about security at the bank itself? Cindy said somebody might be hanging around the main lobby."

"I'll call Choate Ellis in the morning and tell him what's going on. He can alert his security people. Also I want a list."

"Oh, Sonny," Cindy interrupted. "You're being great about this little mess of mine and I really appreciate it. But I'd rather meet my stalker at midnight in an abandoned warehouse than have this broadcast all over the bank! Some people would think I was just after attention, some would think it was funny or that I deserved it. Most would feel sorry for me and try to help...and what a muddle *that* would make!"

"There's this, too, Sonny," I chimed in. "What if one of the guards is the stalker? This would give him—or her—fair warning."

Shrugging, Sonny said, "Choate can tell them that the first one who leaks it is out on his ass. And, besides, the reason I want a list of his security people is so Nacho can run really thorough background checks. If we don't get any hits, we can assume, for the present, they're all clean. Look, guys, just one more question and then I've got to run. Trish will think I've forgotten all about dinner."

We looked at him expectantly. He looked back at us uncomfortably. Finally he spoke.

"This is kind of embarrassing, Cindy, and I don't want either of you to take it the wrong way...Cindy do you—or you, Sis— have anyone in your background who might want to do this for any reason...like giving one or both of you a good scare?"

I knew he was reluctant to pry into Cindy's and my private lives. He only called me *Sis* when he was under stress.

I answered first. "No woman, and certainly no man, has shown any unusual recent interest in me. And I haven't been coming on to anyone in my wildest dreams. As for my exes...I think they are all many miles away and glad to have said farewell. My latest damsel of disaster is, as you know, in no position to stalk anybody—she's still in prison. That's it for me. Cindy, my love, if you'd feel easier talking to Sonny alone, Fargo and I will gladly take a walk around the block."

"Not necessary." She gave me a weak smile. "You know my

latest calamity ended just before I moved up here. She found a gorgeous, wealthy French-Canadian replacement for me, and if she's back looking at me, the mighty have indeed fallen. And I'd know her anywhere. Otherwise—very few affairs and none with scars that haven't totally faded."

"Good enough." Sonny stood and stretched. "Cindy, I'll see you at noon tomorrow. And we'll have a car going by here fairly frequently at night until we get this bird. Be of good cheer."

At the door he turned back. "Have you two thought of a vacation? Between stalkers and builders, you could use a rest. And maybe they would all go away while you cavorted around …oh, let's say, historic Italy."

"The opera!" Cindy cried.

"The gorgeous women!" Sonny and I chorused.

CHAPTER FIVE

Sonny was on the phone bright and early Tuesday morning. Cindy's watchdog, Edgar Fountain, had to take his wife for a doctor's appointment in Hyannis this morning, but would be happy to start his new temporary job tomorrow. So everything was moved back a day. Could we deal with that? I said I was sure we could, and asked about the bank security people.

Choate Ellis, I was informed, had called an early morning meeting and was advising them of the situation as we spoke, and warning them against spreading the news. The list of employees would be faxed to Nacho sometime this morning. The Peres siblings parted as cordially as either could manage at that early hour.

Cindy tried not to look disappointed as she ate her health cereal with skim milk and half a banana. I tried not to look desperate when I noticed she had fixed me the same fit fare while I was on the phone.

But I soldiered on. "Look, Cindy my pet, I got a fairly large check from the art gallery down in Wellfleet. I'd like to get it into the bank. I was going to ask you to do it, but I think I'll do it myself around noon, and then stick my head in your office and suggest lunch. That way, if anyone *should* be checking my movements, it will all look quite casually normal. We do this from time to time anyway. What say you?"

"I say I'm delighted. I don't care what Sonny says, I feel better when you're within hollerin' distance. It's strange, now that you and Sonny are looking out for me—along with various patrol cars and bank guards and friend Edgar is in the wings—I feel a little shaky. Before that, I was just kind of uneasy. I guess yesterday I was still telling myself it could be my imagination. Now it's for real...or I guess it certainly better be...I'm kind of scared." She managed an almost normal laugh.

"Didn't we tell you?" I asked. "Starting tomorrow, whenever you leave the house or bank, there is a lead car with siren and flashing lights, then two cars exactly like yours, so no one will know which one you're in, and two tail cars, so one can follow you whichever way you turn. People will remove their hats and hold them to their hearts, soldiers will salute, children will wave flags and cheer. And your stalker will run behind the motorcade, panting, 'Wait for me, goddammit, Cindy, wait for me! You wouldn't be having any of this parade if it weren't for crazy old me!'"

This time I got a real laugh, and she left for work still grinning.

After watching the news and comforting myself with a second cup of coffee plus a jelly doughnut, I went into my office and began a serious task. I took my Glock 9mm pistol from the safe and began to clean it. It was my heavy-duty artillery, and it would not be far from me, and I would not be far from Cindy until this event ended. What Sonny didn't know wouldn't upset him, and I could guarantee no one would spot me, no matter what he thought.

Almost finished, I was just reloading the clip into the pistol when Orrick's 17th Symphony in Clash-A Major began. I stifled a wild desire to run out, waving the gun and shouting, "The next man who makes a noise...*dies!*"

Instead, I leaned under the bed, where Wells was muttering curses in a low hiss, and dragged her out at great personal peril. I called to Fargo to go to the car, and we headed for the cottage.

The *kinder* leaped joyfully from the car when we arrived. I followed more slowly but just as happily. Wells began a critter hunt among the reeds. Fargo ran to the end of the dock and stood guard against invading waterbirds. I strolled through Aunt Mae's garden, pleased to see that her peas and radishes, along with some herbs I could not identify, were bright with that special tender green of April. Soon it would be time to plant my tomatoes and summer squash! I went inside smiling.

While I made some coffee, I put a load of laundry in the washer, praying as I did that it would not pick today to give its final gasp. Gasp it did, and clank, and grind. But it staggered through its mission, and at last the little arrow triumphantly pointed to *end cycle*. The dryer was a bit quieter, but I wondered if it were not just waiting sneakily for a moment when we weren't looking to burst into flames.

I poured some coffee and went out on the deck, thinking of Cindy's cryptic *Lifegard* note telling her not to worry. Maybe there really were two stalkers. I supposed it was not impossible that some friend had spotted the stalker and followed along to be of help if needed. But why not simply announce him/herself, give a description of the stalker to the cops—or even a name if he knew one—and bring the little adventure to a quick conclusion?

Then I wondered if our note writer were both stalker and lifeguard in one. He could then come forth with information that he had seen the stalker approaching Cindy and chased him away. And who could prove he was lying? Like you read of a fireman starting fires so he can rescue someone, or a nurse disconnecting a patient's oxygen so she can be Johnny-on-the-spot with CPR when the patient goes unconscious.

I tossed various scenarios around—each one becoming more bizarre. When I got to the one where the stalker was really an alligator and Cindy was afraid she was going crazy imagining things…I quit. It wasn't Cindy I was worried about.

Finishing my banking chore, I walked upstairs to Cindy's aerie, where she was saying goodbye to a tall, gangly boy I put at fourteen or so. I hung back, not wishing to intrude, but curious as hell what business a boy whose voice was still at the unreliable stage had with a financial planning manager. Was the bank reduced to making loans against next week's allowance?

Cindy saw me and waved me over. "Alex, meet our valued customer Larry Wismer. Larry, this is my good friend, Alex Peres."

I said hello and extended my hand. He took it in a good solid handshake. Someone had taught him that neither the limp fish nor the bone crusher makes a good impression. He said it was nice to meet me and added that he'd better run along, his grandmother would be waiting in the car.

As he left, I went into my little act in case anyone was paying attention.

"I had some business downstairs," I said, "and I thought if you were free, we might have lunch."

She thought that was a fine idea, retrieved her purse from her office and we left. As we walked toward the center of town, I tried a few tricks of the trade to see if anyone was following us. I knelt suddenly and retied my sneaker. No one fell over me or suddenly stopped to view the year-old display in the Land-Ho hardware store. We walked slowly, and then fast, but no one seemed to keep pace with us.

Finally, we went out on the pier to one of the food stands and ordered, and nobody seemed to care. Cindy cared that I had ordered a hot dog and fries…a cholesterol mother lode if ever she had seen one. I told her the sauerkraut on the hot dog would negate the cholesterol. She said all it might accomplish was a good case of heartburn, which I richly deserved. She actually looked at her grilled veggie bun with pleasure.

I wanted to get off the food subject, but did not wish to get onto stalkers. Finally, I thought of the kid.

As we settled at a picnic table, I remarked, "I see your customers are getting younger."

"Oh, you mean Larry? Don't laugh, he takes his portfolio very seriously."

"A kid his age has a *portfolio?*"

"Well, kind of. His parents were killed several years back in some bizarre accident in Kenya, of all places. He lives with his grandmother—quite happily, I think. I've met her; she seems a very cool character and also an affectionate grandma. Larry will come into some money at eighteen for college, and some more at twenty-five. So he wants to be sure he handles investments knowledgeably, and he is learning."

"I see." I surreptitiously scooped some ketchup onto a golden fry. "You mean he has a 'pretend' portfolio to see what would happen if he really owned the stock. Good idea. Good way to learn."

"No he has real stock. The bank charges no fees on investments for kids under eighteen, with, of course, a guardian's approval. Larry now owns a big five shares each of three stocks which he bought from money he's earned doing odd jobs. He is as diversified as three stocks can be, and he watches them carefully." She laughed. "I'm glad there aren't too many Larrys—I wouldn't have time for adult customers."

"Still sounds like a good idea. I may give it a try."

"Despite some of your behavior and your eating habits," Cindy informed me, "I believe you are over eighteen. If you are telling me you are not…I'm moving out tonight."

"Gosh, you can be so particular about unimportant little things!"

"Well, I always remember that fine old adage from my grandfather: Fifteen will get you twenty." She gave me a sad little smile. "What's it to be, free stock trades or me?"

"Oh, you, by all means. What's a million more or less?"

After lunch I walked Cindy back to within a block of the bank. There I leaned against a phone pole and went over an imaginary shopping list in the little notebook I always carried with me. No one seemed interested in Cindy, and I went on to retrieve my car from the bank lot. As I backed out of my parking space, I caught a quick glance of Larry Wismer sitting on the concrete rim that surrounded the fountain and thought vaguely that his grandmother was running awfully late.

Driving back to the cottage, I resolutely blocked stalkers from my thoughts and considered the several suggestions we had received recommending a vacation. Maybe we should get away for a short while, and now might be a good time to do so—come the summer season, we probably wouldn't have the time.

I tried to think of someplace simple and inexpensive and couldn't. Maybe we should just spend a day or so in Boston picking out the furniture and carpeting and draperies for our ever-expanding Master Suite. Of course, that wouldn't be simple or inexpensive either.

In the pre-Cindy days, when I had thought merely of adding a bedroom and bathroom, I had noticed several furniture store ads touting free decorator service. I had planned to pick one of them and tell the decorator to show me something plain, comfortable and cheerful…all of it affordable. I figured on getting the whole thing settled in maybe an hour…a maximum of two hours. Now I imagined we would not use a decorator and would doubtless visit a dozen stores at least twice.

I braked the car in front of the cottage, making an abrupt stop that sent gravel flying and brought Aunt Mae flying out of her garage, where she was beginning to set up shop for her popular herb market.

"What on earth is going on? Are you all right?"

"I'm fine. I hit the brakes a little hard, that's all. Aunt Mae, do you know a good furniture store in Boston?"

"Certainly. Several, in fact."

"Ah, good, I thought you might. Would you be kind enough

to give me the address of one?" I asked.

"No need, dear." She smiled. "I already gave the entire list to Cindy. I'm sure she has it somewhere."

"Thanks. I'm sure you're right." I managed not to slam the car door and gave my dear aunt a smile and a wave as I turned to the cottage.

CHAPTER SIX

Wednesday morning I walked Cindy out to her car as she left for work and wished her well with her introduction to Edgar Fountain at noon.

She grimaced and shrugged. "I'm sure he'll be fine, if Sonny recommends him. But I feel very strange knowing someone is *definitely* watching my every move, even though he's on my side. It's a weird feeling—being watched because you are being watched. I'm sure I won't be able to do a thing naturally. I'll probably overact like a nineteen thirties Grade B actress."

"Yes," I laughed. "I can see you at the Diggity Dog, waving a white gloved hand: *Oh, yass,* my good woman, I'll have the soup *du jury* and salad *Niceswazz* and a glass of *peanut blanc.* And the waitress will answer: Right, honey, one dog with mustard, one fries and a diet Coke."

"In your dreams." She started the car and leaned out the window for a kiss. At least she was grinning.

I watched her turn at the corner and saw one of the police department's unmarked cars pull out behind her. I wondered if the stalker were watching and if he knew the police car as well as I did.

That evening Cindy got home in a very up mood. Edgar was quite nice and rather fatherly. He was most reassuring and teased her that he turned into a pet dog who simply followed his mistress everywhere and nobody paid any attention to him and neither should she. Just forget he was there, but remember she was safe.

He sounded great and I had hopes of a speedy end to this whole thing.

We actually enjoyed a movie on TV after dinner. We went to bed and laughed and sighed and growled at the late news. I was feeling more relaxed than I had in days. Apparently my lady love was also, for she was giving forth those little signals which we each possess in some way, that say, "I'd like to make love, how about you?" Obviously I was replying in the positive, for she suddenly clicked off the TV and rolled into my arms, sighing, "It's been too long."

I was teasing Cindy over breakfast. "Well, at least there's one thing you still seem to do quite naturally. All is not lost."

"If you're telling me the stalker was looking through the window and Edgar was behind him in the tree—you will find me as celibate as Mother Teresa from now till they hang the bastard and we return Edgar to his nagging wife."

"Goodness!" I took a sip of coffee. "You're in bloodthirsty form this morning."

"You bet." She pushed aside the remains of her half grapefruit and went to work on the twigs and hulls she calls cereal. "He's disrupted our lives long enough. And I don't want him to get spooked and just quit...so he can surface again later, scaring the hell out of me again, or some other woman. Any woman should be able to walk down a street without some lunatic drooling behind her! I say hang him!"

She looked across the table at me, suddenly solemn. "Seriously, I think he should go to jail. He's had us both on edge, reacting to every little noise, jumping when the phone rings, and I know you go through the mail. He's taken up Sonny's time and police department funds. He has worried my boss and involved bank security people. I don't think he should get away with just saying he's sorry, that he was simply carried away by my great beauty. 'Go and sin no more,' is not in it for this guy."

I grinned. "You tell em', tiger, I'm with you!"

And I was. But I wondered if she had considered the stress of a public trial, with all its ramifications. Probably not. On the other hand, she would likely go through it with admirable composure, at least on the surface. I recalled a phrase my grandmother sometimes used that made me snicker as a little kid. "So-and-So has great intestinal fortitude." Meaning, of course, great courage. Sonny used a phrase I liked better: "He has grace under fire." Whatever you called it, Cindy had it.

While I accepted Sonny's and Cindy's faith in Edgar, I wanted to see for myself. So Thursday after Cindy left I set out to keep tabs on our retired cop. Sometimes I cruised the block in my car, sometimes I walked, other times I stood or sat, letting him pass me by on foot or in his unexciting, mature gray Hyundai.

I had to smile. Edgar and I were doing much of the same things, right down to changing our clothes sometime around midday. He had started the day dressed for business. Around eleven he surfaced in bright blue shorts, Hawaiian shirt and a sun hat. Not the same man at all. And early afternoon I graduated from a denim skirt and yellow blouse to my most ratty jeans, baseball cap and a T-shirt boasting that "Hockey players do it with a big stick."

Mid-afternoon I graded us both an A-Plus and headed home, feeling that between the two of us, the love of my life was in good hands.

Driving toward home, I realized that I had been so involved with Cindy's problem I hadn't seen Harmon, nor had I contacted

Cassie about her possible trouble with the strange Pennsylvania customers.

I figured I should see her for some firsthand information and wondered if she were at the airport. I pulled into the first parking spot I found on Commercial Street and fished around in the glove compartment until I actually found my cell phone. And Cassie, in fact, picked up her phone. Two rarities. I told her I was on my way to the airport if that suited her schedule. It did, and I carefully jammed the phone in my pocket.

I found Cassie in the hangar on a ladder, changing the oil in the port engine.

"Don't you have a mechanic now to do things like that?" I asked.

"Hah! If you mean that sweet child Sonny sent out here, he doesn't know the difference between a propeller and a dipstick. I forbade him to do anything other than check the air in the tires, and I wouldn't rely on that. My dear, I love your outfit, and I'm sure Cindy does." Her eyebrows curved upward and her mouth curled in a sarcastic angle.

"Uh, yeah. I have some dirty yard chores this afternoon," I fibbed. "Have you heard any more from the three Pittsburgh pirates?" I opened a small refrigerator and took out a can of Budweiser. "You want one?"

"Yes to the pirates and no to the beer. Get me a Snapple iced tea. I'm flying tomorrow morning."

I knew she maintained a strict no-drinking-for-twenty-four-hours-before-a-flight rule, so as I handed her the tea, I waved the can of Bud. "This going to bother you?"

"No," she lied, looking wistful, so I was noble and took a bottle of tea instead.

"The pirates seem okay," she remarked as she climbed down the ladder and motioned us to her tiny office in a corner of the building. "The men belong to some veterans club in this little town near Pittsburgh. And they are having a big benefit dinner to raise money for a new clubhouse. They figure everyone is sick of hamburgers and hot dogs or spaghetti and meatballs, so they thought up a shore dinner. They figure they'll get maybe four hundred people instead of two hundred by advertising something new and different. So they came out here to line up the food."

"Why here and why in person? Wouldn't a phone call to a Boston or even a Pittsburgh wholesaler have been easier?"

"Sure." Cassie laughed. "But this guy Frank loves an excuse to fly and he's got a nice four-seater Cessna, so they piled in it and headed east. And before you ask, why Ptown...one of the men was here with his wife last summer and had a delicious lobster dinner. Are you getting the picture...three little boys off on a lark."

An ashtray on the rickety table between us told me I could smoke, so I pulled one out. Cassie lifted it from my fingers, so I pulled out another and lit both. "I thought you were quitting," I mentioned casually.

"Uh, not really, but my pack is out in the car. I smoke less if I have to take time to go get them. It kind of keeps Lainey off my case."

And mine were right here, handy. Sometimes I think I supply the entire eastern seaboard of non-smokers, wannabe non-smokers and occasional smokers. I wished I had taken the beer. I wished I had stock in whoever makes Virginia Slims. But I got back to the reason for my visit. "Wasn't there something about renting your plane, and landing in the dark in an unlit cornfield?"

"My God! What is Harmon spreading around? Yes, Frank wanted to rent the plane and fly it himself. It would be a bit cheaper for them, but I think he really would just like to fly it. He's licensed for twin engine and checked out in a plane like mine. However, I told him: where my plane goes, I go. They want the seafood to arrive just before or just after dawn, so the cooks can start cooking in the morning and be ready to serve by noon. Frank has his own little grass strip on his farm with limited lights. It's plenty long enough and nice and smooth, he says. The lighting is more or less adequate, especially with someone on board who knows the approach. For heaven's sake there's no mystery about this."

I took a drag on my cigarette. I was beginning to feel foolish. "So you think it's all aboveboard? That Frank was being truthful?"

"Alex," her voice was heavy with patience. "The man is hardly going to ask me to land a plane in some dark, rutted field where I'm going crash and kill him and his two friends, and make chowder out of all his seafood."

"Yeah, I guess not. Did Officer Hatcher overhear any of this?"

She took another cigarette. "Yes, every word, while he tried to look busy with the tire gauge. He also thought everything sounded legit. We agreed they were all ignorant about seafood—they thought you cook scallops in their shells—but that Frank was knowledgeable about planes. Okay?"

"I reckon. It just sounded kind of funny the way I heard it. When is this great shipment taking place, and where are they getting all that seafood?"

"In about three weeks. They're going to firm up the date next week so I can lock in my schedule. I gave them the address of Cape End Wholesalers here, and Phil Pino's phone down in Wellfleet. If he doesn't have all the scallops they want, I guess he can get them. Satisfied, mother?"

"Just trying to be helpful," I said, somewhat miffed.

"I know, darlin', and I love you for it. Seriously, you look tired, Alex. Have you and your lady thought of grabbing a few fun-filled days somewhere before the season really starts?"

"Yeah, yeah."

I tossed my tea bottle into the recycling bin and went on my way.

At home I buried my hockey T-shirt into my catchall bureau drawer where Cindy never goes and put on a sloganless tan one. Knowing there were no twenty-four hour drinking rules before going to the supermarket tomorrow, I snagged a cold Bud and bid good-day to the departing Orrick Philharmonic as I hit the deck chair for the still-warm rays of sun.

CHAPTER SEVEN

My wardrobe was running thin on clothing to make me look appreciably different when I went out on my patrol to check up on Edgar, and keep an eye out for the stalker as well. Edgar had been in place for nearly a week now, and I didn't check up all day every day as I had at the beginning. But I did go out once most every day.

He had reported to Sonny as of yesterday that he had spotted no one showing unusual interest in Cindy. I wanted to make sure he was doing all he should before we began to wonder if somehow Cindy had imagined her follower. I found that solution hard to accept, anyway. Cindy is not afraid of men as such. Indeed, she gets along well with most men and likes them, gay or straight.

And she is not imaginative when it comes to fancying rapists under the bed or kidnappers lurking in the shrubbery. Something had frightened her and I had no doubt it was real. We had been careful not to spread word of her problem around. Not even Mom and Aunt Mae knew. I hadn't even told Cassie, and I certainly hadn't told Peter and the Wolf…our two good friends who ran a B&B which catered—in every sense of the word—to gay men. Peter's first name really was Peter, and Wolf's last name was Wolf—someone coined the sobriquet and it stuck.

So, I needed a new disguise. I had a brilliant thought. I went outdoors and asked one of Orrick's electricians, who was about my size, if he had an extra pair of coveralls in his van. He allowed as how he did, having picked up his laundry only yesterday.

I asked if I could borrow a pair, assuring him I would have them laundered and back in place tomorrow. Puzzled but agreeable, he went to his van and pulled out a pair with one or two paint spatters, a varnish stain and one knee worn through. Perfect.

Standing in the yard of the courthouse, along with several other idlers, I realized I must have misjudged the height of the coveralls' owner. Both the legs and arms were too long, and I had to cuff them both twice to get them the length they should be for me. They looked a bit clumsy, but I was sure that, accessorized by old sneakers, white work socks, my Red Sox cap and a pair of wire-frame glasses with clear glass lenses, no one would recognize me.

I lazily watched Cindy disappear into the health food store for some lunch hour shopping, while Edgar sauntered across the street to admire the window décor of The Catch fishing tackle mart. I was taking a sip of my lukewarm soda when peals of girlish laughter drifted across the grass to me.

Looking up, I saw my mother and Aunt Mae, collapsed against each other and pointing at me with great delight. I could cheerfully have strangled them both, but I managed to shake my head and to mouth the words, "I don't know you." They looked confused, but at least stopped their sophomoric act, as I walked over to them. I loudly gave them directions on how to get to a restaurant near the Wharf Rat, along with many gestures, and then muttered, "Go to the Rat. I'll meet you shortly." Chastened, they hurried away, and I sauntered to my car.

There, I wiggled out of my failed costume, tossing it and my cap and glasses into the backseat and revealing the jeans and shirt I had fortunately worn underneath. I may have looked a little sweaty and disheveled, but at least I was me again—if indeed I had ever been anyone else.

As I approached their table at the Rat, both women looked quite relieved to see me in something like normal garb and began simultaneously to babble apologies for blowing my cover. I had no choice, of course, but to tell them what was going on and why. Over my beer and their white wine and salads, we sorted it all out, apologies were accepted and we all returned to something like normal.

Both women were naturally concerned for Cindy and outraged at whoever was causing her, and peripherally me, such distress. Both my mother and my aunt had been widowed young, but under very different circumstances. Aunt Mae's husband had died in his late forties of a sudden cerebral hemorrhage. Aunt Mae had never remarried, being unable to find a man she considered even half as wonderful as Uncle Frank had been. She began raising herbs to fill some of the painfully empty time, and became so good at it, she now had a large herb garden and had converted her garage into a small but well-known shop where she sold both dried and potted herbs in season. She had even published two little books on the subject, and actually sold a fair number of them.

Mom's widowhood came along much more dramatically. My father died when I was twelve and Sonny fourteen, which would have put Mom at about thirty-seven or -eight. As I remember him, my father was a heavy drinker and not a merry one. Although he never abused any of us physically, he was sarcastic, critical and withdrawn. He hated his job. Although he was good at it, he always left the impression that he was much too intelligent to be manager of the local supermarket and that somehow Mom, Sonny and I had entrapped him there.

The summer that changed our lives for the worse and then for the better, had Provincetown sideswiped by a powerful hurricane. Dad had closed the market early, seen to it that the large glass windows were covered with plywood, that the generator was set up to kick in if—when—the power failed, etc. He then visited his favorite bar and fortified himself and finally came home, angry at the many inconveniences he had suffered already that day.

By then Mom had pulled her car into the garage, and the three of us had dragged the outdoor furniture into the basement and closed any windows, doors and attic vents we could find. We had just gathered all the candles in the house when Dad drove into the yard, obviously and vocally pissed that he had to get out and re-open the garage door in the pouring rain.

The night was a horror. Dad blew a gasket when he found that dinner consisted of do-it-yourself cold sandwiches. Mom was worn out from helping move all the furniture, and making the house as secure as possible; hot food was out of the picture anyway, as the power had long since failed. Dad retired to the den and sat in front of a black TV screen with his scotch.

Mom, Sonny and I sat in the kitchen, listening to sounds we did not realize the house could make and survive. The building that was always so cozy in winter now presented us with chill drafts it had never before allowed to enter. The rain sounded like people throwing rocks at the windows, and we were sure they must break and let the rocks fly in to hurt us. There were unidentified crashes from time to time: Trees? Utility poles? Objects sailing into other objects riding a demon wind? The dark was palpable with no lights in the house or on the street. And the candles provided a few little islands of yellow that brought no comfort.

None of the three of us wanted to go upstairs to bed, so we spent the night at the kitchen table. Sometimes we turned the battery radio on long enough to be told the storm was expected to diminish by a dawn we feared would never come. Sometimes we dozed in the straight chairs, wakening every few minutes as we lost balance. Finally, we put our heads down on the table, having digested all the terror we could hold, and simply became numb.

Daylight finally did come, as it inevitably must, unless it is truly, finally the end of the world. The wind had slackened to a mild gale; the rain was a manageable downpour. We realized we had survived and were overtaken by a silly lethargy that made us giggle at nothing and satisfy our hunger noisily with the stale leftovers of last night's banquet.

Dad came in from the den where he had slept on the couch, expecting a steaming mug of coffee and a trencherman's breakfast. He looked with distaste and disdain at our sandwiches with the curling edges and hardening streaks of mayonnaise, at the glasses holding flat soda or smudged with congealing milk. He poured a hefty shot of scotch, added a bit of water from the tap, and sat down, turning on the radio only to curse the announcer who warned of flooding in low areas and downed wires which could still kill.

Finishing his drink, he declared he must get to work and see what damage the store had sustained. He didn't question what his house or his family might have sustained. Sonny informed him that a large branch from our neighbor's tree blocked our driveway.

Dad told him to put on a coat and help him move it. Mom said that it could have live wires tangled in it and that Sonny wasn't going anywhere near it. Sonny looked relieved. Dad shrugged and said she'd turn her son into a fairy yet at the rate she was going, grabbed his slicker and went out to drag the branch aside.

The radio announcer had been right.

We were now a family of three with no breadwinner. Mom got a job, Sonny and I helped as and when we could. There may have been additional aid from Aunt Mae and our grandmother—I never knew. I did know that, financially strapped or not, we were more lighthearted and content than we had ever been. Eventually Mom got promoted, first Sonny and then I became independent…and everyone's checkbook now looked reasonably healthy.

Over the years, Mom had several invitations to marriage that

I knew of. She turned them down gently but firmly. Now—it still seems strange to use these words in reference to my mother—she is in the midst of a very successful affair with an actor several years her junior. She had met Noel Fortnum when he was appearing in a play here last summer and they were immediately attracted. Neither seems especially interested in marriage, but they obviously care deeply for each other. At first I thought the long-distance relationship might not work. Now I think perhaps the distance makes it work better. All that really matters to me is—Mom is happy.

Aunt Mae looked at her watch, caught Joe's eye and made a "check" motion with her hand and said, "Jeanne, we'd best stir ourselves. Being late will just make it drag on longer."

"What's dragging on?" I asked.

"The bi-monthly meeting of the Ladies' Altar Guild," Mom answered for her. "I'm chairwoman this year, so I guess they can't start without me, but I do hate being late. It just makes it look as if you consider your time more valuable than anyone else's. Now listen, you two girls be careful and call either of us if you want some extra company. Any time."

I waited till they were safely out the door before ordering another beer and lunch...and then canceling both. I decided to go home and take the furry ones to the cottage so they, too, could have some peace. I'd call Cindy later and tell her where I was.

Ordinarily I don't fall for advertising gimmicks. A gizmo that usually sells for a hundred dollars, but is available right now for nineteen ninety-five doesn't snare me. Telling me that if I order this very minute, you will send me *two* gizmos for the price of one doesn't have me running for the phone. Advising me that the gizmo is guaranteed for life leaves me unimpressed, for the simple reason I have never been able to figure out whose life they mean. The announcer's? Mine? The manufacturer's? The gizmo's? The TV station's? And exactly what constitutes *life* in this circumstance?

But about three weeks ago, I was trying to ignore the Orrick

Concerto and turned on the telly. The movie I got must surely have been a loser even in 1950 and was no better some sixty years later, but in desperation, I left it on.

One of the commercials that seemed to pop up about every five minutes, advertised a sound-activated long-range mini tape recorder which you wore on your wrist, like a handsome sports watch, and batteries were even included. It was valued at more than twice what they were charging for it and—yes—if I called now, they'd send me two...both guaranteed for life!

I figured it might come in handy in my work at some time. I saw no need of two, but figured I'd give the extra one to Sonny, who might also find it useful. I went briskly to the phone and placed my order and promptly forgot about it.

Today, when I took the mail from the mailbox, it included a small carton with a generic company return address, and I had to go in the house and open the damn thing before I remembered what it was. The printed instructions and lifetime warranty, written in elegant script, reminded me what I had ordered. And made me wonder what in the name of heaven I had been thinking of.

A handsome sports watch it definitely was not. It was bulky as hell and looked more like one of those ankle bracelets some unfortunate people have to wear to prove to the police they really are at home.

Wondering if it worked as well as it looked, I followed the instructions to get it ready for action, backed off about eight feet and spoke a few words at my natural volume. I rewound the tape and hit the *Play* button. And I heard my voice, a bit scratchy and tinny, but easily understandable say, "Hi there! I'm about to rob the jewelry store. Want anything?"

I was pleasantly surprised with my new techno-toy. Only the looks of the thing disappointed me. It was about as inconspicuous as walking around with a grenade on your wrist. I'd have to think of some other way to carry it.

At this point, Fargo pushed the carton off the table, checking to see if it contained food. And I got my bright idea.

Scrabbling in the kitchen junk drawer, I pulled out a roll of tape. Then I took Fargo's collar off, taped the recorder to it and returned it to his neck. He didn't like it. He shook his head, then he rubbed his neck along the carpet, next he tried scratching it and finally he sat and looked at me accusingly.

I petted him and told him it wouldn't be for long. Actually I was dying to try my gizmo out in an area with background noise and various people talking. I promised him a hot dog and his ears went up. I apologized to Wells and promised her the cottage later and dragged Fargo out the door.

After parking downtown on McMillan Wharf, I walked Fargo, still stretching his neck from time to time, over to one of the hot dog stands.

A smiling face appeared at the service window. "Hi, Alex. Good afternoon, Fargo. What will it be?"

"And a good afternoon to you, Ginny. A plain hotdog for my furry friend and one with mustard and relish for me, plus a coffee, please."

Minutes later the order appeared on a little cardboard tray, with Fargo's hot dog neatly cut into bite-size pieces and a small bowl of water beside it. Service was first-class here if you were Fargo.

I looked around the area, deciding which of the benches in the grassy strip along the edge of the concrete wharf to choose. Finally I spotted a bench about ten feet from a young couple just starting their own lunch and walked over to it. Placing Fargo's meal and water on the ground, I put the gizmo on *Receive* and addressed my own hot dog.

I couldn't quite hear their conversation...something about whether to go home tomorrow or the next day...something about a place that was closed on Saturday. I wondered if the gizmo was getting any of this. The couple soon left, and we were not far behind. I decided to wait until we got home to see how the recorder had worked. I turned it off and let Fargo into the car.

As we progressed up Commercial Street I spotted Cassie's car several blocks ahead of us. Suddenly she pulled over, got out and started down the alley to the Rat. I pulled in behind her and followed her down the alley. Near the door I hitched Fargo to the big old anchor there and gave him sufficient lead on his extension leash to relax in sun or shade—but not enough to follow me inside, which would have been his first thought.

Once in, I sat down at the bar next to Cassie. "How's the Red Baron today?"

She turned. "Well, howdy, Sherlock. Join me for lunch? I know it's a little late. I just got back from taking a couple of guys down to Teterboro airport in New Jersey, and I'm starved."

"No, thanks. I'll settle for a Bud. Any news from the Pittsburgh pirates?"

"Not yet, and they'd better not take too much longer. I'm already getting bookings. It looks like an early season, thank God. And I'm not going to cancel flights with people I know, to accommodate three lunatics throwing a clambake! Although," she added wistfully, "it would be a nice piece of change."

"Well, you're good at juggling. You'll manage to fit everybody in, even if you have to fly somebody to Augusta via Pittsburgh."

"Maine or Georgia?"

"Don't be a wise-ass!" I grinned.

"Okay. I'm amenable," she replied. "Tell me, how's Cindy dealing with this stalker thing. It must be nerve-racking."

"Dammit!" I set my beer down sharply. "We've been breaking our necks to keep this quiet. Even my mom didn't know about it till an hour ago. How do *you* know?"

"Hey!" She spread both hands in front of her. "Don't be so touchy. I'm not about to call the *Enquirer*. Sonny talked to the shrink at the clinic about the stalker. The shrink hadn't dealt with many stalkers and thought Lainey might be of some help—she nursed at Bellevue a couple of years before coming back to the Cape, you know—so he called her in on it. Sonny was just trying to get some sort of profile on the guy...in fact I think he mainly wanted some reassurance the man would most likely not turn violent. It won't be spread all over town. Take it easy."

"Yeah, sorry. I'm just on edge. Maybe more than Cindy at

this point. God, between the stalker and the Orrick workmen, and two pets barking and hissing—I'm beginning to resemble a snapping turtle, and Cindy is worse. In her mind, it seems to be my fault she can't crowd her entire Catherine the Great wardrobe into the little closet at the cottage. Even that's a dubious haven nowadays." I took a long drink of my beer, and didn't say no when Joe took another off the ice.

Cassie's lunch arrived. And we sat silently for a few minutes while she knocked off the outer reaches of her hunger. Finally, she put down her fork and spoke.

"You know, a change of scenery wouldn't hurt you two at all. Now, Nova Scotia is vastly underrated. We were up there last year, stayed in a wonderful B&B. It was originally an inn, owned in the eighteen-fifties by the parents of the woman, Anna, who became famous in *The King and I.*"

"I thought she was English," I interrupted.

"So did I, but she was Canadian. And our room itself was once occupied by Oscar Wilde on one of his tours. Two enormous double beds so high there was a little stool beside each one to help you get in and out. And the bathroom was mammoth, with a tub bigger than Lake Erie. I had loads of fun pretending Lainey was a rubber ducky."

"Should I mention that little game and its source when I tell Cindy about this great vacation place?" I asked seriously.

"I wouldn't bother. Then we rented a car and drove out to the Acadian forest—the pines and the hemlocks are still murmuring. Then down to Fort Louisburg...we toured the old governor's mansion and there was a double-banked harpsichord—like an organ. I'd never seen one like it, and luck was with us: some woman happened to be there playing it. It was fabulous!"

"The whole thing sounds fabulous," I agreed. "But we are not on a fabulous budget at the moment."

"Yeah, them fancy bathrooms and fountains you're putting in don't come free," she mused. "Well, if you bought the gas, I could run you straight across to Halifax, save you something over an airline flight from Boston...in time *and* money."

"You're a sweetheart, but we couldn't do that. Not this time of year—you're too likely to miss a handful of money from real customers." I finished my beer, put some money on the bar and slid off the stool. "Gotta go rescue Fargo and pick up Wells. I've been headed for the cottage since mid-morning and keep making detours. Wells is doubtless on the phone to the SPCA as we speak."

"Well, think about it. We could make it mid-week, when I'm not as busy. Just let me know."

"Will do. Thanks for the offer." I patted her shoulder and left to pick up Fargo.

He was lying in the shade, looking longingly across the alley at a couple of gulls bobbing in the shallow edge-waters of the bay.

As I untied him from the anchor, I noticed two men sitting on the bench nearby. They had been deep in conversation, but quit talking when I came out, and watched me reclaim my dog. The skinny one smiled and nodded; the chubby one scowled at the interruption. So much for fat people always being jolly.

CHAPTER EIGHT

With the motor left running, and Fargo left in the car, I went inside to get Wells, hoping she was not installed under the bed in its geographic center. No, she sat unmoving beside her water dish, giving me an evil look. I checked it, and—mea culpa—it was empty. I checked Fargo's, two feet away and it was two-thirds full.

"I'm sorry, Lady Astor, that I forgot to fill your crystal water dish. But you could have tried Fargo's. It all comes from the same spout, so if you are dehydrated it is definitely your own fault."

She started to walk away, but I scooped her up and headed for the car, dumping her unceremoniously into the backseat, butting a protesting Fargo out of the driver's seat whence he had moved, and backing rapidly out of the driveway. I felt I was living surrounded by difficult divas…or, I should say, two difficult divas and one prickly baritone.

When we reached the cottage, Wells leaped from the car window and hightailed it up the hill to Aunt Mae's, where she was assured of her own private water bowl and food dish, both of which would immediately be filled and kept filled. Wells would weigh a good forty pounds if she lived with Aunt Mae. I kept Fargo on lead into the house, wanting to get the tape recorder off his collar before he tested its waterproof-to-one-hundred-feet claim.

That done, I was left in welcome solitude to take some chicken breasts out of the freezer and slop some marinade on them and splash some iced tea into a glass for me, first having lovingly filled both animals' water bowls. Finally, I left a message on the phone mail of the leading diva, that I was at the cottage and that dinner was under control and I was headed for the deck. I placed tea and tape recorder on the table, turned the recorder to *Play* and plopped into a chair, my feet propped on the deck railing…and waited…and waited.

After a rather frightening silence, there came the sound of a sort of slurpy clicking noise, which I at last identified as Fargo chewing the final bite of his hot dog. Then a car door slammed nearby and a noisy engine started. Finally, my young couple continued their conversation.

They had at last agreed to leave Provincetown early on Saturday morning, which would put them in Fairfield in time to pick up poor Madison, so he wouldn't be stuck for the whole weekend in confinement—nor would they have to pay not only for Saturday, but for Sunday as well. That settled, they began to discuss how to spend the evening…she leaning heavily toward the Poly-Cotton Club, he tending toward the Atlantic House.

Abruptly their conversation was interrupted by the overpowering sound of large quantities of paper being forcefully crumpled, with rather flat-tuned bells ringing in the background. What in the hell was that? I didn't recall any nearby sounds even vaguely resembling those. I stared at the recorder, as if it could explain.

Then Fargo came in from his swim and immediately clarified

all. He shook himself, and then began to scratch his neck and collar. If he had been wearing the recorder, sounds would have been magnified by it. His nails rasping on the leather would make the paper noise, and his jingling tags provided the bells. I had a whole new frame of reference to learn.

I smiled, amused at Fargo's various sound effects. But they did interrupt whatever conversation I was attempting to record, and some day, some conversation might be important and need to be captured in its entirety. Of course, the chewing noise was easily avoided, but the scratching was spontaneous. There must be some solution. I would think of something.

Out of the blue, a woman's shrill voice with a strong midwestern accent resonated in my ear. I was so startled I almost turned my chair over, jumping to my feet and looking all around for the voice's owner.

"Well, I'll tell you, Fred, I am *not* going to sit all afternoon in a stuffy bar smelling of beer and stale cigars because you didn't have the good sense to bring comfortable shoes."

"Pauline, the problem is not my shoes, we must have walked five damn miles a'ready. Just one cold beer won't hurt either of us. Might even improve your humor. Sure couldn't hurt it."

"Well, I'm telling you, Fred, just one and I mean just..."

The voice trailed off about the time I got my breath back and the lovebirds must have entered the Rat. But I am a trained investigator, and I figure out things like this. Obviously, during one of his collar scratches outside the Wharf Rat, Fargo managed to hit the *Receive* button and catch the touching dialogue between Fred and Pauline, doubtless two of the tourists we are annually so happy to see.

I found myself hoping Fred indeed rested his feet all afternoon with at least three beers, while Pauline plodded ever onward, collecting plastic bag after smiley-faced plastic bag of clever souvenirs and sticky, made-right-before-your-eyes saltwater taffy for the grandkids, the next-door neighbors, Fred's boss and Cousin Betty, who could never be pleased no matter how you tried.

But my handsome sports watch had still more clever tricks in its plastic case. Next I heard the voice of one of the Blues Brothers—coming or going—stop to pass the time of day with Fargo.

"Hi there, Fargo, won't they let you in, boy? Now I call that a cryin' shame. You got better manners than most of the people already in there. Well, you be good, and Alex will be back soon." Footfalls crunched on the gravel path but I couldn't determine the direction.

There had been a brief jingle of bells as the Blues Brother scratched Fargo's chin, and a continuous soft thump throughout the conversation as Fargo's tail wagged against the old anchor. I was getting pretty good at interpreting the stylish sport watch's ancillary sounds. And as I thought of it, I shouldn't have been surprised at Fargo changing the mode of the recorder. The buttons were small and close together. One good swipe with a paw and it could easily go from one function to another.

Still, I was unprepared for the next sound my new techno-toy belched forth across the cottage deck.

"Nice looking dog," a pleasant male voice remarked.

"Likely to take your hand off," a grumpy tenor replied.

"I doubt it, but I guess he could. That's a funny looking collar he's wearing."

"It's one of those electronic ones that keep the dog in his own yard. You know, it beeps real loud in his ear if he goes too near his boundary. Or I guess maybe you wouldn't know, being a city fella."

Our tenor sounded condescending. I wondered if these were the two silent men I encountered on my way out of the Wharf Rat. If they were, I'd bet that the tenor was the unfriendly chubby guy.

"Did Frank call?" Mr. Nice Guy asked.

"Yes. He'll be out in two weeks from today. Says he's been scoutin' and has the perfect place. And he says two weeks gives us plenty of time out here to do some scout work on our own—you know—to check schedules, busy times, whether they have a good sized staff, amount and weight of cargo we'll have. He wants a complete picture," The tenor finished importantly.

Nice Guy sighed heavily. "Oh, that's our good old nit-picking Frank. If he had his way there'd be a printed, illustrated book of instructions for every job we do…with a quiz at the end."

"Has it occurred to you," the tenor asked sarcastically, "that just possibly that's why every job we've done has been a success?"

Suddenly I knew them…I was sure of it! They had to be Cassie's Pittsburgh pirates…two of them anyway. One average looking, one rather fat and a missing one named Frank!

"Can it," Mr. Nice muttered. "Somebody coming out."

And I heard my own voice asking, "So, big boy, ready for a swim?" Followed by a click. Most likely me hitting the *Off* button as I gave Fargo a pat and freed him from the anchor. Followed by silence.

My God, I breathed. Maybe Harmon was going to prove right for once! That conversation did not have one reference to seafood, or a benefit lunch and dinner or a veterans group or their brand-new clubhouse back home in dear old East Burnt Elm Tree, Pennsylvania.

Maybe they really were going to meet up with one of our incoming fishing or "tourist" boats and pick up a big load of dope. And they might want to make sure the incoming boat did not carry a large enough crew, so that they had to worry about getting stiffed by them.

With only Cassie and the three passengers, they wouldn't especially need to know about weight and bulk of the "cargo." That's if they were sure of using Cassie's plane, but what if they were thinking they might have to try and get it all aboard the smaller Cessna? They might well have to leave at least one man behind to drive or fly home commercial. And if they did have to use the Cessna, they'd doubtless need to refuel at least once en route, so they'd want to make sure their cargo looked innocuous.

By damn, Harmon! I think you've done it!

But Cassie! Cassie would be a problem to them from the get-go. She would immediately realize that the "cargo" was not packed in coolers. And even if they *did* put it in coolers as a disguise, they would probably not be met by a refrigerated truck at the cornfield...if, indeed, that was even their destination. My joke to Mom about their flying to Florida—or anyplace else— might well have been more truth than fiction.

And Cassie. She would never accept a payoff. So at whatever obscure landing field they used, the plane would be quickly painted a new color and given fake registration numbers, and Cassie...Cassie would be dead.

CHAPTER NINE

My first thought was to dash back to the Rat. Just possibly they had gone in for a drink or something to eat, and might still be there. But I could hardly hold them there by my great good looks alone. I could yell for help from any local men who were in the bar, but what if someone—anyone—got hurt?

I had no legal right even to try to detain them verbally. They had done nothing wrong that I knew of. They were almost certainly conspiring to traffic in an illegal substance and possibly even to murder, and I had the tape to prove it. But I was not a cop with a badge and pistol allowing me to cuff them and take them in for questioning.

So, call police headquarters and hope Sonny would be there. He was not.

Nacho said he and Mitch were following some tip they had gotten on the recent hit-and-run, and she did not know when they would be back. She would have him call me. I bit my tongue and thanked her. I did not have the right to ask her to send out cops on my request unless someone was in imminent danger.

Shit. I put the old-fashioned phone back in its cradle on the bedside table and walked back through the kitchen, out onto the deck where Fargo lay contentedly, watching Wells serpentine through the reeds on a critter hunt. I wished my only problem were an empty water dish, with an alternate one at hand.

Damn Sonny! Why did he personally have to follow up the hit-and-run tip? He was the one who talked of how valuable Mitch had become, what a gifted detective he had become.

Surely Mitch could ask the necessary questions, look at the suspect's vehicle and decide whether or not to impound it, whether to check any persons who might prove the suspect was or was not the errant driver, whether he or she had been drinking, whether…oh, hell, *I* wasn't the one interviewing the suspect.

I dragged the gas grill out from under the shelter of the deck and into a level area of the yard and wiped it down. I washed a couple of potatoes to ready them for the little microwave oven we had bought for the cottage a couple of weeks back. Small though it was, it still took up about a third of the kitchen counter space, making me quite careful as I cut up a salad.

I still loved the cottage, but I was beginning to take its shortcomings seriously. I looked upon them as ongoing irritants rather than laughing at them as part of getting away from the workaday world. And I think Cindy was doing the same thing. She seemed very temperamental these days, and I rather imagine she would have said the same about me.

I hoped we would get back into the real house soon and would find the new bedroom, etc.—I refused to call it the Master Suite—all we had looked forward to. And I hoped we would both survive—both emotionally and financially—the furnishing thereof. One part of me wanted to buy a bed and call it quits for a while on the house, and have Cassie fly us to Halifax, where we would rent a car and get lost for a couple of weeks. But I had the feeling Cindy would either collapse or strangle me if I even suggested that alternative.

And here was my opportunity to find out if I dared. I heard her car…no, I heard two cars. Now what? I hurried to the living room window; it was Sonny and the two of them were looking at something in Aunt Mae's budding garden. Good, it gave me a chance to get another chicken breast into the micro a minute to thaw it and then into the marinade. I washed another potato and put it with the others. The salad would do for three. Bingo!

I was innocently putting out the animals' evening food when they came in.

"Hi, darling!" Cindy gave me a hug and a kiss. "Guess who I found loitering along the way?"

"He looks suspicious to me," I replied.

"He is suspicious," Sonny stated with a phony grin. "These days he seems to get more calls from his sister than he does from Harmon. That is enough to make anybody suspicious. What's up?"

"Nothing that won't wait until we sit down and enjoy what's left of the sun. What are you drinking?"

Sonny opted for beer, Cindy for a scotch and soda, me for a bourbon highball. I played bartender while Cindy changed clothes and Sonny played with Fargo. We soon gathered on the deck, and I asked Sonny if his anonymous tip regarding the hit-and-run had proven fruitful. I wanted him relaxed before I brought up Cassie's pirates. His opening crack about the phone calls hadn't sounded entirely joking.

"Yes, I think it is the vehicle," he said. "Just as our anonymous phone call told us, we found it on a side street in Orleans. It has front-end damage, with what looks like blood and some fibers caught in the headlight…could be from Mr. Alves' clothing. We'll know in a day or so."

"Did you find the owner?" Cindy sipped her drink and pronounced it just right.

"Yes, and there's no joy there. He lives in Eastham and swears the car was stolen. But he didn't report it until yesterday, which is strange at best. We're trying to verify his whereabouts at the time of the accident."

"How's Mr. Alves? Have you heard?" I rescued my cigarettes from Sonny's side of the table and lit one.

"Yeah. I was just at the clinic. Dr. Gloetzner says the old fellow still thinks he's Napoleon, but he did manage to ask where he was and why he was there. So I guess there's hope."

"I'm glad, he's a nice old codger. His wife must be frantic."

"You're not far wrong," he admitted. "But their daughter is here from Worcester, so at least she has someone with her. Look, Alex, I've got to get going. Want to tell me why Nacho said you sounded a little frantic yourself this afternoon?"

"Yes, but why don't you stay for dinner? We have plenty."

"That sounds like a winner. I guess I'd better start up the grill, then." When there was a grill in sight, nobody cooked but Sonny.

We got ourselves rearranged and I showed Sonny and Cindy my new toy. When I told Sonny I had a duplicate for him, he gave me that big brother look and simpered, "Oh, thank you ever so!"

I told the two of them of my experiment downtown with the young couple and my inadvertent recording at the Rat. I had set it to start with Fred and Pauline to make him laugh, and he did, along with Cindy.

Then the Blues Brother came on and again he was amused. "That's Bert McMichaels," he chortled. "I'll have to tell him to watch what he says around Fargo."

I explained the two men I had passed on leaving the Rat and what had been picked up while I had been inside. Then I hit *Play* again.

The tape ended, and I turned it off triumphantly.

"There! Doesn't that prove Harmon's initial guess? Those men are no more staging a charitable clambake than I am."

"It doesn't prove a damn thing. I swear you get more *like* Harmon by the day. Every person who stops someone to ask directions is setting up a million dollar dope trade." He stood and walked out to put the chicken on the grill.

Cindy went inside to finish dinner. She was obviously staying out of this.

Sonny returned, freshened my drink, got himself another beer and came back out.

"Alex," he spoke carefully and softly. "I know you have been under stress lately, but you really are getting a little far out. You can't reasonably expect me to arrest two men just because I don't quite understand a conversation you shouldn't have taped in the first place. Think about that young couple you taped at first. You said they wanted to get home and get Madison out of some lock-up. We assume Madison is a dog or cat, but what if he is their three-year-old son, locked in a cage under the care of a twelve-year-old, while they have a getaway weekend? Believe me, it has happened."

"Everybody was sitting on some sort of public bench," I argued. "None of them had a reasonable expectation of privacy. And the pirates didn't mention seafood or their club or vets or anything bearing on what they told Cassie. I tell you, Sonny, they are dangerous phonies."

"I gotta turn the chicken. Right back." He loped across the lawn, flipped the meat and came back. "Okay. Look at what they probably meant. They want to make sure the suppliers will have enough clams and lobsters and whatever to fill their order, even though demand is getting heavy here in town. Do they have trucks available to go to the airport? Do they have enough employees to catch, process, pack and deliver it to Cassie at a given hour? Surely Cassie will need to know the approximate weight in order to figure her fuel situation, and size so she will know how to balance them in the plane. So Frank is a nitpicker, which may account for their mutual success on various jobs. What job? Installing vinyl siding? Painting a house? Fixing a car? Installing a furnace? Come on, Sis, the list is endless."

"Well, I suppose it could go either way," I admitted. "But think of Cassie. If it *is* dope, they've got to kill her somewhere along the way even if they just push her out over Lake Erie."

"And we can't let that happen," he placated. "If she gets a

definite time and date from these guys, I will personally inspect every cooler to make sure it holds nothing more than tomorrow's dinner. Okay?"

"I guess." I sighed. "But for Cassie's safety can't you have someone keep an eye on them?"

"My dear sister, I do not have the entire NYPD at my command. First I would have to assign people to find them, if they could, then use at least five people to tail them, et cetera. In the meantime restaurants could be robbed and old ladies mugged...all because of Harmon's imagination and your Star Wars gizmo. C'mon, let's eat."

"Sonny." Cindy had dealt herself back into the game. "Am I taking up too much of your time—and budget—with this stalker of mine? Apparently he is proving to be harmless." Her voice quivered a bit. "If he even exists. Maybe you should just send Edgar on home."

Sonny—always gentle with Cindy—reached across the table to pat her hand. "You let me worry about when to send Edgar home. Right now he's doing what should be done."

We all agreed that dinner was very good, but somehow none of us seemed terribly hungry.

Sonny didn't linger after dinner. I don't know if it was business or pleasure...or just a desire to get away from his bothersome sister and her bothersome friend. Cindy and I cleared up the deck and moved inside, leaving the aloof half-moon to make its chill, still progression across the pond. Cindy must have started the wood stove earlier, for the small living room felt warm and friendly. She came in bearing a tray with coffee and two small glasses of brandy—the snifters were at the house.

"I figured we might enjoy this with a little light conversation." She smiled. "We have a choice of something over one hundred TV stations—and nothing to watch. I'm sick of meerkats— their problems are all too human. I am not smarter than a fifth grader—we didn't have all that science stuff in fifth grade, did we? The only thing worse than *American Idol* is *Don't Forget the Lyrics*.

In the cops 'n robber shows they're either busy screwing each other—one way or another—or lying on the floor bleeding. The sitcoms make the *I Love Lucy* reruns seem deeply intellectual. And the nature shows are all too depressing…the more so because I know it's all true. So talk to me, baby."

"Gladly. I only wish I had taped your little speech and sent it to every TV network. It's a scathing commentary, and like your nature programs, all too true. First, my love, a question."

I sipped my brandy and mentally snuggled in its warmth. Then I asked, "Has everybody you know been recommending that we should take a nice, long vacation…and soon?"

"Just about." She laughed slightly. "Are we in that bad a shape? Do we need one of those old rest cures my grandma used to talk about? I think rest cure was a nice way of spending a couple of weeks in a pseudomental hospital. You figure that would help? Brisk walks before breakfast, calisthenics before luncheon, inspirational reading and a glass of warm milk and one small cookie at bedtime?"

"We're probably not there yet, but it's close. Seriously, I do think we need a break." I steepled my fingers in front of my mouth for a second. "Nova Scotia sounds fabulous. But we'd really have to watch our pennies."

"New York?"

"Hell, we could *buy* Nova Scotia for a week in New York."

"Well," she continued. "Personally I feel a little Vermonted-out for a while."

I nodded agreement. "Same with Maine. It's kind of like camping out in the backyard."

"Yes." She sounded discouraged and then brightened. "Then let me float this past you. Close your eyes and listen."

I did as I was told.

"Visualize tall mountains, but not the harsh Rocky-mountain type. Softer, gentler ones with moss to lie on beside a small stream, with tall pines and oaks standing guard. In the distance the mountains seem to blur a little, as if a light, fragrant smoke drifts between them. Then you realize the fragrance is closer, and the whole mountainside has a pink cast from blossoming mountain laurel and rhododendron. Far up the stream you may luck out and see a mama bear teaching her cubs to fish. And lower down is a beaver dam. When you get anywhere near they slap their tails like a rifle shot and all disappear. Below the dam in the white water, otters play—that seems to be all they do, all day long. And in a nearby meadow polka dotted with yellow blooms, fox kits play-fight with mama serving as referee."

I felt myself drifting as she continued.

"At the foot of the mountain is a sizeable lake where boats are limited to sails or small electric trolling motors, slow and barely audible. The lake is loaded with various bass and bluegill. The inn there will even clean and cook your own catch for your dinner. And at the top of the mountain is a small icy tarn, loaded with crappie that are the most tender, sweetest fish you ever tasted, and water so clear that when you look into it, you aren't sure whether the clouds are above you or beneath. I'm sure you'll want to make the hike up to it." She gave me a sweet, totally sarcastic smile.

"And," she added, "you hear the clop of horseshoes and look up to see riders on tall mounts with kind eyes and long, delicate legs, moving at a rapid, even pace they can continue for hours with no strain on them or you. Most comfortable ride in the world. Give 'em an apple and they're yours for life. They're Tennessee Walking Horses."

"My God," I breathed. "Cindy, are you suggesting suicide because you've made reservations for us in heaven?"

"Not quite." I heard her pouring more coffee and opened my eyes, rubbing them and peering between my fingers like a child who has had a dream too good to be true.

She spoke briskly now. "Remember my cousin Ken and his wife Frances?"

"Yeah, I met them at your parents' house once. He was something in politics and she was something in horses. Nice people, I thought."

"You thought right. He's in the Tennessee Legislature—

probably governor in the next election. And between you and me, I think the two of them are practicing a fancy waltz for the Presidential Inaugural Ball down the road a piece."

"Wow!" I sat up straight. "He asked me for a signed print of the picture of Fargo on the beach, leaping for a seagull. I sent it to him. You think he might hang it in the Oval Office?"

"No. But it may be in his log cabin."

"He's got a log cabin? He's bound to be elected. These guys with a condo in Aspen, and a mansion at Westhampton, and a modernistic abortion at Malibu...they're a dime a dozen. Ain't nobody got a log cabin no more! Where is it?"

"It's in Tennessee, you idiot. He's smart enough to keep that local boy image—just a simple mountaineer. It's near Beulaland."

"Beulaland. Is that a town or the Promised Land?" I asked.

"Sort of both. The nearest real town is Elizabethton."

"Elizabethton, er...that's exactly...where?"

"It makes kind of a triangle between Kingsport and Johnson City." She was grinning openly at my discomfort.

"Kingsport, of course! Oh, yes, on the...uh, river! I've got it now."

"Sure you do, darling. When you drag out a map tomorrow, find Knoxville and go kind of northeast."

I didn't deign to answer that. And her thoughts fortunately took another tack.

"What I'm trying to get to is this: Ken and Frances have been after me for ages to come down and use the cabin—now that he's in Nashville so much, they rarely use it except in July and August, but they hate to see it just sit there empty. And their two kids are not quite old enough to let them go there alone. I don't think I've been there in almost fifteen years, but it's unforgettably beautiful and peaceful and fun in a bucolic sort of way. Should I call Ken and see if it's not in use for a week or so?"

I got up and returned with the phone. "Here. Call."

"Get my address book out of my purse while you're up, please." I was delighted to comply.

It was all settled in about two minutes. We would vacation in Tennessee.

After that it turned into a lengthy family gossip session and I took the animals out, trying not to yell *hot damn!* loud enough to startle the neighbors.

We finally got to bed, feeling as if large weights had been removed. Cindy struck a seductive pose.

"If we're going into the woods, I'll have to learn to be foxy."

I put my arms around her. "Get a load of my bear hug."

"I'm a big mouth bass; now where should I nibble?"

We carried on this rustic silliness into more and more graphic suggestions and the obvious conclusion.

Personally, I think it was a lot more fun than pretending Cindy was a rubber ducky in the bathtub.

CHAPTER TEN

Our getaway would have been a credit in speed to Scarface Al Capone with Elliot Ness in hot pursuit.

Cindy got Choate Ellis's hearty permission to take two weeks off, and did everything ahead of time at work that could possibly be done in three days. And in the evenings, of course, she house-cleaned. "So we won't come home to a mess." I wondered if she had looked at the yard recently. It was my firm contention that Hadrian's Wall had been a simpler endeavor.

I got Harvey Weinberg to cover my accounts and informed my insurance companies of that fact. I dropped off a bunch of clothes for our dry cleaner's offer of *Special 24Hour Service*. They lived up to their ad, but it was the biggest scalping party since the Mohawks calmed down. We had decided to take Fargo, and the vet provided a booklet listing motels that accepted pets. Wells would go to Aunt Mae's the night before we left, to begin a posh vacation of her own.

Cassie had an absolute library of maps and helped me plot our course. We wanted to avoid all large cities if possible; we wanted the most direct route available, but we wanted some of the lovely scenery we had been told lay along the way.

At first I thought it worked out rather well. We would take the Massachusetts Turnpike to its end, clip off a small corner of New York state, drop down to Scranton and pick up Interstate 81. From there we just stayed on I-81 in a more or less straight south-westerly shot across Pennsylvania, took a tiny bite out of Maryland and West Virginia, crossed the suddenly enormous-looking State of Virginia…and were in Tennessee.

Then I examined the length of the route Cassie had highlighted on the map, and looked up at her in considerable dismay.

"We thought we could make this in two days' driving. This looks more like a week," I groaned.

"Sure you don't want me to fly you down? You can always rent a car, or maybe a pickup, at whatever airport we may find down there. Lit or unlit."

"Plowed or unplowed is more likely. Anyway, we both want to see the country. I've never been in that part of the world. The last time Cindy was there she was about fifteen, and her father was still teaching at University of Chattanooga, so it was a fairly easy day's drive—from the other direction. And if we fly, Fargo can't go. He's scared of airplanes, as you know."

"Yeah." She pulled out a pair of calipers and walked them from Ptown to Elizabethton. "Close to a thousand miles. You can make it in two days if you don't linger. You'll be over the worst of it when you clear Scranton."

"Fine. That just leaves most of the Appalachian chain to negotiate, and probably cows and pigs all over the road," I grumbled.

Cassie laughed. "Interstates are not designed to have steep grades or sharp curves…that's both their beauty and their eventual boredom. You may see the occasional deer or little critter, but I doubt you'll get cows and piggies in the road until you get off of I-81 and over to...what was the name again?"

"Beulaland, and if you laugh I'll clock you. And don't ask me again if I know what a big patch of land called Kettlefoot Wild Animal Management Area means—although you might think of retiring there."

I pushed my coffee mug toward her. "Get me a beer. What the hell has Cindy gotten us into?"

Cindy had gotten us into a vertical position at approximately three thirty a.m. We were hoping to leave a half hour later. Wells had been taken to Aunt Mae's the night before. I had loaded Cindy's two suitcases and my one into my car trunk while she was gone. I had also loaded dog food, doggy blanket and two favorite doggy toys plus a tennis ball.

This morning I had—I hoped—concluded the loading process. Our two gym bags holding cosmetics and other small necessities were now in the trunk.

In the car proper was a jug of water for Fargo, a small cooler holding ice and fruit and soft drinks for us, a bag of cookies for us and a smaller bag of cookies for Fargo. He wasn't certain he was going, so he sat in the driver's seat to make sure.

Mom would be over later to clean out the fridge.

Cindy concentrated on her morning health cereal while I washed down two of yesterday's croissants with a cup of coffee. We cleaned up the kitchen and left. The Orrick crew would presumably lock up every night.

I took the first driving shift, expecting some excited commentary from Cindy along the way and perhaps some nuzzles and tail wags from Fargo in the backseat. It didn't work quite that way.

Just before we left I had booted Fargo over to the front passenger's seat, assuming Cindy would see to getting him out and into the back. Instead, she climbed into the backseat herself with a cheery, "Okay, darling, up, up and away! Let me know when you want to swap driving. Anytime, love." She thereby stretched across the seat, turned on the little overhead light and opened the morning paper. Well, she was on vacation.

It was, of course, still dark, but I knew every inch of Route 6. Traffic was light at that hour and as Cassie had recommended, I didn't linger. After a few miles of staring at darkened trees and buildings, Fargo had curled up beside me and began to snore lightly. Cindy had switched off the little backseat light and let the paper fall across her chest. Maybe she was snoring lightly too. I was beginning to get that I-am-the-last-person-in-the-world feeling.

It began to get light, turning from black to an ever-lightening gray, finally tinged with pink. It wasn't a bad time to be alone. You felt not only relieved, but also triumphant that you had again achieved victory over the forces of the evil blackness and lived to fight another day.

I yawned and stretched, although I wasn't sleepy; I was just greeting the day. But I awoke my passengers. Fargo mimicked my stretch and yawn and resumed looking for something of interest.

The other felt guilty and began apologizing, but I was generous.

"Vacation means never having to say, 'I'm sorry I fell asleep,'" I forgave my penitent partner.

"You're a love. Do you want me to drive? Where are we?"

"I'm fine. We're coming up on the Sagamore Bridge. It's still early and a little foggy down low along the canal. This is when I dream I may look down and see FDR in the stern of the old presidential yacht, wearing a big straw hat and holding a fishing rod."

"What a wonderful image! Have you ever seen it?"

"Once or twice, when it was thick fog I think I got a glimpse. Apparently he really used to come through the canal often. The canal was one of the feats of his administration. I think perhaps somewhere he is still proud of it."

"I should think he would be. I shall look closely as we cross."

"Alex. Sweetheart. Are you awake?"

"More or less." I had been slouched in the front seat, not exactly asleep, but far away somewhere. I straightened and rolled my head around to get the neck muscles back in line. "What's up?"

"We've been making really good time. If we detoured about twenty miles east, we'd be in Pennsylvania Dutch territory. Maybe we could find a restaurant that serves some of their wonderful food. The turnoff is coming up."

"Take it."

Fifteen minutes later we were in a clean little town, dotted with the famous black buggies, pulled by a single muscular horse, reins handled by a black-clad man with a flat black hat, or perhaps by a woman in a long gray gown, with a hat looking to me like an old-fashioned nightcap.

We stopped in front of a small park. While I took Fargo for a brief run, Cindy asked someone about a restaurant and was referred to the Family Kitchen.

We were seated at a table for six, with four places already taken. We introduced ourselves and began the rather forced conversation of strangers thrown together by chance. We exchanged information regarding hometowns. We spoke of destinations. Just as we were getting to the weather, large platters were placed on the table by rather pretty young women in gray uniforms that came just below their knees and had spotless high white collars, with white cuffs just below the elbow. 1930's design, I was sure, and still worn by these "plain" young people.

The largest platter held tender roast beef with gravy. Fried chicken was piled high on another. Ham with a honey sauce actually came with a little fat around the edges, and the slices were not even. Good grief! It had not been spiral cut! And it actually tasted like…real ham!

There were sweet potatoes and white potatoes, spinach and red cabbage. Covered baskets held biscuits and cornbread. After I thought I couldn't eat another bite for a week, here came the applesauce cake and shoo-fly pie—which even Cindy had to try. Conversation collapsed under the largesse. Strong coffee got us all moving again, but with difficulty.

I drove, with a tape of *The 1812 Overture* blasting from the speakers and strong hot coffee in a cup in the dashboard rack, poured from a newly filled thermos. We had asked about a doggy bag and they had given us a meal for a tiger. In the backseat Fargo burped. And half his meal was still in the cooler. I burped, which did not surprise me. Cindy burped, which did.

The motel that night was a motel...period. I didn't even remember the name of the town it was in.

But it could have been on any major highway in the contiguous United States. Pseudobrick and clapboard on the outside, pseudohominess on the inside. It was clean, comfortable and utterly forgettable. There was a restaurant attached, with waitresses in the more familiar brightly colored uniforms with short skirts and sleeves. They served a completely forgettable meal. I momentarily considered dipping into Fargo's doggie bag, but figured it wouldn't be fair. We walked the dog, fell into bed and all three fell asleep over some forgettable TV.

We found ourselves in the Shenandoah Valley and were enthralled. Surrounded by protective mountains, the valley was somewhat warmer than the nearby areas. Already it was lush with growing crops. Comfortable farmhouses and the occasional mansion flashed by. Well-kept lawns with early flowers and blooming shrubs were the norm.

Suddenly Cindy tapped my arm and said, "Look."

I did, at a tall, blackened chimney standing alone in the midst of an overgrown, weed-filled yard, surrounded by unmortared low stone walls. No one was behind me and I slowed the car and pulled over.

"I think solitary old chimneys and their fireplaces are so lonely and sad." Her lovely eyes clouded slightly with a prelude to tears. "They seem to be reaching up, begging God please to bring back their house or barn…they provided warmth, perhaps meals were cooked on their grill. Babies were born beside them and the old died in warm, loving comfort in front of them. And now they stand alone, bereft and guarding nothing, no warmth left in them. Useless."

I had no answer to that, but anyway, Cindy had another thought.

"Do you think that one is left from the Civil War? Perhaps someone deliberately has left it there as a sort of reminder of what Sheridan did to this beautiful land?"

"I suppose it could be." I shrugged dubiously. "What happened to this valley is a shame. But whether you agree or not, Sheridan said the fastest way to end the war was to destroy southern crops. If they couldn't feed their army, it couldn't fight. He said he was actually saving lives."

"There may be a valid point in there somewhere, but burning families out of their homes isn't just burning crops. And did you know that members of Sheridan's own staff wanted him relieved as being insane? They said he acted like a maniac anytime he was involved in killing and destruction. He loved it. But Lincoln and Grant said he was indispensable. How do you like them apples?"

"I don't," I shook my head. "But Lincoln and Grant wouldn't listen to me either. I said crops: yes, houses: no."

"Idiot!" Her mouth tightened.

But then, honest little scholar that she was, she muttered to herself, "Of course, they said the same thing about Patton."

I turned my head away until I got control of the smile.

And then we were in the mountains. They were everywhere. If we were at a high altitude we could see them lined up as far as the eye could see, like giant ocean waves suddenly frozen in time. If the road took us lower they towered above us, seeming to lean a little away from us, to allow us safe passage. The mountain laurel flirted, pink and lively in the breeze and the larger, deeper toned rhododendron bobbed and nodded in matronly greeting.

The big trees were not yet fully leaved, but were recognizable. Oak, maple, pine, hickory, dogwood, others I did not know.

A small brown critter running right in front of the car brought me to reality with a jerk. Automatically I hit the brakes and cut to the right. The rabbit—I had ID'd it by now—finished its frantic run across the highway safely and disappeared into underbrush. But a much larger creature careered out of the forest, and only its desperate scratching, clawing, twisting one-eighty allowed it to miss running full tilt into the right side of the now unmoving car. It gathered itself and trotted shakily back into the woods.

Feeling pretty shaky myself, I leaned my arms and head on the steering wheel. I was almost crying in relief. Cindy was half-out the passenger door, looking for casualties. Fargo was barking loudly and irritably for having been dumped off the backseat and on to various coolers and grocery bags.

"Hush, Fargo!" Cindy ordered. "Alex, are you all right? Are the rabbit and that big dog all right? Should we follow them and make sure?"

"I'm okay, or I will be in a minute. The rabbit is out of breath but grateful to be off the luncheon menu. The big dog is a coyote who is, like me, simply recovering from his considerable scare. We'd never catch up with him, anyway."

"A coyote? I'll be darned."

"Yeah." I put the car in gear and pulled back onto the highway. The Appalachians were not all pink blossoms and stately green trees.

Finally, finally! We saw the sign. "Welcome to Tennessee." I had begun to think we were a four-wheeled flying Dutchman, doomed forever to traverse an endless Virginia. Already I felt less tired. Cindy took the wheel, however, in the hopes she might have retained some teenage recollection of the local roads.

We left Interstate 81 for a state road, left that for a county road, left that for an unmarked asphalt road that could have used a little TLC. We passed through a small two-street town, marked by a slanting sign informing us we had entered Beulaland,

Population 1237. I could not believe it was real.

Cindy slowed the car to a crawling twenty miles an hour. After the speeds we had previously been going, I felt I could get out and push the vehicle faster. My feelings must have showed.

Cindy laughed and said, "Can't help it. Speed trap. Always has been for any pesky furriners—and a furriner is anybody from farther away than Elizabethton. Look subtly to your right, a sheriff's car should be waiting behind the gas station. Or it used to be."

It still was.

Even at our snail's pace we had passed through the town. About a half mile farther I saw a bunch of big mailboxes lined up along the road next to a turnoff onto a gravel road.

"Hey, look!" Cindy pointed. "There's Ken's mailbox, and I reckon that there is his road. Yup! Now all we have to do is go on down this road to the Bromfield Inn and get the keys. Darling girl, we have *made it!*"

CHAPTER ELEVEN

We turned and went through a large ornate gate with the words "Bromfield Inn, 1884" forming the top of the wrought iron span. Just inside was a neatly painted sign reading "Welcome to the Bromfield Inn and Country Club. Please drive slowly." So we did...past what looked like a three-hole chip and putt golf course, then a double terrace with tables and umbrellas, ending beside a sizeable lake.

A couple of tables were occupied. From behind the hotel itself I heard the *thonk* of tennis balls. Two small kids played in some sand that bordered the water to form a small man-made beach. A girl of maybe fourteen lay propped on her elbow in the sand, watching the kids. Three sailboats cruised the lake, along with several small boats that had to be motor-powered, although I could not hear them. It made a nice postcard scene.

We pulled up in front of the prestigious three-story shingled building, complete with veranda and comfortable chairs. Immediately a young man stood beside Cindy's window.

"Good afternoon and welcome to Bromfield. My name is Jerry. May I park your car for you?"

Cindy hesitated. "I don't know that you need to bother, Jerry. I just have to run in and pick up something."

Jerry cocked his head, surveying the rather messy interior, the car-weary dog and the two of us who were a bit messy also.

"Are you two ladies by any chance headed for Mr. Willingham's cabin?" At our nods, he continued. "I know our owner, Mr. Bromfield, wants to welcome you. Maybe I could just pull the car over there where it's handy, and maybe this nice doggy would like a little stroll by the water."

They sure loved the word *welcome* here at Bromfield's, but his offer to walk Fargo sold me. "Fine," I said. "We'll do it your way."

We walked into the elegant lobby with its marble floor and impressive chandelier, and I assume Cindy felt as scruffy as I did. A young lady at the registration desk greeted us with a professional smile. "Welcome to Bromfield. May I help you?"

"I'm Cindy Hart, Ken Willingham's cousin. I believe he left an envelope for me."

"Indeed he did." The receptionist turned to a bank of cubby holes behind her and extricated a manila envelope with Cindy's name on it.

As she took it, she thanked the clerk and turned to me. "We're in. One more mile to the cabin and we are out of that car for at least twenty-four hours."

"Oh, please," the clerk sounded distressed. "Don't leave quite yet. Mr. Bromfield wants to meet you both. He's coming right down and asked that you wait in the bar."

"Oh, of course. We'd be delighted." Cindy had on her social voice. I don't know where she found it. I could feel fatigue suddenly settling on my neck and shoulders like a giant pouting toad.

We followed the clerk's pointing finger into the large room with a beautiful curving mahogany bar and comfortably sized red leather barstools with black backs and arms, and a dozen matching tables. We looked at each other and headed for the bar. A table looked more like you were going to set and stay a spell and I hoped we'uns would be movin' shawtly. I was getting into my mountaineer mode. I also might just have been overtired.

"Good afternoon, Ms. Hart, Ms. Peres." The bartender smiled as he placed napkins in front of us. "Welcome to Bromfield, my name is Joe. And what is your pleasure?"

Well, at least I could remember his name. I just had to think of Joe at the shabby old Wharf Rat, for which I felt a sudden wistful pang. And I wondered how this Joe knew our names...probably a fast phone call from the receptionist. One more "welcome," though, and I might say something I'd regret.

"Do you serve anything but beer?" Cindy was asking. I wondered what she thought all those bottles along the mirrored wall held, cleaning fluid?

"Oh, yes, ma'am," Joe reassured her. "The county is dry except for beer, but we are a private club and can serve drinks and wine. Mr. Bromfield says you are his guests this afternoon. And if either of you wish to use any of our services or facilities later on, all you have to do then is sign the tab. It will go to Mr. Willingham's account. Do order whatever you please."

Cindy ordered a Cosmo; I opted for a bourbon old-fashioned. Nothing had ever tasted better. Joe moved away, having the good sense to let us recuperate in silence.

After a sip or two, I looked around me to note our fellow customers. There weren't many in this still off-season weekday afternoon. A woman and two men at one table, an elderly woman at another, a tough-looking man at the end of the bar, and standing at the other end of the bar, a young man in jeans and T-shirt, whose gaze drifted from Cindy to me and back again.

He looked to be about eighteen, with unruly blond hair and a sweet face. His clothes were clean, but damp in spots, and at his feet was a canvas bag that seemed to be leaking something that looked like water. I looked at him more closely, and his expression made me think he might be slightly mentally challenged.

When I caught his eye, I spoke. "Hi, young man, I'm Alex. Can I help you with something?"

He blushed and grinned. "Oh, no ma'am. I am sorry if I was staring but you must be Mr. and Miz Willingham's cousins, and I wanted to tell my mom you're here, and how pretty you both are. And Jerry says that big black dog is yours. He's pretty, too."

I laughed. "He may be the prettiest of all. His name is Fargo. Mine is Alex, and the other lady's is Cindy. She's the Willingham cousin. I'm a friend...no relative, though. What's your name?"

Before he could answer, a short, pudgy man from the table behind us jumped up and came toward us, calling out, "Jesus X. Christ, Marbles, you've done it again! You're bothering the ladies and that bag full of fish is leaking all over the floor."

As he approached, I could hardly keep from laughing at his attire: a violently vivid green blazer, lighter green pants, a bright yellow collarless shirt and sneakers that looked like the same brand as mine, but a lot cleaner. He was still muttering to himself, when Cindy announced which side she had chosen in ringing tones.

"The young man was not bothering us at all. Unless you are an employee, the small leak is not your worry, and if you *are* an employee, why don't you wipe it up?"

A flash of anger crossed his face, quickly replaced by a wide and contagious grin.

"Now, forgive me ma'am, I just didn't want anyone to slip and fall. Allow me to welcome you ladies to beautiful Beulaland. I know you're going to love our countryside, and you'll certainly enjoy your accommodations. In fact, after a day or two, you'll be begging me to put a binder on one of the condos I'm going to build up on Crooked Creek Mountain, so you can enjoy it year-round. I understand you are Ken Willingham's cousin. Ken and I are the best of friends, so you just call on me if you need the tiniest thing." He waved a business card in our direction. Neither of us moved to take it, so he placed it on the bar.

The young man got back into the conversation. "It's just water. Joe, hand me a bar towel and I'll mop it up."

"Don't worry about it, Tommy, I've already called housekeeping. But you better get those fish out to the kitchen and ready for dinner." Joe turned and explained to us. "Tommy makes sure when our menus advertise fresh-caught fish that we're telling the truth. He catches them and brings them in every afternoon."

"I see, that's a very good policy," I said. "So your name is Tommy...much nicer than Marbles, I think."

Once again the black look came and swiftly left the man in green, and I noticed a sardonic smirk on the fellow at the end of the bar. "Oh, I just tease him that his head is full of marbles, it don't mean anything. We're family."

Cindy sipped her Cosmo and looked innocent. "Well, now we know Marbles is really Tommy, really who are you?"

"My full name is Carter Branch Redford, but everybody calls me Branch. Now please do remember that I'm just friendly ol' Branch, at your service, ma'am."

Cindy placed her index finger on her chin and pulled her mouth slightly open. "Oh, I can't be sure. I'm just a silly ol' female. But if I forget Branch, I can probably remember Twig."

"Well, now, while I do hope you remember Branch, Ah'm happy to answer any lovely lady."

A roar of laughter had gone up from Joe and the two people left at the table. If I knew small towns, half the people in beautiful Beulaland would be calling Branch Redford Twig by tomorrow. A middle-aged man made his way toward us, hand outstretched and still chuckling at Cindy's riposte.

"I'm Carl Bromfield, you must be Cindy and Alex." He introduced us to the woman at the table, "Lou Jackson, one of our two dedicated vets in town, who's had a rough afternoon with a foal who got herself headed the wrong way in the birth canal."

"And Clay Rodman, who was afraid he was going to lose one of his beloved—not to mention valuable—mares. And, of course, you seem to have met Twi—er, Branch Redford." I noted that the tough guy was not introduced.

Bromfield turned to where Tommy still stood, taking it all in. "And I think you've met Tommy Blackstone. Son, you'd better get those fish out to the kitchen. And when you get home ask your mother to call me, I need vegetables for the weekend."

"Oh, yes sir. Right now. And have Mom call you." He pulled a booklet and pencil from his shirt pocket and made a note. If I was right about his handicap, he was dealing with it well.

Bromfield ordered a round of drinks for everyone, and we moved over to the table with the others, except for Branch, who claimed an important appointment, and the rough character, who left—I thought—with Branch. I personally was not sorry to see them go. The vet and her client seemed pleasant, but fatigue was winning. In a short while we made our farewells, and I could tell even Cindy was struggling to be gracious. We collected Fargo and gave Jerry a tip that made him smile and invite Fargo to return anytime.

The gravel road indeed led to Ken's and Frances' cabin. When we pulled into the parking area we saw that a dusty red pickup was already there. We looked at each other with dismay at the thought of more people and slowly climbed to the front deck.

A middle-aged woman packed into slacks that matched her truck came out of the house and across the deck.

"Ah, good. I was hoping you might get here before I left. I'm Florence Fouts—ha-ha, jack of all trades I guess you'd say. The beds are all made up and towels are out.

"I got you some coffee and bread and eggs, all that kind of stuff. Also some hamburger—it's Black Angus, raised right down the road, can't be beat. And a piece of ham—from over Oaktown way. Acorn fed, the best around. I'll be back on Friday to straighten up and change the linens. You need anything bought at the store, call me by Thursday. Number's on the kitchen corkboard. Good day to you."

She was gone before I could ask her what we owed her for the groceries. Well, there was always Friday.

The cabin was pretty typical from the outside. There was a generous deck attached to a sizable building of dark logs interspersed with yellowish gray mortar and topped with a red brick chimney. The view was marvelous. Along the back and side of the house a frisky stream about twenty feet wide splashed its way down toward the foot of the mountain, where I lost it among the trees. I had the feeling it emptied into Bromfield Lake, sparkling in the distance.

The interior did not meet expectations. There was no sagging couch covered by an Indian blanket, no bearskin rug leering at us, not a single deer head moulting over the fireplace. The kitchen was not primitive and conducive to paper plates and pizza dinners. The bathrooms held no rusty tubs without showers. And when we peered into the bedrooms, not a single bunk bed peered back.

The kitchen had an up-to-date stove complete with grill, a large refrigerator freezer and a gleaming dishwasher. The two baths—one upstairs and one down—had tubs with showers and—honest—heated towel racks and bidets. We stared at each other, and finally Cindy said. "Well, I'll call Orrick. It may not be too late."

The master bedroom had a queen-size bed. Upstairs, the kids' rooms each had twin beds, as did what was obviously a guest room. The living room and the dining area were tastefully and comfortably furnished in traditional style. For a log cabin, it wasn't too shabby.

I looked at Cindy and said, "Nap?"

"Oh, thank God. I was afraid you were going to say, 'hike.'"

She flicked back the bedspread and Fargo leaped into the middle of the bed, stretching all four legs as far as he could. Look, Ma, no chintzy car seats. We arranged ourselves on either side of him.

I was awakened by a low growl from Fargo, as if he weren't sure whether to bark or forget it. It was very nearly dark; I could just about make out the furniture in the unfamiliar room. But the windows were all open, and I thought I heard voices talking quietly on the deck.

I turned to Cindy, who was stirring. I whispered, "Be very quiet, honey, I think someone is on the deck. Fargo, you be quiet, too." He rumbled deep in his chest but didn't bark.

I had fallen asleep with my clothes on, so I simply swung out of bed and stood up in my sock feet, collared Fargo and started for the deck. Passing by the living room fireplace, I acquired a small shovel. It was the first thing I touched, and I didn't want to fumble around for the poker.

Reaching the front door I felt along the wall to the right side of it. Sure enough: light switches. Not knowing which switch controlled what, I simply pushed all of them up at once. The living room lights went on, the deck lights went on, the parking area lights went on and the back and side yard lights went on. It was as bright as the county fair.

At that moment Cindy obviously reached the fireplace utensil holder. It went over with a resonating clatter, Fargo—who hates being collared—began to bark furiously, and Cindy arrived at my side clacking the fireplace tongs together like a small irritable alligator.

Swallowing a giggle at Cindy's ferocity and managing to hang on to Fargo so that he would not climb into my arms, as he is wont to do in times of stress, I stepped out the front door.

"Well, well, if it's not Twig Redford. To what do we owe the honor of this visit?" I gushed.

Branch and the man with him seemed frozen, immovable and silent.

Cindy joined me on the deck. "Yes, Twig, how about an answer. I don't believe the deck is a public park."

Branch still did not speak, but his companion did. "Jesus Christ, Branch, what the hell is wrong with you? Of all the places to meet in the State of Tennessee, you pick Ken Willingham's. And if that ain't dumb enough, you pick a weekend he's got company. I thought you said the broads were staying at the Bromfield!"

"I thought they were, Mickey. Just shut up." Branch finally looked at us, as I quieted Fargo. "I'm sorry if we frightened you ladies, but honestly I had no idea you were here."

"Didn't you see our car?" Cindy wanted to know.

"Yes, but I just figured you parked here to avoid tipping the valet every time you went out. Oh, God, it's all really simple. I wanted to meet my business partner, Mr. McCurry, privately, and this seemed a nice quiet place. I told you, Ken Willingham is a good friend, so I figured he wouldn't mind if we sat on his porch for a while."

McCurry snorted a sarcastic laugh, which told me about how good a friend Ken really was.

"Don't you *live* somewhere?" Cindy snapped her tongs impatiently.

"Uh, well, I have an apartment behind my office in Beulaland, but I had to close it a few days for…for renovations. I'm staying with my brother for a day or so."

"Or forever," I muttered sourly. "Who's your brother, just in case we want to confirm all this?"

"Clay Rodman," he answered reluctantly. "You met him at the Bromfield."

"Why the different last names?" I was beginning not to like any of this.

"Actually we are half-brothers. Same mother, different fathers."

"And just what is your business, Twig?"

Branch managed a parody of his winning smile. "Why, real estate, honey. I told you earlier. Mr. McCurry and I are helping to develop a wonderful nature lovers' community all along the crest of Crooked Creek Mountain—that's this mountain here." He waved up the mountainside behind the cabin.

"Yeah," Mickey agreed. "If you ever get off your ass and get clearance for a road."

"That's all moving right along," Branch soothed. "And I think we should do the same, Mickey. These ladies have had a long drive. Good-night ladies, good-night."

He stood and actually bowed. I smothered a grin. Bowing and scraping in his absurd clothing, he looked more like the

89

Court Jester than a hotshot realtor. They both finally got off the deck and down the steps, Cindy clicking her makeshift castanets to urge them on.

As Branch fumbled for his keys and for the ignition, I could hear Mickey hectoring him.

"...the hell away from them. They're too damn sharp. All them questions—you'd think they was cops. And I can tell you, that dog is a killer."

Fargo the Killer Dog and I sat on the deck, lights still blazing, just to make sure our company had indeed moved on. In a few minutes Cindy put a platter on a nearby table. Fargo and I didn't have to be invited to move over to it. We had scrambled eggs with a slice of acorn-fed ham, the best around. There was toast and some kind of homemade jam I couldn't identify but found sweet and tangy and good. Cindy returned with coffee and mugs and a sweater for me, all of which was quite welcome.

"What do you think of that little scene," Cindy asked.

"I think they were genuinely shocked to find us here. I think they are as crooked as our musical mountain stream over there, and I wouldn't want to buy a condo or cabin from either of them. I think new condo owners would find out that Branch's road washed out with the second rain. But that wouldn't matter much, because the plywood condos will have washed away with the first one. And Mickey will have skipped with their down payments."

"Uh-huh." She poured us more coffee. "Mickey looks like a hit man."

"A facial scar will do that for you," I temporized.

"I'm afraid of him."

"Darling," I urged, "don't be. Even if he is some sort of tough guy, lots of people in the 'development' business are. But we are no threat to him. It's just his way, he has no reason to have anything to do with us."

I moved around the table to share her picnic bench and put my arm around her. She tilted her head onto my shoulder.

"Alex, lately I've been kind of afraid of most men I don't know...and even a few that I do. I think that stalker business has got me really screwed up. I hate feeling like this!"

"Now, angel, it's no wonder that you—"

"No!" she said sharply. "Listen to me. Last month…remember all the trouble they had at home along Commercial Street with that broken water main—they couldn't find the last, smaller leak? The street was torn up for weeks."

I figured this was just background and simply nodded.

"Well," she continued, "it was right between the bank and downtown where I usually went to have lunch, or do a little shopping, or just walk a bit. There were always three or four young, wet and dirty idiots working there, and they always called out something silly—overgrown boys. I pretended to be deaf and went my way."

Her voice grew a little shaky at the end. She cleared her throat and sipped her coffee. I remained silent, not wishing to interrupt her thoughts.

"Sometimes there was an older man there…maybe a supervisor. He wore some kind of name badge. One day, one of the kids yelled something that struck me funny. I didn't turn around, but I laughed and waved as I went. Then I heard an older voice say something. A car was passing and I didn't get it all. But it was something about throwing me in a van and giving me a good fucking. I turned around—I couldn't seem to help it—and looked straight at him. He had an absolutely evil grin on his face and made that gesture with one hand on his bicep and his other fist going up and down." She demonstrated.

"My sweet girl, why didn't you tell me?"

"I was afraid. Afraid he really planned to do it. Afraid you might go after him and get hurt. Afraid Sonny would go after him and he would kill me when he got out of jail. I saw him everywhere. Watching, planning."

She was crying now and I pulled her closer.

"Cindy, this will be settled within an hour after we get home. Even if he never followed you a foot, he threatened to rape you, and that's a crime. The bastard *will* pay. And one thing is for sure—he ain't in Beulaland! I'm freezing. Let's go in."

We took two snifters of Ken's VSR brandy to bed with us, and I must say it worked wonders for both of us. I made a mental note to invest in a bottle when we got home.

CHAPTER TWELVE

We decided to have breakfast out and headed the mile or so down the road to gay, mad, metropolitan Beulaland.

Along the way we passed several houses, each with a barn or two, larger than the house. One pasture area was filled with square-built Black Angus cattle, augmented by two or three lovely little Jerseys, which I assumed kept the family and employees in plenty of milk and butter. Real butter.

Across the road, breakfast was being enjoyed by nearly a dozen handsome horses, nibbling almost daintily on tender-looking grass—or forage—or whatever you called it.

I didn't think it was hay while it was still growing. The horses came in a variety of colors, and except for some obvious colts, looked quite tall and wonderfully graceful to me. I wondered what breed they were.

Cindy solved my mystery. "Look at those beautiful Tennessee

Walking Horses! I haven't seen any in ages!"

"Walking horses? They take their time in Tennessee?"

"Hah! They could probably give the Derby winner a run for his money—they're part Arab. But when you ride them, they have three gaits. A slow walk, which is self explanatory, a running walk which is about as fast as a trot, but smoo-oo-th. And they can keep it up all day, and you will not have a single ache tomorrow. Thirdly, they canter, called the rocking chair gait, because that's what it looks and feels like. You don't go very fast but it is fun to do and pretty to watch—almost like dressage."

Pulling in front of a rather long, gleaming white concrete block building entitled Gertrude's Gourmet Coffee Shoppe and Delly, I said "Goodness, love, I didn't know you were a horse expert."

"I'm going to spend a couple of hours on one of those while we're here. One way or another," she answered enigmatically. My Cindy—ever a surprise. For all I knew, she could ride bareback while turning summersaults.

The food at Gertrude's was also a surprise. A wide choice of flavored coffees, which pleased Cindy. A wide choice of hotcakes, which pleased me. I settled for regular coffee and buckwheat cakes with wild cherry syrup, while Cindy reveled in Kona coffee with a dollop of real Jersey whipped cream. Plus of course, some grass clippings and small roots which she called cereal and topped with skim milk.

The place was fairly full, mostly, I thought, with locals in for the morning coffee break. A few, like us, furriners from the scattered cottages and cabins around. Only one person looked familiar.

Lou Jackson stopped by on her way to the cash register. She looked tired and admitted she had been up very early to visit a sow who had delivered a "pretty little litter," but whose milk had not come down, so she had had to go out and give her a shot—and wait around to make sure it worked. It did, she laughed, and said the hungry little piglets weren't even coming up for air when she left.

"By the way," she added, "My partner Gale said if I ran into you, to be sure to remind you of the buffet and dance Saturday night at the Bromfield Inn. If you don't have other plans, why don't we reserve a table for four and meet you there around eight o'clock?"

Cindy and I looked at each other, and Cindy said, "That sounds very nice. How thoughtful of you both!"

Lou smiled, "Well, it's kind of stodgy, but this ain't New York. We do have a couple of young lawyers who are gay—and forgiven by our Bible Belt contingent for the same reason we are…we four are the only veterinarians and lawyers within about fifteen miles, and we're good. Of course, there's Clay Rodman and Carl Bromfield but they usually take their pleasures in Bristol or Knoxville. And they come from old families. Around here, that covers a multitude of sins."

"I wonder how the local Bible Belters would feel about personal financial advisors and private investigators," I smiled, silently wondering at the accuracy of her gaydar.

Lou laughed. "No problem. A lot of us could use the first one and the other could run for sheriff—Jeffie Johnson has an IQ about the same as the Beulaland speed limit and a belly that ain't gonna fit under the steering wheel much longer. As the man said, C'mon down! We've a few gays renting or building out here now. We'll get a majority yet."

She looked at her watch. "Oops, I gotta go. We've got surgery this morning on a real sweetheart of an English setter. He got his foot caught in a trap. We'll be lucky to save the leg."

"What a shame!" Cindy cried. "Is there much of that around? Do we need to watch our dog?"

"No." Lou was counting out the money for her breakfast. "Very little, actually. The Rangers, and all of us really, keep a close look, and it's quite rare that some fool even sets one. This one is strange, too. Jasper had an electronic collar to keep him in his yard. It was found neatly unfastened at the edge of the property. Like somebody called him over and took off the collar so he could get past the signal. I reported it to the sheriff but he says he's not the dogcatcher. And by then so many people had handled the collar, fingerprints were impossible. Well, 'bye now."

"Good luck with Jasper!" I called after her.

A surprising number of heads turned toward me with approving expressions.

We had decided over breakfast to take a look at Ken's fishing tackle and, if it wasn't too complicated, to try our luck for a couple of trout in Crooked Creek. When we got to the cashier we saw the register was manned—or I should say—womanned by a hefty woman of about sixty whom I judged to be the proprietress.

I had earlier noticed a number of nature photos framed and hung on the walls. A few were excellent, others I felt I would have handled differently and maybe better. Behind the cashier was a very good photograph of a big gray owl with piercing eyes and a large beak. I did not comment on the strong family resemblance, but contented myself with asking the woman I presumed to be Gertrude if we needed a license to fish and if so, where did we get it.

Yes, we needed one, there weren't no oceans here where you could just wade in and kill fish. We could get them at the Post Office down the street if we wanted to waste the money on them. We probably wouldn't catch anything anyway.

Cindy mentioned she had seen a bunch of fish Tommy Blackstone had caught in the lake yesterday, and that her cousin had assured her Crooked Creek was rich in trout.

Gertrude issued what may have been a laugh and opined that there was a far cry from what Tommy and Ken would catch to two city women who would probably just catch their lines in the seats of their pants. She handed me my change and muttered a barely audible, "Thankyoupleasecallagain," lending new profundity to the word "insincere."

Walking toward the Post Office, a tiny clapboard building with a sagging door and worn paint, but a bright flag waving proudly on a clean white pole in front of it, I asked Cindy why

Gertrude didn't like us.

"Oh, that one is easy. We didn't ask for separate checks and she heard at least part of our conversation with Lou. She managed to be near our booth almost the whole time Lou was there."

"What the hell does she care? We spent some money, we tipped her waitress well, we didn't smear food on the wall. Business is business."

"What the hell do *you* care? The food is good, and it's the only show in town, if you don't count a poisonous diner out on the State road."

"It pisses me off, that's all." I opened the Post Office door with a vengeance and nearly hit Clay Rodman with it, so small were the federal environs.

I began to apologize profusely, but Clay waved me off.

"No harm done! You learn to enter and exit very carefully here. What brings you two abroad so early?"

"Trout," I replied. "We came to get fishing licenses."

The postmistress had perforce heard the entire conversation and said, "I guess you want temporary visitor's, right?"

"I guess we do if they're good for a week or so."

"Thirty days. Ten dollars apiece. Going after anything special?"

"Just some trout and—uh, whatever they have in the lake. Does it matter?"

"Not a bit." She smiled. "Just curious."

While the postmistress and I transacted our business, Cindy and Clay had moved outdoors and were having an animated conversation when I joined them. Cindy looked excited, and Clay explained.

"I breed Tennessee Walking Horses—you saw some of them earlier, I understand. In the summer, I rent some for riding the trails around here. I, or one of my men, always go with the renters, to make sure nobody gets lost or mistreats one of the horses. Still, I won't rent out a pregnant mare. I have three of them right now, and this morning I'm taking them up to Crooked Creek Mountain to spend the summer at my sister's place. You met her son, Tommy," he added.

Cindy could not stay quiet. "Clay was going to ride one horse and take the other two on a line, but now—*now!*—we can all ride one and his sister will drive us back down here to our car!"

I was thrilled beyond belief. Horses are not only large and strong, they always look as if they know something I don't.

"Great. I thought you wanted to go fishing." I could but try.

She waved her hands as if clearing away an entire hive of bees. "Oh, that can wait. We're going to ride Tennessee walkers! You are in for an experience!"

That's what I was afraid of.

I had to admit they were beautiful. If they were pregnant, they weren't showing it yet. They looked sleek and muscular... and high. Clay's stable man already had one of them saddled and ready. Now he put saddles and bridles on two more and we were as ready as we would ever be.

Clay gave Cindy a knee up, and she swung gracefully onto her mount.

"This is Princess Palomino." He introduced Cindy's mare. "She's bridle-wise and easy-tempered. You lead off, Cindy. We'll stay in a single line till we get to the private road that goes beside Ken's place. Slow walk."

Cindy started slowly for the gate, and Clay cupped his hands to give me a boost. I did something wrong, dragged my foot across the horse's rump and felt frantically for the right-hand stirrup. Clay came around and literally put my foot in the stirrup. The horse gave me a disgusted look and started after Princess.

"Her name is Ladybird. Stay in the middle," Clay called after me. I had to stay in the saddle first.

I was a nervous wreck at the traffic on the main road, but fortunately our mounts were not, although I did hear Pride and Joy, Clay's mare, do a little tap dance when a noisy truck passed us. I didn't look.

But we reached the turnoff without incident and left the macadam road for the smoothly bulldozed gravel road. We were three abreast now on the gentle slope, and when Clay and Cindy nudged their mounts into a running walk, Ladybird stayed even with them.

Far from being bounced up and down, as I had anticipated. I felt as if I were gliding over a dance floor, yet covering a lot of ground swiftly…and there was nothing frightening about it. I leaned forward and gave Ladybird a couple of pats.

We were on the west side of the mountain, and the sun had not yet cleared its peak, so we were in shade as we looked down on the sun-quilted valley. The air was still cool, but fragrant with laurel. Clay put his finger to his lips and then pointed down to a quiet strip of backwater along the creek. A bear was teaching two cubs to fish. It looked to be a long, wet process, with the cubs swatting happily at every little wavelet. She looked up alertly, but the road curved away at that point, and after a moment, she returned to her patient schooling.

Farther up, a mockingbird claimed his special tree with complex trills and piercingly sweet notes to put most opera stars to shame. And suddenly I understood how people could feel about mountains the way I felt about the sea.

Eventually, and yet too soon, we turned onto a narrow driveway leading to a house and sizeable barn, with a natural meadow behind it and, doubtless the work of years, two terraced truck gardens below it. Three horses and two colts grazed the meadow, and our horses nickered in recognition.

At that moment a car shot from in front of the house and roared down the driveway toward us. I was almost sure it was going to hit us. Automatically I pulled Ladybird to the right and kicked her sides with my heels. It may well have been her own sense of self-preservation, but she reacted with a leap and a scramble up the slope beside us. I was off-balance, but safe, and so were my two companions.

As the car passed, I had recognized Branch's loutish "associate," Mickey, behind the wheel. Another person was beside him, crouched low in the seat, and I assumed it was Branch. I was furious. The damn fool could have killed any or all of us, horses included. Clay stared after them, face white with anger.

Cindy was dismounted and stroking Princess's head. "I think she turned her ankle," she explained. "She's limping a bit."

Clay swore bitterly under his breath. "If one of these mares miscarries, I'll kill him...and that thug he calls his business associate."

We led the animals to the barn and into clean, airy stalls. Clay began to examine Princess's ankle and leg. Cindy found some large towels and tossed me a couple, plus a halter.

"Unsaddle Ladybird and replace the bridle with the halter. Next wipe everything dry, including the horse. Then when they're a little cooler, we'll water them." When had she become an expert in the care of horses? When would I ever plumb the depths of this person?

I did all those things as ordered. Clumsily, I admit, but without the least tinge of fear. I had come a long way, Ladybird.

CHAPTER THIRTEEN

Entering the back door to the kitchen, we met Clay's sister Sara, coming from another part of the house. Apparently she hadn't heard our arrival, which was a bit surprising. I noticed that her eyes looked red and wondered if she had a cold—or had been crying...perhaps over her visitors? Clay introduced us and asked for coffee for the three of us. Under happier circumstances, I thought she would be attractive with her light brown hair, eyes to match and good strong features tanned by her outdoor life.

As Sara began making the coffee, Clay could hold his anger back no longer. "Branch and that effing pal of his! What the hell were they doing here? Goddamn Mickey damn near killed us all and Princess has hurt her ankle—I'll strangle them both if she's seriously injured. Jesus, I bring them up here to be safe from careless summer riders, and before I can get 'em in the pasture we're all nearly dead!"

"Clay, please. Please just don't badger me." Sara had tears in her eyes, and her hands were shaking. "Please."

Cindy and I had already taken chairs at the kitchen table, but I stood up again. "Look, Clay, obviously you and Sara have both had a difficult morning, and don't need guests while you deal with it. Why don't Cindy and I just hike on home, and you can bring the car back this afternoon?"

I figured we could walk the couple of miles, mostly downhill, with no great trouble. Of course there was the bear, but hopefully she and her cuties would have gone by now.

"No," Clay waved me back to my seat. "Please stay. You're not personally involved in this mess so maybe you can see it more clearly. What's your opinion?"

"Not complimentary," I answered. "*Development* schemes like this one are usually a scam. Branch obviously thought he could pay a little cash fee with one hand to get easements from property owners in the area so a road could be put in, leading up the mountain. With the other hand he sold the idea of a vacation community to whatever construction people he's dealing with. Equally obviously, most of the property owners around here don't want cheap time-share condos and rickety houses cluttering up their mountain...lots of traffic, destruction of animal habitat, air pollution and total loss of charm. Give 'em two years and they'd have a Walmart next door to the Bromfield Inn."

I nodded my thanks to Sara as she set a mug of coffee in front of me and I took a sip before going on.

"The construction people have now spent a bundle on surveying most of the mountain, on engineers to plan where the road could go, where switchbacks will be necessary, how to get power in. They are probably out of cash and can't get more financing without at least showing that they have access to the development area. They may have to have architects provide models of the whole shebang to 'prove' to the state and county that everything is ecologically friendly—which the finished product will not be, anyway. Five will get you ten they'll have some sort of runoff somewhere that pollutes Crooked Creek and consequently, the lake."

I took a chance and lit a cigarette. Sara smiled and produced an ashtray, plus her own cigarettes. As an afterthought she reached back and turned on a small exhaust fan over the stove.

"So," I concluded, "they blame Branch for not coming through. They are now in considerable debt with a cash-flow problem; they are bogged down and don't know how to rectify it. And they have now sent Mickey along as a 'closer' to convince people they had better sign those easements on the dotted line. And I must admit, he is really an intimidating figure."

"Advantage Construction Company is a sleazeball outfit, all right," Clay agreed. "They are out of Knoxville, but they put up an old-folks complex in Kingsport only about a year ago. The main building now leans at an eight-degree angle, and it's on level ground, and another building has a swimming pool in the basement, probably from an underground spring. No one is sure."

We all laughed, and Cindy suggested getting photos of the Kingsport buildings and showing them to property owners on Crooked Creek Mountain.

"It would certainly inspire *me* not to let them build a road across *my* property, much less a housing development nearby that might come sliding down the mountain into my front yard the first time it rained."

She smiled at her imagery and then added, "Getting a lawyer to represent all, or at least most, of the property owners would be better yet, and I understand you have a couple of good attorneys in town. Actually, it wouldn't cost much when you divvy it up among the owners."

"Oh," I put in, "make sure to have the lawyer's letter include that any harassment by Mr. McCurry or other parties will be considered illegal trespass and threat of gross bodily harm and any other nifty phrases your lawyer can think up."

Clay gave his sister a meaningful look. "We should hire these two as landowners' representatives, Sara. They know how to fight fire with fire."

Sara responded with a weak smile. "Well, we need all the help we can get. On a day-to-day basis, I usually can handle whatever life hands out. I've managed pretty well since Tom Senior died. But something like this comes along…frankly, that Mickey turns me cold with fear."

I deliberately did not look at Cindy. Instead I asked quietly, "In what way does he get to you, Sara?"

She lit another cigarette with shaky hands. "Just this morning, Branch was trying yet again to get me to sign that damned easement thing. I wouldn't do it, and finally he was about to leave when that Mickey turned back and said, 'Well, Ms. Elegant Lady, you and your stubborn neighbors have got us crying the blues right now, but you may do a little crying yourselves down the road.' I tell you, it went right through me! All I could think of was my darling Tommy and my precious horses. I think I would die if any of them were…hurt."

Clay shook his head in disbelief. "I can see Branch mixed up with a sleazy company, but I can't see him with a man like Mickey. Branch is stupid with money, so he's always looking for an easy quick deal to make him rich. But he would never hurt anybody, much less family."

"I believe you," Cindy answered. "But I don't think he can control Mickey's actions. I think Mickey's orders come from Knoxville. And who knows whether he's even sticking to *their* instructions? I think he enjoys scaring people. At least so far he has limited himself to verbal abuse. Let's hope he keeps it that way. And your ineffectual Branch may end up as much a victim as anyone else."

"I'll tell you one thing." Clay slapped his hand on the table. "I'm going to see Peter Minot, my lawyer, when we leave here. I want photos of that Kingsport mess and the strongest letter he knows how to write sent to Advantage Construction in a hurry. Copies of both will go out to every property owner on Crooked Creek Mountain, so they'll know just what we're dealing with. If the owners kick in on the attorney fees—swell. If not, I'll pay the damn bill myself. And if he bothers you again, sis, I'll shoot the son of a bitch!"

He stood up and put his coffee mug in the sink. "Let's move it."

Cindy and I bounced around in the back of Sara's truck on a couple of folded horse blankets until we reached the cabin, where I de-trucked. Cindy bounced on to Beulaland to get the car.

I let the very angry Fargo out. His entire demeanor told me that I had been gone a lot longer than just breakfast, I had not even brought home a doggie bag, I smelled of some strange creature and if I thought forgiveness was near, I was dead wrong.

This lasted until I threw the first stick into the creek.

As we played, I thought of Sara and her horses, and how I would feel if anything happened to Fargo. I wondered if I would be mad enough to kill in vengeance if someone killed Fargo. I wasn't sure. I think maybe you go a little insane when someone kills a loved one, especially a pet or young child who can have no idea why anyone would wish to hurt them. The killer has taken away—forever—something innocent and loving and beautiful, and you can never, ever get that particular thing back.

Yes, I think I might well kill, and consider the planet well rid of a piece of virulent garbage.

Fargo came out of the water, shaking and spluttering. Apparently he'd had enough of the frigid stream. I took him into the laundry/mudroom and dried him off. He immediately spotted a sunny area on the back porch and curled up for a snooze. I would keep a close eye on him for the rest of our visit.

I tossed the damp towel into the washer and as I did, my eye caught sight of the bunch of fishing rods and reels propped in the corner. I started sorting them out, picking the lightest and simplest as being best for us. On the floor beside them was a tackle box with all those items that find their way into tackle boxes. Flies were mixed with lures and sinkers and leaders. Various hooks were tangled in a small clear plastic box. A stringer dominated one corner of the large box, and on that optimistic note, I decided we'd better just take the whole thing upstream with us.

My dark philosophy had disappeared with the thought that we were on vacation, we had no easements to sell or buy, and Advantage Construction had no bearing on our lives.

I was, of course, dead wrong.

Fargo heard the car first and ran to greet Cindy. He was particularly attentive to the paper bag she carried, and shortly, so was I. From Gertrude's she had procured a luncheon designed to please us all.

Finishing our goodies, we put on the smallest rubber boots in the mudroom and slogged up the road with our fishing gear, already planning what to have with our trout dinner.

Some boots may be made for walking, but these were not, and by the time we reached the little pool Clay had recommended, we were both out of breath. The big tackle box grew heavier by the step, and my camera banged uncomfortably on my chest. Fargo barked at and chased everything that moved.

As we reached the pool, Cindy managed to grab him before he leaped into it, put him on his lead and tied him to a small tree, where he immediately went into his second sulk of the day. He serenaded us with whimpers, whines and the occasional howl.

Cindy chose a fly, added it and a leader to her line and cast. She flicked it neatly right into the center of the pool, as if she did this every day. I smiled and followed suit, except that I held the rod a little too high, and the line went back over my head into a bush of mountain laurel. Was Gertrude a witch?

It took some time to get the line free, during which time Cindy had gotten a strike and reeled in a fair-sized trout. Suffice it to say that the only thing I caught that afternoon was a terrific picture of Cindy, with a triumphant grin, trout held high.

Suffice it also to say, sometimes God is good. On her next cast, Cindy slipped on one of the brick colored river rocks that eons of water friction had given smooth rounded shapes, lost her balance, and sat down in about two feet of water.

Before I went to her rescue, I made the mistake of shooting my second great picture of the day. I helped her up, retrieved her rod, released her catch, since it would not feed the two of us, and dumped the water out of her boots. Our walk home was quiet. Even Fargo had the sense to pad silently at my side while Cindy squished grumpily behind us.

In the process of rescuing—well, assisting—Cindy, I had noticed that the rock which had been her literal downfall had some interesting quartz patches in it, sparkling from time to time when the light hit it right. If I could find another like it, or just another interesting one about the same size, they would make a unique pair of bookends. So I crammed it into the tackle box, although it added a good three or four pounds to my burden. Cindy did not offer to take turns.

All the meat we had was frozen solid, and neither of us was in a cooking mood, anyway. Going out apparently was not on the menu, either. After her long, hot shower Cindy's attire consisted of pajamas and an enormous terry robe she had found somewhere.

I made one of my famous grilled cheese sandwiches, served with pickles and potato chips. I offered to make one for Cindy, but she opted for a can of Campbell's chicken soup, of the type that was probably meant for one of the Willingham kids. We watched the news, which eliminated the need for light dinner-time conversation, and afterward Cindy retired to the bedroom with a book. I remained with Fargo in the living room to watch *Victor Victoria* on TV for the third or fourth time. I was beginning to know the dialogue.

About an hour into the film, Cindy padded into the room and knelt beside me with her finger across her lips.

"Someone is trying to get into the bedroom," she whispered. "I can hear them fooling with the screen."

I removed my shoes and followed her down the hall. Poised at the bedroom door, I could hear the scraping noise she had described.

"Let's give them a nice surprise," I murmured. "We'll go into the bedroom and over to the window. When I nod, you yank

107

up the blind, I'll yank up the screen and punch him one in the nose."

We followed only part of my plan.

As the blind went up and the screen went up and I pulled my fist back, Cindy screamed and I realized my face was about three inches from that of a large, strange-looking black bear. Behind him in the night I could see other dark shapes moving in the trees. Did bears travel in packs? Could they break down a door?

It was no time for questions. Quickly I slammed the screen back down, catching the bear with a smart smack on his large black nose. He let out a loud, startled, feelings-hurt...*moo-oo-ooo!*

"Oh, my God! Cindy, it's a *cow!* It's one of those Angus things, and his buddies are all up among the trees. You can barely see them, but they're there. This poor guy was just scratching his back on a rough log, and I walloped him on the nose. I thought it was a pack of bears."

Cindy was laughing helplessly at my face-to-face encounter. "Bears don't travel in packs, they're pretty solitary," she managed to gasp. "Oh, Lord, the look on your face was priceless!"

"I'm glad you enjoyed it. It was you and your 'intruder' who put it there. What do we do now? I've no idea who they belong to, do you?"

"No." She sobered quickly. "But we can't let them go farther up the mountain or a bear may well nab one of them. I guess the best thing is to call the sheriff's office—they'll probably know the owner. Get a big flashlight out of the mudroom and try to head them off, while I phone. I'll be right out."

"Cindy, there are ten or twelve of those things out there."

"Yes, just get above them and point them downhill and kind of shoo them gently. They are tame, Alex, they are tame."

They may have been tame, but they were also stubborn. I fought a losing battle. I'd just about get one of them turned around and five others would saunter past me, nibbling noisily at delicacies along the way. Cindy soon joined me, announcing that deputies were en route along with some people named Dermott who owned this errant ebony herd.

Once we accumulated our full complement, the chore was easier. Perhaps recognizing their owner's raspy voice, the now-docile black blobs turned downhill and went home. Mr. Dermott thanked us all profusely, and shook his head when the deputy asked him if he knew how they got out.

"I didn't stop to look. I've got electric fence all around that pasture, it's always been foolproof."

"Could the wires have been cut?" I asked.

"Now who would do a thing like that? But I thank you again for your help. Weren't for you ladies I coulda lost a steer, maybe more than one."

I tried another question. "Did Advantage Construction offer you a fee if you'd sign an easement allowing them to put a road across some of your property?"

"You mean that crazy idea of a nature lovers' commune or something that Branch Redford's tryin' to sell? Him and that bully boy he's got with him?"

I nodded and the deputy looked at me sharply.

Dermott laughed. "That guy with Branch told me I really oughta sign, that I could use the money to put up stronger fences. I told him if he thought my fencing was weak, just to grab aholt of it on his way out. He did, and jumped about three feet. Guess that shut him up."

"Or made him buy some insulated cutting pliers," Cindy suggested. "You might want to talk to Clay Rodman. He's trying to get some injunction against the bully boy—his name is Mickey McCurry, by the way—and get Advantage Construction to take their plans to some other area. Preferably in North Dakota."

I turned my flashlight back on and shined it over one of the insulators. The copper wire lay limply on the ground beside it.

Dermott swore long and loud, and this time the deputy made a note.

We went home to a worried Fargo and Cindy took him out on lead, while I made some tea. The night had grown chilly, and I had grown tired. I realized that tea just seemed right. Especially with a wee tot of rum. Cindy agreed, her earlier snit forgotten. "We spoke too soon this morning," she said thoughtfully. "Mickey has now destroyed personal property and endangered livestock."

CHAPTER FOURTEEN

I awoke ravenous. Cindy was already up, dressed and drinking coffee in the kitchen.

She put her cheek up for a kiss. "I thought you were going to sleep all day, my love, and I am getting weak from hunger. These cattle roundups really take it out of you."

"Indeed they do. I'm hungry, too. And the fridge is loaded. So what are you making for breakfast?"

"Reservations. People who have worked long into the night do not make breakfast."

"Do we have to go to Gertrude's?" I asked.

"The only decent place in town…Gertrude's. Perhaps she will grow to love us as time goes by."

"That's a ghastly thought, but I suppose you're right. Their food is good."

"I knew greed would triumph," she said loftily.

Gertrude's seemed even more popular this morning than when we were last there. They weren't the breakfast crowd; these people had an early breakfast at home. They were here at this hour for coffee, maybe a pastry and news. I imagined the Dermott's late-night roundup had been recounted countless times by now.

It was a little strange. It started with Gertrude approaching us with menus and a toothy grin, asking, "What'll it be, girls, booth or table?" Then several people I didn't know nodded and smiled or said hello.

Lou approached us, in obvious good spirits. "I understand you two earned your spurs last night."

"Yep." Cindy tucked her thumbs in her waistband and added, "Next week we start lasso lessons."

A number of people smiled, and one man said, "I saw you riding Clay's Princess yesterday. This time next year you'll be in the Johnson City horse show."

I turned to Lou. "How did Jasper the English setter make out?"

"Barring complications, he's got his leg. But he'll also have a permanent limp. Oh, don't look so sad, he'll get around fine. Dogs—most animals—adapt better than people. He's a great boy, he'll handle it."

"That's wonderful, really. I'm sure his owners are grateful. This town is lucky to have you and your partner."

She bobbed her head in thanks and moved on to pay her bill.

Greed did win out. Surprisingly I saw cheese blintzes on the menu and—wary but hopeful, I ordered them. They were delicious, with crisp bacon and a peach chutney to die for. I asked the waitress if I could buy a jar and she brought one to the table. The professionally printed label read: Homegrown Peach Chutney from the kitchen of Sara Blackstone.

She raised horses, she raised vegetables, she made preserves. Did she ever sleep? No wonder she stayed so slim.

Cindy—for her—also let greed have its way. A Denver omelet

complete with home fries. Amazingly, she left Fargo only about half of everything. I generously added a bite of one blintz to the doggie bag.

I started toward the door, while Cindy paid the check, and I noticed a woman struggling to open the door as she juggled a rather large carton. I took a couple of quick steps and pushed it open for her.

"Thank you." She was a little out of breath. "You're one of the women who saved the cattle last night, aren't you?"

"Well, I helped a bit. I'm Alex Peres and..." I turned to Cindy, now beside me. "This is Cindy Hart, who also helped. Probably more than I. Being originally from Tennessee, she is apparently a natural farmer and livestock expert."

"I'm Sophie Dermott. Robert, my husband, and I just wanted you to have a little 'thank you' for all your efforts. There's a couple of nice steaks in here. Oh, and I must tell you. Rob fixed the fence this morning and said to tell you, there'll be an alarm put in tomorrow to go off if it happens again. And he's warning the neighbors to be on their guard."

She held the box out toward me and I automatically took it— and nearly dropped it. It felt more like half a cow was in there.

We thanked her profusely, and then Cindy inquired, "Sophie, how did you know we were here?"

"Oh, a friend stopped by, happened to mention she seen you going in. I figured I could catch you. The steaks are frozen, so you'll probably want to go straight home. I must run, Rob will be needing the truck."

Ah, the joys of a small town.

At home we opened the box, and no longer wondered at its weight. Six *filets mignon* and six glorious T-bone steaks were still frozen solid as we popped them into the freezer. We left two filets in the refrigerator to thaw; dinner was no longer a question mark.

The question was what to do for the rest of the day. I felt lazy after the large breakfast but knew I wasn't going to get away with it. I was right. Cindy suggested we take Fargo and climb up to the tarn near the top of the mountain.

"What, exactly, is a tarn?" I wanted to know.

Cindy smiled. "Well, according to my grandmother it's a body of water larger than a pond and smaller than a lake, whatever that may be. It's kind of like her recipe for devil's food cake: you start with a large cup of flour. My grandfather said tarn was short for tarnation, because the water is always so tarnation cold. I believe both are basically correct. But if you are the scholarly type, you will wish to know it's an Old English word left over from Anglo-Saxon days—meaning small mountain lake."

What none of Cindy's family, nor she, had mentioned was that you reached a tarn by one helluva hike. Uphill.

But the climb was beautiful. The trail ran beside the creek and then away and then back to it. I discovered three more river rocks of the right size, so we had two pair of bookends now—or would, when we picked them up on the way home. Periodically, the trail was covered with last year's pine needles. Our hiking boots caused them to give off a clean, slightly acrid odor.

I saw a small flat piece of wood that looked like it might have been part of an orange crate. It had a nail hole in one end. What it was doing here, I couldn't guess. But I picked a large oak leaf, jammed the stem of it in the hole and set my sailboat on the water.

Cindy picked a nearby dog-tooth violet and laid it on the craft, intoning, "I christen thee the Argo II." We watched until it sailed jauntily out of sight and I wondered if it would make it to the lake far below. I looked at Cindy and we both laughed: it was fun to play.

We passed a small meadow dotted with some yellow flowers. Across the far end of it trotted a fox, dutifully followed by her two kits. Fargo wanted to play and barked twice. As smartly as a unit of the Marines, the threesome made a right turn and disappeared among the trees.

A blue jay flew low over us, squawking loudly at our trespass upon his territory. Less aggressive, a red-headed woodpecker ceased drilling on a dead pine limb and watched us warily until we passed, and then went back to his lunch.

Finally, we reached the tarn. It was a deep blue even as it reflected the lighter blue and white of the sky. I wondered how deep it was. I unclipped Fargo's leash and he ran forward to get a drink. Then he decided to wade a few steps forward and suddenly found himself swimming. Obviously it shelved off quickly, and obviously it was too cold even for the intrepid Fargo. He clambered out, shook himself and found a sunny patch of grass to roll in.

We had been warned against taking any sort of real picnic into the uninhabited areas where bears might get a whiff and decide to join the party. Consequently, all we had with us were a couple of peaches and two chunks of cheese, which we hoped would lack the charm of fried chicken or ham sandwiches or whatever for Br'er Bear. Even so, we ate rapidly and kept Fargo close beside us as he devoured his biscuit.

Our only "garbage" was the pair of peach pits, which we put back in their plastic bag and returned to the backpack. Then Cindy produced her surprise.

"Reward time!" She announced and pulled a peanut butter jar from the pack. It was filled with claret, and as we took turns sipping it from the jar. I lit a cigarette and figured it really didn't get any better than this.

I waved my arm around. "Now who in their right mind would want a bunch of cottages and condos added to *this* landscape? And who would want a nice paved road where fox babies go to play?"

"Greedy people who don't endorse the rights of animals or other people," she replied. "And stupid people who think they can buy a house in the middle of a forest and that nothing will change."

"It would be a crime." I dipped my cigarette in the water, fieldstripped it and put the filter in my shirt pocket. "But how do you stop it?"

"Well, the people who have bought property along the foot of the mountain fall into two groups, mainly. They are either farmers who have bought as far up as pastures and land good for crops or pigs can be found. Or they are people like Ken and Frances. They bought a lot of extra property to block off access to the wild part of Crooked Creek Mountain. It will work for a while, anyway. In the meantime, you try to get protective laws."

"I've noticed a bunch of signs like *No trespassing, No hunting, No motor vehicles.* Do they work?"

"Fairly well." She reached for our elegant wineglass. "The Rangers do what they can. They pretty well keep the little four-wheelers off the trails. Even the sheriff shoos furriners away, although he turns a blind eye to the farmer who takes an occasional deer on posted property."

She took a sip of wine and set the jar back on the ground between us. "The sad thing about this whole mess we now seem to be involved in, is that a lot of people would lose money on these houses even if they weren't jerry-built."

"How's that?"

"Think about it. The bears are not going to move out overnight. Would you send your child out to play over there?" She waved an arm toward the woods. "Especially if she were eating a fat tuna salad sandwich?"

"No," I answered. "And I wouldn't want her deciding to take a little wade in this tarn, either. It shelves off so fast even Fargo had to work at pulling himself out."

"Not only that," Cindy added. The water is terribly cold and never really warms up and is very deep. The old locals still call it bottomless. You can get cramps in no time. All you need is one kid mauled by a bear and another drowned and this place would be a ghost town. No one would be able to sell the houses or condos they had bought but no longer spent time in, and Advantage would be stuck with any they hadn't already sold. And in a month, half of the bears would have been shot on sight."

"So everybody loses, including the animals." I shivered and took the last sip of wine.

Fargo gave a low rumble in his chest, and following his line of sight I spotted mama bear and the two little teddy bears watching us. Thinking they might be thirsty, I suggested we vacate the pond-site. We quickly put the water bottles and jar into the backpack, and slowly walked back to the trail.

As we went over the crest, I looked back and—sure enough—mama was on her hind feet giving us a final look. I waved and started the downhill trek.

Along the way, we picked up the three river rocks I had set aside earlier. Cindy put one in the pack and said the others were all mine. I carried one in each hand, and we reached the cabin just as my knuckles were about to drag the ground. My calves had already turned to Jell-o from the downhill hike, and visions of deck chairs danced in my head.

I did manage to hose the dried mud off of the rocks and line them up with the other one along the edge of the back porch. I could hear Cindy talking to Fargo on the front deck. I headed for the shower and happened to notice Cindy's bottle of bubble bath stuff.

With absolutely no guilt I poured a slug of it into hot, hot water and disappeared from the chin down.

CHAPTER FIFTEEN

Why is it bad habits are so pleasantly easy to adopt? Thursday morning found us back at Gertrude's caloric trough, smiling at familiar faces, saying good morning to people we now knew—at least casually.

As we made our way past the counter to the tables area, I said good morning to Deputy Spitz, who had been a member of our cattle roundup team a few nights back. Usually, the few times I had seen him in town, he reminded me of my brother Sonny... with a perfectly pressed, spotless uniform and boots polished to a shine that made one blink. Not this morning.

His uniform was spotted with dirt, the knees of his pants stained by grass and the handsome boots a muddy mess. More disturbing than the condition of his uniform was the strained look on his face.

"Good morning, Deputy Spitz. Rough night?"

"Hi. You know, I thought about calling you. You got a coupla minutes?"

"Sure." By now Cindy had chosen a table. "Bring your coffee and come on back."

He flopped tiredly into a chair. "Well, ladies, we've got real troubles brewing around here, I think."

Whatever the trouble was, it waited a minute while we both ordered breakfast.

"Please." Cindy tapped her chest and said, "Call me Cindy," and then pointed at me and said, "and Alex. What on earth has happened now?"

"And I'm Dave. You know the Lauters?" he asked.

I laughed. "No, but I think I know their sheep. I noticed them the other day. It must have been right after shearing time. They looked like a big, wrinkled bunch of aging nudists caught at the church fair…all huddled together like they were embarrassed at being seen in public. I noticed their name on the mailbox."

Cindy smiled, but Dave just nodded. "That's them all right. Well, there's one less of them this mornin'. Somebody shot one of them last night and, we think, tried to shoot the herd dog… Sammy, scrappy little border collie and smart as a whip. We believe he heard the first shot and started trying to get the others into the shelter. He's got a scrape along his ribs that looks like a bullet just grazed him. He's okay. Thorina is dead."

With an alarmed breath intake, Cindy asked, "Who's Thorina?"

"One of the sheep. Would you believe the Lauters have got every one of them named, and they know which is which. I got there last night to find Elsie Lauter sitting in the middle of the field beside Thorina, cryin' and rockin' Sammy in her arms. She looked up at me, and I swear that woman is heartbroke. She said, 'Dave, they're killing my babies. You got to stop them.' She damn near had me cryin' with her."

"Do you know who did it?" I sipped my coffee and tried to look casual.

"I think so, but I can't prove it. Nobody saw him. I crawled around on my knees half the night and finally found one of the bullet casings. That will tell us something; the state police have it now. I got Mickey McCurry out of his motel bed at daybreak, but I had no cause for a search warrant and he wasn't thoughtful enough to leave the gun on his night table."

"Do you know where he was when all this happened?" I moved my arm to let the waitress serve my ham and eggs.

"He said he was over at Jake's Dew Drop Inn till about midnight and then came back to the motel and went to bed. Well, I just got back from the Dew Drop. Jake says McCurry was there at the bar from about eight o'clock till they closed at midnight. The cook swears McCurry ordered a hamburger and fries, the last order before he shut down the kitchen, which would have been about eleven thirty. That pretty well clears him except for two things."

He snagged a piece of Cindy's uneaten toast and waved to the waitress for more coffee. She gave us all refills.

"And the two things are?" I prompted.

He swallowed a large bite of toast. "Excuse me. One thing is: I asked the cook to show me the order. They're numbered, and it should have been the highest number and the top slip of paper on the spindle. He said there was no written order, that Mickey had stuck his head in the window and ordered it himself. The other thing is: for a twenty-dollar bill, either Jake or his cook or both would swear in court that Jesus Himself dropped in and had a dance with one of the women who hang out at the bar."

Cindy grinned and then looked serious. "Where was Branch?"

"I just talked to Clay a little while ago. Apparently Branch was in Knoxville all day yesterday at Advantage Construction, and got back to Clay's a little after ten. He's livin' there now, couldn't pay his office/apartment rent. He helped Clay filling out some pedigree papers on a couple of colts he's got for sale. They watched the news and went to bed. Branch is clear. He wouldn't do this kind of stuff anyway. He'd promise you anything and lie like a trooper, but he wouldn't kill an innocent animal."

"Everyone seems to credit him with being nonviolent. What's with Branch, anyway?" I had begun to find something both sad and likeable about the guy.

"Oh, let me make it brief, then I got to run. First there was Clay and Sara and their mom and dad, all-American family. Clay Senior had a tractor and farm implement franchise and did real well. Then one day they were unloading some hay balers from the delivery truck and one of them tipped off onto Mr. Rodman. Bye-bye dad. Fortunately the money was mostly in trust for Sara and Clay. Sara was a farmer from the time she could lift a hoe, and Clay loves every horse that was ever born. They both went to U-Tenn, and learned what they needed to know and it has paid off for them."

Dave yawned and checked his watch. "Anyhow, their mom was none too bright and let Branch's father sweet-talk her into marrying him. Branch came along about the time his father was slipping into alcoholism and losing his job. He managed to drive off the side of a mountain in the fog and Mrs. Redford was left with little Branch and even littler money. They both felt deprived, although Clay and Sara were both generous. Branch has always figured he was left out somehow. Sara and Clay sent him to university, but he didn't like the work, and quit. He's been lookin' for the end of that rainbow ever since. And I am looking for a hot shower and some clean clothes. If you'll excuse me…"

"Just one thing." I held out my hand to stop him. "My brother is a cop, too. Detective lieutenant in Provincetown. You've probably thought of it, but let me say something I imagine Sonny would be thinking right now. Mickey *definitely* has made some threatening verbal statements to property owners. He *may* have set the trap that caught Jasper's leg. He *probably* cut the wires on Mr. Dermott's fence. He *almost certainly* killed the Lauters' sheep and tried to kill their dog. What do you think, Dave?"

"I think he is escalating, Alex. He's escalating and I am frightened for my town, because I do not know how to stop him." He turned and walked away.

Cindy and I had stood up to follow him out, but we were

now trying to cobble together a tip—neither of us could find any small bills or much change. We didn't notice Mickey McCurry approaching until he had reached our table. His eyes were bloodshot, his hair uncombed, his face unshaven, and his clothing a mess. His breath could kill from three feet out. Either he had really tied one on or had spent much of the night raising hell on the Lauters' farm. Or both.

I looked up as he slammed some papers onto the table. I noticed we were about eye-to-eye. In some way I had thought him taller than I was. Perhaps a bully always seems bigger than he really is. He had a hefty build, but was no taller than I. Somehow I felt better.

He spread the papers on the table. "I suppose you seen all this shit. I understand it was your bright idea to begin with."

I looked down at two eight-by-ten photos. One showed a building leaning slightly to the right, looking rather raffish with its tilt. The other was a picture of what looked like a basement after a flood. A man stood in water that came just above his knees, holding a measuring stick that indicated a depth of slightly over two feet.

Then I picked up a sheet of stationery from the law offices of Peter Minot and Paul Aspen. It was a letter to all owners of property in the Crooked Creek Mountain vicinity, warning them that some of their neighbors had recently suffered verbal threats and others actual injury and/or death of livestock and/or pets, possibly connected with easements sought by Advantage Construction.

The letter went on to urge them to refuse to speak with any representative of Advantage Construction and to demand that he leave their property at once. If he did not, they should call the sheriff and report a threatening trespass. They should take extra security measures around their properties and families. They were urged to attend a meeting at the Baptist Church, Monday at eight p.m., at which the discussion would include a demand that Advantage recall its representatives in the Beulaland area and pay damages to owners who had been coerced into granting property easements, or suffered any out-of-pocket expense or emotional distress.

It was one pisser of a letter and I was grinning by the time I handed it to Cindy.

I picked up the last letter—a fax that had come in over Clay's line addressed to Branch. Apparently Minot had overnighted a letter similar to that of the owners to Advantage, and they were boiling.

Their fax ordered Branch to be in the Knoxville office at nine sharp on Monday and have McCurry with him. Meantime, McCurry was not even to say hello to anyone in Beulaland. Had they both lost their fucking minds? Signed by the CEO. Obviously Clay and his attorney had wasted no time.

Grinning even wider, I handed the fax along to Cindy.

Mickey wasn't smiling.

I shrugged. "Sorry, Mickey, I'm not responsible for your comeuppance. I do not know Mr. Minot, I do not know many of your victims—and none of them well—and I certainly do not know the CEO of your employer."

White with anger, he turned to Cindy. "Just because you're Ken Willingham's cousin you figure you can come down here and just run things and have people bowing right 'n left. You think you and your smart-ass friend and your junkyard dog can tell me what to do? Well, you fucking well can't! Understand? You'll pay for this!"

He grabbed her shoulder and shook her so hard she lost her balance and crashed into the table, scattering papers and dishes.

I brought my half-filled coffee mug down on his wrist with my full strength. He yelped and grabbed his wrist; I hoped it was broken in a thousand pieces. I grabbed the front of his shirt and threw my weight against him, backing him against the wall. I got my arm across his throat and leaned hard.

"Listen, you no-good son-of-a-bitch, you ever touch my girl again, you ever touch me or my dog—hell—you ever touch a dirty sock of mine, and you will live just long enough to be bloody sorry that you did. Now get out of my sight." I removed my arm, which was choking him, kicked his feet out from under him and turned to find myself face-to-face with Gertrude as she wielded an enormous iron skillet over Mickey's head.

She pulled him upright by his shirt. "Get out, you lowlife, and don't never come back. Less'n you want to be wearing this skillet around your neck!"

He scuttled out, clutching his left wrist with his right hand.

I turned to Cindy, now sitting down again. "Are you all right?"

"Fine, just a little out of breath—and surprised." She covered my hand with hers. "My God, Alex, I've never seen you like that. I thought you were going to choke him to death."

I put my finger to my lips. "Don't tell the audience, but I couldn't have held him much longer. I'm as tall as he is, but he's a lot heftier. Another few seconds and I'd have had to break a chair over his head or run for it."

I turned and began to apologize to Gertrude for the ruckus, but she held up her hand to stop me.

"No need. He started it. Guess those pictures and letters has got him crazy...he must know he's fired...plus whatever trouble he's into up here. I saw them all early this morning. Minot and Clay had them hand-delivered late last night. I figured it was prob'ly you girls' and Clay's ideas plus Paul's fancy words. But you two be careful. That bastard would be mean on Christmas Day.

"Now." She looked almost benign. "You've had a hard mornin'. What you need is some of my special tea. It will fix you right up."

The last thing I wanted was tea and the sympathy I knew would be forthcoming from many of the Delly's customers who had witnessed the scene. But I could think of no way to refuse. Cindy was equally mute, and we just sat for a few minutes until Gertrude returned with a tray bearing three tall glasses of iced tea. Apparently she, too, had had a hard morning.

When I saw the frosted glass, I realized something cold looked good and noticed I had been sweating. I took a long swallow of good Darjeeling tea…heavily laced with the smoothest rum I've ever tasted.

Cindy took a sip and her eyebrows did their trick of climbing halfway up her forehead. Then she smiled and clinked her glass against mine.

"Here's to you, my dear—protector of the innocent, woman in shining armor against the forces of darkness, and the toughest cream puff I've ever known!"

CHAPTER SIXTEEN

We had the canvas roof rolled back on the boat, enjoying the early afternoon sun. The little electric motor hummed quietly to itself, racing us across the lake at about four miles an hour. These were the only "power" boats allowed on the lake, and sailboats used their motors in emergencies only. It was delightfully peaceful.

Gertrude's "tea" had helped us over the hump of shock after our set-to with Mickey McCurry, but we felt the need of something pleasant to offset the morning in general. And we didn't want to rehash it a dozen times with people we'd run into at the Bromfield. And so, the lake.

Cindy had the tiller, and I took the occasional picture of her, of the billowing cumulus clouds, of the infrequent sailboat looking condescendingly elegant as they always do. We edged along to where Crooked Creek entered the lake with the last few feet of its bubbling mountain creek personality.

Also enjoying the tiny waterfall and slow-moving pool beyond it were three—I think—otters. They moved so fast it was hard to tell. I was snapping pictures as quickly as I could, and still couldn't keep up with their antics. They leaped and chased and dived, and then popped up here and there like bright-eyed, mischievous periscopes. I have no idea as to the life span of the otter, but I will give you ten to one they have more fun within it than we do in the three score and ten allotted us.

We left them, finally, and began our leisurely progress back to the docks at the Bromfield Inn. We had fishing tackle and bait with us, but by some unspoken agreement, we did not use it. I think neither of us wished to take anything from the lake that day.

I was at the tiller when Cindy turned, finger across her lips, and pointed. I cut the motor and we drifted a little way toward a deer and her fawn, standing at the edge of the lake and drinking daintily of its cool waters. I took several shots of them, and I'm certain that one of them will be our Christmas card. We were close enough to hear them drink. The only other sound—and one I wished I could record—was the territorial song of a cardinal as he staked out his summer locale.

I am not sure why deer and their offspring are so loved by so many. Perhaps they epitomize the gentle serenity most of us yearn to glean for ourselves.

The rest of us shoot them.

We docked the boat and paid the pleasant young woman at the shelter for the time we had been out. We had left Fargo in Jerry's care, and from his lack of excitement at our return, I had the strong feeling he had been well entertained—and probably well fed—by the Bromfield valet corps. I made the executive decision that he would survive another hour while we polished off our delightful afternoon with a couple of Joe's perfect cocktails.

As he placed our Cosmo and bourbon old fashioned before us, I took his picture. I wanted it partly as a pleasant memory of our vacation, partly to tease Joe at the Wharf Rat that he had competition deep in the hills of Tennessee, and with the thought that if it turned out well, I'd enlarge it and send a print back to the Bromfield.

At that moment Tommy came around the corner from the kitchen. He gave us a startled, almost frightened, look and went quickly back the way he had come. I wondered why he did not come out to say hello, but then assumed he was just one of those people who are allergic to cameras.

That was a mistake.

While we were at the bar, I remembered to ask Joe about what one should wear to their buffet and dance Saturday night.

"Just about anything," he replied with a laugh. "There are two alternating bands," he explained. "One is regular music, the other is square dancing."

I winced. Thus far in my young life I had managed to avoid square dancing, which seemed to me a bunch of people tapping their feet and milling around in circles while some man stood in a corner and hollered where they should head next.

Joe gave the bar a fast swipe with a clean towel. "Most of the ladies wear slacks or jeans, although some wear old-fashioned dresses and funny hats like that lady who used to be on *Grand Ole Opry*...Minnie Pearl, wasn't it?"

I shrugged my ignorance as Joe continued. "Some people dress up sort of formal, so you really can just take your choice."

Relieved at tomorrow night's wide choice of dress, we finished our drinks, collected a yawning Fargo and went back to the cabin.

After dinner, Cindy straightened up while I took on another chore. I went into the laundry/mudroom and looked closely at the three guns hanging on the wall. One was a .22 rifle, one a 16 gauge shotgun and the third an old 40mm Smith & Wesson automatic pistol housed in a moldy holster. From the looks of all three of them, their last usage had been at Gettysburg.

I eliminated the .22 as being too small to do the damage we might need done in a hurry, and too hard to handle in close quarters. The shotgun had the drawback of being likely to hit not only the person you were aiming at but also anyone else standing fairly near him.

That left the Smith and Wesson. It probably had a kick like a mule, and I imagined I could miss the QE2 broadside at a hundred feet. But I wouldn't miss at twenty-five feet, I thought, and since the thing doubtless sounded like a cannon, noise alone might help turn the trick.

So, finding a cleaning kit in a drawer below, I set to work. It took me over an hour and made a mess of the kitchen table, but finally I was satisfied it would not blow up in my hand if fired. I loaded it, put a bullet into the chamber, moved the safety to *on* and placed it in my night-table drawer.

Cindy frowned, but I felt better.

We each had just enough of a sunburn to make us sleepy, and neither of us quite made it through the eleven o'clock news. I surfaced sometime later to the sound of soft rain on the back porch roof, turned off the TV and went back to sleep, never having been quite awake.

In my ensuing dreams Cindy and I were at the Bromfield Inn, doing a Fred Astaire/Ginger Rogers version of the square dance…galloping gracefully around the dance floor, hopping onto chairs and then onto tables, the tapping of our feet becoming louder and louder. Some of the onlookers were calling out to us. *Cindy! Alex!* The tapping grew louder still. Finally it woke me.

It was Tommy, pounding on the back door and yelling, "Cindy! Alex! Wake up. Frank Allen is bad hurt!"

CHAPTER SEVENTEEN

I noticed their pickup truck slewed to a stop in the middle of the gravel road, but figured there would be no traffic at this hour. It was shortly after six and barely light. I yelled at him to wait a minute, fought my way into a pair of jeans, left my T-shirt hanging out and rushed to the back door.

"Come in. Who did you say was hurt?"

"Frank Allen. Half his ear is gone and he's bleedin' something fierce."

I must have looked blank, for he elaborated. "Frank Allen F-17, my mother's stud horse. He's her baby. She'll die if anything happens to him."

By now Cindy had found a robe and joined us. "How can we help? Have you called Lou and Gale?"

"No. Our wires are cut and the phone is dead. That's why I'm here. Please, can you call them right away?"

"Sure." I picked up the kitchen phone. "What's the number?"

He rattled it off to me and I dialed. After an eternity a sleephusky voice muttered, "Highway Animal Hospital."

"Gale? Lou?"

"Gale. Who's this?"

"Alex Peres. I've got Tommy Blackstone here at the cabin. Their phone is dead and Frank Allen—uh, seventeen something —is hurt...Tommy says half his ear is gone and he's bleeding heavily."

"Jesus. Tell Sara to keep calm, and put a cold towel on it. He's her baby. I'm on my way right now."

I hung the phone up. "She's on her way, and says put a cold towel on the ear. Tommy what does Frank Allen 17 mean? You surely don't have seventeen horses named Frank Allen?"

Tommy and Cindy laughed, and I felt a combination of stupid and irritated at their in-humor.

Tommy explained, "Frank Allen F-1 was the foundation sire of the Tennessee Walking Horse. Frank Allen F-17 means he's foundation stock, the seventeenth generation direct descendent of F-1. He's pureblood and a champion, Alex. He's never come in lower than second at any show. His colts are among the best ever bred, and he's...he's the sweetest guy in the world, gentle as a lamb, not a mean bone in him. And I know he's in pain." His voice broke. "Why would that man want to hurt him? Frank Allen loves everybody...why, Alex, *you* could ride him!"

Cindy stifled a snort, and I gave her a cold stare as she said to Tommy, "Mickey would hurt Frank because he's got enough mean bones for the whole county, I guess. Now you go home and tell your mom Gale is on the way. We'll be along shortly in case there's anything we can do. Now scoot, it's going to be okay. Don't forget the ice-water towel."

"Tommy, wait one second," I interjected. "Yesterday at the Bromfield. You seemed to be avoiding me. Had I hurt your feelings or something? Had I made you angry in some way?"

He edged toward the door, not meeting my eye.

"Tommy? What's wrong? Let's set it right."

He mumbled, "I was afraid to tell you."

"To tell me what?" I pursued.

"I was cleaning fish and I heard Uncle Branch around the corner on the veranda, talking on his cell phone. I don't know who to—all he kept calling him was 'sir.' But he was telling them that he was worried about Mickey. That Mickey had scared old Miz Armand so bad she went to the hospital with chest pains and..."

"When was this?" Cindy interrupted.

"Yesterday morning. Mom saw the EMTs come by and went out to see where they went. But I guess the old lady is okay now. She was just scared. Anyway Uncle Branch then told this 'sir' that Mickey had already hit one young woman and got beat up by another one in a fight that followed, and that he didn't know what Mickey would do to get even. He said you both had heavy-duty connections—whatever that meant. Then he saw me and walked down by the lake."

My mouth was dry. None of what Tommy had told us was any way to start a day.

"Well, thanks, Tommy. I appreciate your telling us about that. We'll be on our guard." I patted him on the shoulder and forced a grin. "Now you can scoot."

He scooted and we got dressed. Soon we heard Gale's SUV spit gravel as she made the turn up the mountain. I figured she must sleep like a fireman, with her clothes laid out in the order in which she donned them. We took the time to call the phone company and Clay. When Clay heard what happened he was so angry I thought he was going to choke. He was on his way. By the time we left, it was light, but the rain looked here to stay.

When we got to Blackstone Farm, Gale had the bleeding under control and was stitching up the ear. I felt so sorry for Frank Allen, half his ear had apparently been cut off with something sharp, like a straight razor. He would heal in time, but he would never again be the gorgeous chestnut showhorse who won all the blue ribbons. It was almost as if he knew it. He stood in the wide

132

aisle of the stables, not causing Gale any trouble, his chin and lower jaw resting quietly on Sara's shoulder…a hurt child asking Mommy to make it better.

Tommy began to feed the other horses, obviously he knew exactly how much of what feed every animal received. He might have been a little slow with sixth-grade math, but, by God, Tommy knew his horses.

Cindy began helping Tommy. I had nothing to do, so I went in the house and made coffee. The others soon came in, with the exception of Tommy. We had just sat down when Clay arrived, the sheriff right behind him.

They pulled up chairs while Cindy poured them coffee and then started another pot. Clay introduced her and me to Sheriff Johnson.

"Ah, yes, ladies. The Willingham guests, aren't you?"

Cindy started to reply, but Sara interrupted. "Excuse me, but I have to get back to Frank." She picked up her mug and began to rise.

Gale gently took the mug and set it down. "No, Sara, have your coffee and some toast or something. Frank is fine. I gave him a shot to make him a little sleepy so he won't shake that ear a lot."

Tommy came in and seemed to report to Gale. "I mucked out Frank's stall and put him in with plenty of fresh straw in case he wants to lie down. I sifted the old straw real careful; there was nothing in it. But I piled it up separate in the lot in case you want to check it, Sheriff."

Gale said, "Good idea, Tommy, and when the other horses finish eating, turn them out so Frank will have a nice quiet morning. A little rain won't hurt them. Put them in the near pasture, where you can keep an eye on them, and please excuse me, I have a busy day. Call me if it starts bleeding again. Otherwise, I'll see you tomorrow," she added as an afterthought. Clay nodded his approval.

Finally the sheriff got a word in. "Before you leave…any idea what could have made the cut, Gale?"

"I'm pretty sure it was a straight razor. Maybe a scalpel. I think not a knife—that would have chewed the skin up more. It's almost a surgical cut. See you later." She was gone.

"Sara." The sheriff's voice was surprisingly gentle. "Can you tell me when you knew Frank was hurt?"

"Sort of. Frank or one of the others woke me up, kicking his stall. I figured it was him acting up a bit, like maybe one of the mares is coming in season. I just yelled out the window and told him to stop that, and he did."

She unthinkingly picked up a piece of the buttered toast Tommy had put in front of her. I smiled at him. He was quite a kid. He looked at me gratefully as if he was afraid I was angry he hadn't told me sooner about the phone call.

Sara took a bite and went on. "Then, I dozed…I'm not sure how long. It started again with all the horses raising Cain. I figured probably a bear was trying to get in the garbage and I grabbed some clothes and went out beating my big pot with an iron spoon to scare him off." She sipped her coffee.

"I didn't see any bear, or anything else, and went to check the stable. That's when I found him." Her voice broke on the last three words.

"Then what did you do? And what time was it?" Johnson asked.

"It was going on five o'clock. I grabbed a clean towel and tried to stop the blood. I screamed for Tommy and he came running. I told him to call the vet and you. Next thing I know he's in the stable telling me the wires are cut and the phone is dead and he's going to your place." She pointed at us. "That was about it."

"Did either of you touch the phone box?" Johnson asked.

Tommy and Sara looked at each other. Sara simply shook her head. Tommy explained, "I tried both phones in the house and they were dead. I was going to try the one in the stable, but when I came out of the house I saw the phone box open with all the wires yanked out and cut. So I said I'd go down to Alex and Cindy's—I mean Mr. Willingham's. And I didn't touch the box."

"Good. We won't get any prints in the stable, half the county's been in there. But maybe the phone box…if I was out cuttin' wires and a mad woman come along bangin' on a big bass drum, I might touch something I hadn't meant to. Too bad it wasn't a thousand watts."

He grinned at his own humor, and I joined him. Nobody else did, and Clay could remain silent no longer.

"Dammit, Jeffie, we *know* who did it! Arrest the bastard before he gets out of here Monday morning and just walks away from his dirty work without paying—in any way—for all the grief he has caused."

"He's leavin' Monday?"

"Yes, real early Monday. Branch got a firecracker from the brass at Advantage Construction after they received Peter Minot's letter. They said for him to have McCurry in their office no later than nine Monday morning. I think Advantage is going to say they aren't responsible for anything he did since he was technically under the supervision—and presumably under the control—of Branch. And that's about like saying I'm in control of Iran."

"Lord," Cindy murmured, "half the livestock in Beulaland could be hurt or dead by Monday."

The sheriff favored her with a nod. "If he sticks to livestock."

Well, well, I thought. The sheriff is not a total dolt after all.

"Jesus, Jeffie, don't even go there." Clay pounded his fist on the table. "Just *arrest* the son-of-a-bitch. Get him for jaywalking if you have to! I know Branch isn't clean in the deal, but he hasn't hurt anything or anyone, and I don't want him blamed for Mickey's malicious mischief!"

"Mickey's malicious mischief," Johnson repeated with a hearty laugh. "That's a good one, Clay, I'll have to remember that one!"

"For God's sake, Johnson! There's nothing funny about any of this! Are you waiting for a murder before you make a move?"

"For God's sake yourself, *Rodman!* I got no grounds to arrest him. Hell, I can't even get a warrant to search that room of his

135

at the No-tel Mo-tel. Now when I get the information on that casing of the shot that killed the sheep—we never did find the damn bullet—if Mickey has registered a gun like it, at least I'll get a warrant. However, if he owns a gun, you want to bet it isn't registered, anyway?"

"Yeah, yeah," Clay surrendered. "Well, can you at least keep an eye on him so nothing else happens?"

"I can try. Lately he seems to be pretty well glued to a barstool at the Dew Drop."

I thought of that nice Deputy Spitz. "Tell your people to be careful, Sheriff. The only thing I can think of meaner than McCurry sober is McCurry drunk."

He gave me a smile that had little warmth. "Yes, I understand you ladies discovered that at Gertrude's yesterday. It's kinda hard to believe…y'all seem so nice and po-lite…it's hard to believe you got him in a choke hold and then had him on the floor threatening on killin' him."

I returned his smile in kind. "I'm sure my so-called choke hold barely caused him to lose a breath, and kicking the feet out from under somebody not expecting it hardly requires a Navy Seal. As for threatening to kill him, he probably hears that promise at least twice a day. Now if Gertrude had crowned him with that skillet, we might have had something to celebrate."

I turned to Sara. "We're going to let you and Tommy relax and get some rest. Obviously Frank Allen is under excellent care between Gale and Tommy."

He squared his shoulders and looked proud.

"Yes," Cindy added. "We are so terribly sorry it happened. It's worse than a crime, it's an evil act, but Frank is still your boy, and he'll be fine. If there is anything at all you need—you have but to holler! We'll see you soon."

"Yes, I'll be going, too," Johnson put in. "I don't know how to make a pretty speech, but I'll have a man out here to check that phone box."

I wondered why he didn't just do it himself. Then I thought perhaps he didn't know how.

He set his car on my tail all the way down from Blackstone Farm to Ken's place, and then gunned it with squealing tires and a burp of his siren as he hit the paved road. Yippee Ky Yo!

We were at loose ends. We flopped in the living room and Cindy lit the fire.

The rain maintained a dismal half-hearted drizzle. Fargo stared morosely onto the soggy deck. A heavy fog was moving in, or was it a low-lying cloud? For lack of a better idea we had more coffee. It tasted lousy.

We had thought of driving down to Gatlinburg today. Sonny had been there last year with the girlfriend du jour. He said it was touristy, but also had some wonderful craft shops and a couple of interesting small museums. Obviously it was not the day for that trip.

Then Cindy brought up what had I had been thinking of, but hadn't quite had the nerve to mention.

"Darling, are you familiar with the old saying: a lady always knows when to leave the party?"

I laughed. "No, I don't think I ever did hear it, but it's apt, isn't it? What were you thinking, my lady? Today? Tomorrow?"

She set her coffee mug on the cocktail table and made a face. "Ghastly stuff. Anyway, I think tomorrow. We're meeting Gale and Lou tonight, which will probably be fun. Anyway, I'd hate to cancel—we'd have to tell them why. And I'm sure most everyone we've met will be there, and we can make our farewells casually. Then early tomorrow morning we can fold our tents and steal away. We can either push along home in two days like we did coming down, or take it a day slower and visit some of the sights on the way home."

"I think you're right." All of a sudden, I wanted to go home, right that minute. "For one thing, I feel that we're getting too involved down here for people who don't belong. It would be different if we owned this place. Of course, I guess the problem with McCurry will end Monday—if Branch can drag him away. Personally I think he's a psychopath who's loving every moment of it."

"He may well be." Cindy looked thoughtful. "And I hope he doesn't work up to a *grand finale* before he leaves. But I don't regret any of the little things we've done. If good people don't pitch in, the bad stuff just goes on."

"Quite true, m'dear." I got up and pushed a loose log to the rear. "There have been a couple of emergencies where we have done the good neighbor bit. But we have to remember we are not neighbors, we are visitors. And Peter Minot is involved now, and the problem with Advantage won't end with McCurry's departure. There will be legal twists and turns for the next hundred years unless Advantage backs down. And we have no part in that. Let's go home. We've got a *Master Suite* to furnish."

Suddenly we were energized. We had things to do. I phoned Mrs. Fouts and luckily found her in. I told her we were leaving tomorrow and finally got the figure we owed her for the original groceries. I sat down and wrote her a check for the food plus a tip before I forgot.

That inspired me to go down to Gertrude's and stock up on several of Sara's jellies and preserves to take home, and a few pastries…just to get us through the efforts of packing and loading the car. Then I hit the small "super" market for some Georgia peaches, cookies, doggie treats and sodas plus that flavored water Cindy likes. That took care of snacks for the road.

I returned home to find Cindy on a cleaning spree. I explained to her that Mrs. Fouts was coming as soon as we left to put things in order for the next occupants.

"But we shouldn't leave her a mess," Cindy insisted.

"Angel, we will not toss the chicken bones over our shoulders, nor will we throw half-empty beer cans in the fireplace or carve our initials in the dining room table. We will depart with dishes washed and bed stripped and Venetian blinds all at the same height. But if you don't leave Mrs. Fouts just a little something to do, she's that terribly honest type who will tell Frances they don't owe her anything for the day, because we did it all ourselves."

"Oh, all right." She looked a little bereft. "I feel all charged up. Now I can't think what I should do?"

"Make us a drink and bring in a log while I set up the Scrabble board I found in the laundry room. Penny a point?"

"Dime a point. I feel lucky."

"Uh-oh."

CHAPTER EIGHTEEN

Fog and drizzle had done little to rain on the Bromfield Inn's parade. Most of the tables were taken with people having dinner. Lou and Gale were already there. Lou stood and waved us to our table.

As we twisted our way to it, I was surprised at the number of people whom we didn't know who nodded or spoke briefly or simply smiled at us. I supposed they had heard of our help with the errant cattle and our temporary triumph over Mickey McCurry at the Delly. And then a small event occurred that made me think perhaps we had a good press agent.

I noticed Gertrude sitting at a table with three other ladies of uncertain age and unstinting of makeup, all in elegant gowns heavy with jewelry. I gave Gertrude a wave and in return received a broad wave, an inviting smile and an absolutely frightening blown kiss from all four dowagers. I scuttled ahead to our table, leaving Cindy to make her way as best she could.

The buffet was typical of country club offerings, but well cooked and nicely served. The band played light semi-classical music at a volume that provided a pleasant background and allowed easy conversation.

We caught up on the animal casualty report. Jasper was coming along, Sammy was doing well; the problem was keeping him away from his beloved sheep for a few days. Frank Allen was still upset and nervous, but not seriously injured.

"Actually," Gale opined, "I think Sara is making him more nervous than he needs to be. It's wise for several reasons to keep him in his stall for a few days, but she's checking on him every half hour, sometimes crying when she pets him, leaving the stable lights on all night…I think Frank by now thinks *he* did something wrong."

"It's a scary situation," Cindy countered. "That damned man—much as I'd like to see him in jail, I'd be very happy just to see him out of town. Of course, that merely foists him onto another innocent town, but I almost wouldn't care."

"A creative police department would help," I added. "I remember when Provincetown was blessed with a guy who regularly beat up on his wife. She was afraid to file charges for fear he'd kill her and their two- or three-year-old toddler. Sonny, my brother the cop, got a friend of his to buy the husband a bunch of drinks in his favorite spa. When the guy got good and drunk, Sonny casually stopped in the bar for a drink, insulted the man right and left until he took a punch at Sonny—who then arrested him for assaulting an officer. That put him in jail for a few days, while they convinced a neighbor to testify against him. And that gave the wife some courage, and they got him good and proper."

"Maybe you should tell that story to Deputy Spitz," Lou said. "That sounds like something he would do."

"What about the sheriff?" I queried. "Couldn't he set up something like that?" I was half-kidding, and Gale took me up on it.

"Sure. The friend would be busy getting Mickey dead-ass drunk. Jeffie would come in and get drunk with Mickey. They would start to fight and the friend would be afraid someone was going to get shot, so he tries to break it up. Jeffie arrests his friend for interfering and forgets to arrest Mickey. Mickey falls asleep while driving back to the No-Tel Mo-tel and drives his car into the reception area, which is being burgled at the time. He accidentally runs over both burglars and gets the Good Citizen Award of the Month."

We all laughed, and I agreed that sometimes it seemed as if justice were indeed blind, if not drunk to boot.

Suddenly Cindy looked keenly toward the outer door and did her eyebrow trick. "Well, well, look who's here!"

As I turned I was thinking that McCurry combined with square dancing could really make my evening. But it wasn't he at all.

It was Tommy Blackstone, looking very handsome in tan slacks and a dark green or navy blazer, with the strobe lights, it was hard to tell. He was escorting two well-dressed women. The older one was absolutely stunning in an Anne Bancroft sort of way, and it took me a moment to realize it was Sara. Her dark hair was attractively styled and her makeup was just enough and just right. Her well-tanned complexion was set off by her soft peach dress and the single strand of pearls that led to an enticing décolletage. The younger woman had blond hair much like Tommy's and wore a pale blue dress that let her hair dominate the scene. Her main touch of color was an orange sash, very nearly matching the stripe in Tommy's tie. I wondered if it was accidental.

"This table excluded," Cindy gushed, "Tommy's got the two best-looking women in the room! Sara looks divine and thank God she's having an evening out. Who's the pretty girl?"

"Tommy's girlfriend, Cissy Milton—probably his wife in another year or so," Lou advised.

"That's great!" I replied. "That family deserves some good things and she looks like a sweetie. Ah, will they be okay living independently?"

"They'll be fine according to Doc Fisher. Tommy is a little—slow, I guess you'd say, but far from seriously retarded—because of a tangled umbilical cord which caused some trouble at birth. Cissy is on about the same level, maybe marginally better, due to an auto accident. Sitting on Grandma's lap instead of in her baby seat, she had a slight brain injury."

Lou sipped her coffee and Gale spoke up. "Since their conditions were accident-caused, not genetic, they can have kids without any more than every parent's worry that the offspring will be normal. And they are far from dumb. Tommy knows more about horses than anyone in the state except Clay. And Cissy runs—*is*—the home delivery part of the Delly…and we all know, our Gertrude don't suffer no fools lightly."

We all laughed, and I asked, "Who are the three Harpies with our Gertrude? Beulaland's retired motorcycle club?"

Lou raised her chin high and pursed her lips. "Honey, you ah speakin' of the very coah of the Ladies' Altar Guild of St. Luke's Episcopal Church. The flowers don't dare to wilt in theyah presence."

We laughed so loud, we got looks from around us. Fortunately, before we could carry this conversation further, waiters began clearing the tables, and the orchestra grew silent and departed the stand.

In a few minutes a whole new group of musicians filed in, wearing blue overalls and workshirts, topped with various styles of straw hats. Last in line was a thin man dressed in jeans and white shirt with a string tie and tuxedo jacket. He had to be the caller.

Tuning procedures complete, the band struck up a brisk tune and the tuxedo man called, "Pick yo pahdners and form in foahs."

Lou and Gale excused themselves and headed to the dance floor. Other twosomes joined them, including Gertrude and her companions—who else would have dared partner them? Cindy looked at me, and I said, "Don't be absurd."

At that moment Peter Minot approached with a wide grin.

"Which of you ladies will do me the honor?"

"Cindywillbedelightedto," I blurted. I was taking no chances.

"I *am* delighted," she said as she rose and took his arm. "See you later, chick-chick-chicken."

The participants made their way 'round and 'round the room, docilely following the high-pitched instructions. I sat happily alone. I love to dance, and I am pretty good at it. But I feel that, unless you are in a Broadway chorus line, dancing is a two-person contact sport, not a groupie affair. I do not like being yelled at while I am dancing, and told what steps to take, when I am perfectly capable of following the music without directions from the sidelines.

I was basking in my superiority, when a figure appeared beside the table.

"Howdy, Ms. Alex, would you do me the favor of the next set?" It was Branch Redford, looking quite gentlemanly in light gray pants and a darker blazer.

"Thanks, Branch, but I don't square dance."

"Don't square dance or don't dance with me?" He sat down, uninvited. "Ms. Alex, I am *persona non grata* in my own hometown. Part of it is my own fault, I freely admit, but part of it ain't. For example, those photos of the old-folks home. Yes, I got the county to pay for half of it and a couple of banks to pick up the slack in a mortgage. But the trouble there isn't that I sold sub-par work." He took a generous sip of a dark highball.

"Then what is it?" I smiled, disbelieving.

He waved at a waiter and ordered a drink for us both. "The units were built on limestone with hollow areas underneath. The weight of the buildings caused some of it to collapse. So now one building slants, and the other opened up a spring. Now, *that* was for the engineers to realize and tell us not to build there! I think maybe they did know and just took a chance. But *I* didn't know it when I sold it! Now the old folks are in 'temporary' quarters I wouldn't wish on a weasel, and I would never have done that to them. I sincerely would not!"

"So why did you stay with Advantage?" I looked for our waiter. By now, I wanted the drink.

"I was so naïve," he explained, "I believed 'em when they said it would never happen again. And this mountain development sounded great. I figured if I did an effective, fast job, it would put me in good with Advantage and be a gold mine for Beulaland. We might well become another Gatlinburg!"

"Didn't it occur to you, not everyone might want to be another Gatlinburg?"

"Frankly, no. I figured property values would go up, businesses would have more traffic. There'd be lots of B&Bs and restaurants and…oh! Just loads of things. But I was wrong. These damned old dirt farmers don't know nothin' about business. And then Advantage saddled me with Mickey."

"Ah, yes. Mickey. Are you aware of what he's been doing? What he did to your own sister?"

"I know what they say he's been doing. I haven't seen him do anything. He's got a rough tongue. He scared the bejesus out of some old people. And I tell you, I wouldn't be surprised if he hurt them dogs and shot that sheep and all…though I can't prove it. You cross him and you're on his shit list forever. Pardon my language, ma'am. But I never *saw* anything, so what can I do?"

I realized Branch had had a drink or three, and I wanted to keep him talking.

"Branch," I suggested, "let's go in the bar. I need a drink, and these waiters are all jammed with orders."

"Dance one set with me, Ms. Alex, and I'll buy you the whole bar."

I finally figured out that he simply wanted to be seen dancing with me. I was staying at Ken Willingham's. I had made friends with Beulaland locals. I would clothe him in my respectability. Okay fine. I'd get what I wanted out of him in the bar.

"All right, Branch, you win." The band was tuning up again. "Just don't blame me if I step all over you."

He offered me his arm. "You can't hurt these shoes, ma'am. Let's go trip the light fantastic."

145

I automatically looked down and saw he was wearing the sneakers like mine, and probably the same size. Even for a short, chubby guy he had small hands and feet. Maybe I couldn't hurt the shoes, but I could sure hurt the tops of his toes. Well, he had asked for it. On whether we would trip the light fantastic or trip each other, the jury was still out.

The less said of our dance, the kinder.

In the crowded bar I managed to get Joe's attention and ordered a bourbon on the rocks. Branch duplicated my order and doubled it, and then leaned forward and said softly, "Run this on Clay's tab, will ya, Joe?" Joe looked unhappy, but complied. I figured it was to the Bromfield benefit.

"Clay was pretty upset about Frank Allen, wasn't he, Branch?"

"We all were," he answered stoutly. "Terrible thing to do to a sweet, beautiful animal! Now there, I have to say I truly doubt Mickey had anything to do with it. After all, he knows Sara and Clay and I are family."

"You think that would stop him? After all, Clay is the one who hired Peter Minot and told him what he wanted done." I sipped my drink gratefully.

"Yes. But family is family." I thought he was trying to convince himself. He was gulping his drink. His hand had a slight tremor.

"Say, how's that big ole dog of yours?" He was trying hard to sound casual.

"Oh, he's at the cabin sulking." Actually he was in the boathouse sixty feet away, being carefully watched by the squad of car valets, who took shelter from the rain there. At least one of them would be with him at all times. They were to bring Fargo directly to me at once—dogs allowed or not—if Mickey showed up anywhere on the premises.

I continued the fairytale. "He always sulks when he's alone, but he gets over it. By the way, I hear you and Mickey are leaving Monday. So are we. We'll be sorry to leave, but I'll bet you won't."

My hope was that if he repeated that our departure was

planned for Monday to Mickey, Mickey would hold off any attack on Fargo—or us—until Sunday night, when we would be far, far out of range.

"No, I won...won't be sorry to leave this sorry town." He was beginning to slur. "They never have appreciated me and I don't 'preciate them. Now, Mickey, thass another ball of wax. Joe! Another round here."

I handed my first glass back to Joe with some liquid still in the bottom and took a very small sip from my second.

"Mickey doesn't want to leave?" I prompted.

"I don't know what the...heck he wants. He stays mad at the world. He takes any disagreement as grounds for a fight. He's nearly always half in th' bag, but he gets so violent, I wunner if he isn't adding something to the booze."

"You mean like steroids?"

"Yeah, or somethin' like that. Makes him think he's God and nobody can't stop him. If I were Clay I'd leave town for a day or so, but he won't leave his precious horses. Even though he's got a bunch of men guarding the stables. I tell you one thing, Ms. Alex, Mickey can be one scary critter."

"I can't argue with that," I agreed. "I was surprised to see Sara and Tommy here tonight."

"They'll be okay. Clay has two men guarding the stables and them, too. Night n' day."

Did he realize what he had said? That Clay had men guarding *them*—Sara and Tommy—not just the stable? What did he think Mickey was going to do? Frankly, a mass murder with an Uzi was not beyond imagination, and I didn't want to be on the six o'clock news.

"Can't you have the sheriff do something to cool him down and get him out of here. I think most people would be happy to cut their losses if he were just locked up until somebody from Advantage—other than you—came and got him. There's always public drunkenness or DWI, or even 'insulting' the women who hang out at the Dew Drop Inn."

He looked at me with a sad smile, and the put-on southern

colloquialisms disappeared. "Ms. Alex, don't you understand? I've tried all that—and more. But Jeffie Johnson is scared to death of him. And after Peter's letter to the Advantage brass, *they* are scared of him. He's a loose cannon and nobody but poor Branch is left trying to hang on to the rope. I wish I knew some Marines."

"How about Deputy Spitz. He seems levelheaded, and he's big."

"He wouldn't interrupt his breakfast to tell me my clothes were on fire. Two of the people in that old-folks home are his grandparents—and you know who he blames."

I was about to ask him another question, when I heard the faint trill of a cell phone. I knew it wasn't mine. Mine was on the kitchen table in Provincetown, where I had put it so I wouldn't forget it. After searching several pockets, Branch came up with his. I listened shamelessly to his end of the conversation.

"Hello...oh, hi, Mildred... What's up?... Where are you?... The Dew Drop?... I thought you would be at the No-Tel by now... What do you mean you were scared to go with him?... Oh, I don't think he would have hurt you...Why would he be planning to teach you some manners?... Well, calling him a foul-mouthed bully is hardly being nice to him—which is what I paid you for... He slapped you right at the bar and Jake threw him out?... Oh, God, well. No wonder you didn't go with him... He's going to take care of what? Who?... Oh, I see... No, keep the money...Where is he now? The No-Tel, you think... Okay, I'll try to calm him down. You go stay with your sister for a while, honey...you hear? Thanks for calling."

He folded the phone and stuffed it back in his pocket. As he spoke, the color had slowly drained from his face as if someone had pulled a plug. Ashen now, and apparently sober, he somehow treated me to his professional smile.

"Well, Ms. Alex, Saint George is off to find the dragon. Wish me luck." He squared his shoulders and walked away.

I did wish him luck. He would need it. He made an almost comical figure of a knight, but seemingly he was the only one this Camelot town had on its roster.

CHAPTER NINETEEN

Returning to the table, I found Cindy sipping a Cosmo. "Hello, darling, I was beginning to think you had eloped with Branch."

"No. I was giving him a bourbon transfusion after our trip around the dance floor." I decided to try to keep it light; there was no point in ruining our last evening here. I just hoped it wasn't our last evening *anywhere*. "I see the regular musicians are back. Shall we risk it?"

"I thought you'd never ask."

We danced well together, and both enjoyed it. We stayed on the floor for the next tune, and had only taken a step or two, when Clay tapped my shoulder.

"May I borrow your lady for a few minutes?"

"I'll be watching the clock." I smiled and started to walk back to our table, when I noticed the sheriff pushing Sara around the floor with great concentration if little grace. Well, why the hell not? The little imp inside me asked. Why not indeed? I answered. I cut in smoothly.

He relinquished her gruffly, and we stepped away. "Thank you," she whispered gratefully.

"My pleasure." She felt supple and sensuous and somehow compliant in my arms, and I would always remember her differently than I would have a day ago. The music was too soon ended, and I walked her back to her table where Tommy and Cissy sat.

Sara and I looked at each other and smiled knowingly. One of us was committed to another, and one of us was a widow and businesswoman in a small southern town. I took both her hands briefly, and she leaned forward to give me a cheek kiss. And the band began to play.

Cindy, Gale and Lou were all at our table, and conversation was general for awhile. Then Cindy said, "By the way, Clay said to tell you goodbye, he's going to Kingsport for the rest of the weekend. He asks us to come back next year. He thanks us for being so nice to Sara and Tommy."

I felt my face turn red, but managed to answer casually. "They're nice people. I'm glad he thinks the Mickey situation is cool enough to take a weekend away. Cindy, it's getting late, m'dear, and we have an early morning. What say you?"

"I say that band is actually playing a waltz, which I don't think I've done since eighth grade dancing school. Waltz me to the coat check and we will make our reluctant departure."

We said a hopefully temporary goodbye to Gale and Lou, and waltzed our way to pick up our raincoats. At the door we were delighted to see we did not really need them. The rain had stopped although trees and gutters were still dripping. The fog was doing its best to climb every mountain. Tomorrow should be clear.

Our car was returned to us, our dog in the front seat, sporting a carnation in his collar, and, after giving Jerry a giant tip to share with his buddies, we headed back to the cabin.

The closer we got to it, the more nervous I got. What had Mildred told Branch when he questioned whom she was talking about? Could it be us Mickey planned to take care of? Clay? Sara and Tommy? All five of us? Was that why Clay left town after posting a bunch of armed guards for all the horses plus his sister and nephew? We had no guard. Any second could catapult us into disaster.

I entered in the parking area, turned out the headlights and let Fargo out. He ran around, sniffing and barking a couple of times, but he did not seem unduly excited. He was merely announcing that he was in residence. I turned off the little overhead light and told Cindy to climb over into the driver's seat when I got out and to make sure the car doors were all locked, and motor idling.

"The lights are on in the bedroom and front deck," I told her. "If I don't start turning on lights all over the house in a couple of minutes, flick the headlights, turn the radio to blast, blow the horn. Wake up the whole neighborhood and call 911. And *get down to the sheriff's office and stay there!*"

I gave her a glancing kiss and got out before she could tell I was shaking. I called softly to Fargo and took him by the collar. The only thing he had ever attacked in his life was a squeaky toy, but he could—and would—growl and bark.

We went silently up the back steps and onto the porch. I tried to unlock the door soundlessly, but with the big old key, it sounded like I was opening the Tower of London. We crept into the laundry room…the mudroom…whatever the hell it was, it was pitch dark. The kitchen door was closed. Had we left it that way? Was he waiting in the kitchen? I could almost feel his big hands around my neck. I could definitely feel the sweat running down my back.

I groped around in the tackle box where I had earlier hidden the loaded pistol. I finally felt it and pulled the gun out, taking off the safety. I let go of Fargo's collar, opened the kitchen door and flicked on the light.

Nobody. I took what felt like my first breath in a week.

Fargo ran room-to-room, sniffing. But he always did that

when we came home—frankly, I think he was checking to make sure no strange dogs or cats had moved in during his absence. His hackles were not up, and there were no barks. I checked the pantry and moved on to the hall light and our bedroom and bathroom. Then I walked into the living/dining room and hit those lights. Nothing.

I went out on the deck and waved Cindy to come in. At this point I figured she was safer inside the house. She scampered up the steps and across the deck and gave me a fast, hard hug.

"Oh, God, Alex. I thought you never would come out. And you are soaking wet. You were sure he was here, weren't you? How could you walk into that laundry room? I would have fainted, I think."

But she was made of sterner stuff than she thought. When I told her I had yet to check the upstairs rooms, she grabbed her trusty fireplace tongs and followed me every inch of the way.

Finally satisfied no one was lurking in the house, we collapsed at the kitchen table and let the shakes take over. Fargo was the only calm one of us. Cindy finally poured us a stiff tot of Ken's expensive brandy, and while it may have stiffened our backbones, tonight it unsurprisingly did nothing for our libidos.

We knew there would be no bed sport and little bed sleep this night. Cindy made coffee, and after the machine finished its gurgle, she got up to pour us a mug. Fargo picked that moment to whine to go out. Startled, Cindy whirled around and caught me with a sharp blow to the cheekbone with an empty mug. I yelped and bent over, hand to face. The damn thing *really* hurt!

"Oh, Lord, you go through an eight-room house where a lunatic might have hidden and you are fine until I almost kill you with a coffee mug!" She began to laugh in a pitch I didn't like.

"Shut up," I muttered—was my cheek broken?—"And get some ice!"

"Yes, yes, of course. Oh, darling, I am so sorry. "She kept apologizing as she wrapped ice in a clean dish towel and held it gently against my cheek.

And so the night went. We moved from the kitchen to the

living room couch and took turns dozing, and finally all three of us fell asleep, tumbled together like a litter of overgrown puppies.

Sometime before we all faded out last night, Cindy had set her little travel alarm for seven a.m., and had put it on the dining area table so one of us would have to be up and moving to shut it off. It woke me with a surprisingly loud noise that sounded almost like a siren.

I worked myself free from pillows, Cindy and Fargo and staggered toward the clock. When I got near it, I saw the time read six fifteen. While I was puzzling that out, I realized the sound I had heard really had been a siren at the foot of the mountain, where the little private road met the main road into town. And it now sounded like two police cars and the whoop-whoop of an ambulance. There must have been an accident—and apparently a serious one.

Beulaland's finest would have to handle it without my oversight. I made it to the bathroom and turned on the cold water. A face-wash and tooth-brush would have to be enough until I had some coffee and maybe something solid in my stomach. When I looked in the mirror I recalled that my headache was not entirely due to Ken's brandy. I had a sizeable, colorful shiner, and my cheek was sore as hell. It even hurt when I brushed my hair.

Just as I poured the coffee and took my croissant out of the micro, Cindy and Fargo arrived. Their timing was always good. I opened a door for one and poured coffee for another.

"Why are we up so early?" she asked plaintively. "Oh, your poor cheek!" she added.

"There was some sort of accident down on the main road. The cop sirens woke me, and I thought it was the alarm clock."

"Should we go down?"

"The cops are there. Leave it to the pros."

At that moment there was an authoritative knock at the front door. As I reached the living room, I could see through the window: our guests were the sheriff and Deputy Spitz.

153

"It's the cops," I called over my shoulder and heard Cindy scamper for the bedroom. I figured they were looking for possible witnesses to the accident, but I did quickly shove the pistol under a couch cushion as I passed. I opened the front door. Fargo scooted in, the two men stood like statues.

"Good morning Sheriff, Deputy. May I help you with something?"

"We hope you may have some helpful information. May we come in?" Johnson looked about as untidy as I did. His clothes were rumpled and sagging, his hair had been hastily combed and his eyes were bloodshot. Dave Spitz looked like a recruiting poster.

"Come on in the kitchen, there's coffee and some pastry if you like." I didn't want them in the living room.

We sat at the kitchen table, and I poured coffee. Jeffie refused a pastry, which surprised me, and Spitz could hardly have one if the boss-man didn't. So I had my second.

"That's a nasty bruise, Ms. Peres," Johnson remarked.

"It feels nasty, and my own dog is to blame. He startled Ms. Hart last night, and when she turned around she accidentally clocked me with a coffee mug."

"Really?" Spitz asked me neutrally.

Johnson didn't bother to comment, but asked. "Is she here? Ms. Hart I mean."

"She's dressing. I imagine she'll be here in a minute."

And she was, looking fresh and well-groomed. I now felt doubly grungy.

"Good morning, gentlemen. I understand there was an accident at the foot of the hill earlier. I hope it wasn't serious."

"Well, it may have been an accident. We haven't *entirely* ruled that out." Johnson gave a wolfish grin. "But it was certainly serious, all right. In fact it was fatal."

"Damn!" I took a sip of coffee. "That's too bad...helluva way to start your day."

Cindy looked concerned. "Was it anyone we would have known?"

154

"Well, now, I don't know. We aren't sure of his identity ourselves." Johnson sounded almost coy, as he removed several credit cards and what looked like drivers' licenses from his shirt pocket and began to read off the names on them. "Do either of you know a Michael Cully of Galveston, Texas?" As we each shook our heads, he moved on to the next. "A Michael Sullivan of El Paso, Texas? A Michael McNulty of Gadsden, Alabama? A Michael McCurry of Rome, Georgia?"

"Well of course, we know a Michael—actually Mickey— McCurry." Cindy stated. "But I thought he was from Knoxville. Is *he* dead?" She was not a good poker player; she looked as relieved as one who has just learned that the giant meteor is going to by-pass the Earth by ten miles.

"Is there really a Rome, Georgia?" I asked. "I guess I stopped with Venice, Florida."

"There is a Rome." Johnson looked irritated. "And Mickey is dead."

I lit a cigarette before replying, and Johnson looked at the pack hungrily. I did not offer one. I figured a senior police officer on an official call should not smoke a cigarette. Especially one of mine.

"Then, of course, we know the man called Michael McCurry. I assume they are all the same man—he stuck with Michael to have a first name familiar to him, and since all the last names are Irish I imagine that's what he really is. Of course any one of the names—or none of the names—could be his real one. Same with the towns. Did he have a car here? The only car I ever saw him in was Branch's. Strange."

Johnson was frowning. Obviously he hadn't figured on the licenses being fraudulent with regard to the cities as well as the names. And I doubted he had picked up on the Irish surnames.

"Car? Yes, he had a car," Spitz put in. "In fact, it's parked at the bottom of the road. Have you any idea when he parked it there?"

"No." Cindy answered. "There were three cars parked at the intersection when we came home. I didn't pay attention to them—I just assumed one of our neighbors was having a party. I'm sorry, I don't remember. I do recall one of them was light-colored."

"Yes, well, hmmn…could have been his. Now, moving right along. Could you ladies give my deputy here your names and home addresses and where you work, while I just have a little look around?"

What the hell was he trying to pull? "Sheriff, we'll be glad to give you our proper names and home address. I don't believe our places of work would be of any value to you. Neither Ms. Hart nor I own or rent this property. We are guests here. While Ms. Hart is a cousin of the owner, neither she nor I have the authority to allow you to search it. To 'look around' the outside grounds or the interior of the house, you'll need a warrant. And just in case you want to shuffle through my car—you'll need a warrant for that, too."

Cindy put her coffee mug down with a bang that made my cheek hurt all over again. "Furthermore, Sheriff," she announced, "neither of us saw a thing. We were both asleep until your sirens woke up Alex. So we have no idea who was at fault in the accident. But I'd be willing to bet you find that Mickey—your Michael McCurry was driving while drunk."

"I may find that he was drunk." The sheriff gently placed his empty mug near hers. "But he wasn't driving anything. He parked on the main road by the turnoff and got out of the car. Then somebody bashed the back of his head in with a rock and tossed him in the creek."

CHAPTER TWENTY

I looked out the living room window as Johnson's car backed out. Spitz's stayed parked, with him leaning against the hood.

"He's obviously making sure we don't take off, or remove anything from the car or house. Well, by the time Jeffie gets back and takes the house apart, we'll never get out of here today. Damn!" I gave the door a kick.

"Alex, I don't care if it's two in the morning, we'll drive twenty miles up the road and find a motel. I'm beginning to hate this place."

"You hate the sheriff and you hated Mickey. The place is still nice."

"Sometimes you irritate the hell out of me, my sweet." Cindy scowled. "Don't you see, that sheriff is getting all ready to blame this on us. That way he won't have to arrest a local who might vote for him next year. Clearly, he's been lousy at the job, but if he makes an arrest right away, he'll be a hero—especially if it's a furriner. Sometimes you are too damn trusting, Sherlock. You'd do better to figure out who really did this."

"Clay," I said. "Or Branch. Or more likely Clay *and* Branch. If Mickey was as drunk as Branch said he was last night, he probably was passed out at his motel. They tied him up and dumped him in a small horse trailer, one of them drove Mickey's car out here and parked it so it would look as if he were coming here and/or to Sara's. The other drove the trailer. They bopped him one and tossed him in the creek to suggest he fell off the bridge. That guardrail is low; he could have overbalanced. They drove home in the trailer, hosed it out, put down new straw. Case closed," I said.

"Not bad," Cindy said. "If he wasn't passed out, but was actually here or at Sara's, why did he leave his car down by the main road?"

"He wouldn't have wanted anyone to see him driving to this place or Sara's and parking nearby."

"Pretty nifty. Now, if you can just convince SuperCop. Where are you going?"

"Only to the living room," I reassured her. "Even SuperCop might find a big revolver under a couch cushion. I want to get it back in the holster."

"Sure. But really what difference does it make? He wasn't shot. Certainly not by that gun."

"Our Jeffie is liable to say we planned to shoot him—which we did—only the opportunity to kill him down by the road somehow presented itself first."

"See how clever you can be? Now, make us a Cosmo and I'll set the Scrabble up on the deck."

"A Cosmo? It's nine o'clock in the morning!" I was shocked.

"Oh, all right. Make it a double."

I actually won two games. Cindy pleaded exhaustion and fell asleep in the sun. I was dead tired but jumpy. I walked to the edge of the deck. Three deputies had arrived at some point and run yellow crime-scene tape all over the place and were now walking slowly *up* the path. Two of them literally had out large magnifying glasses and occasionally one of them would stop, pick something I couldn't see off a bush and put it in a glassine envelope. The other had a camera and took shots here and there.

Then there was great pointing and gesturing and picture taking. Spitz even risked leaving his squad car and trotted up to where the path and creek made a left turn and disappeared up the side of the mountain. Eventually the men all came back down and all but Spitz left.

I was thoroughly confused. Johnson had clearly said Mickey was found near the intersection, which was *down* the mountain from Ken's cabin. Had Mickey walked past our cabin and gone on up to Sara's? Had her guards belted Mickey in the head and brought him to the foot of the road? Were she and Tommy all right?

I picked up the phone. Sara was as relieved as the rest of us that Mickey was dead, though she tried not to sound too happy. No, they had had no sign of a trespasser during the night. She was horrified at my tale of the sheriff and his men.

"Watch Jeffie," she warned. "He thinks everyone considers him the fat, stupid country cop from the movies. The fact that it is true has not yet dawned on him. And he particularly dislikes people who are not locals. You might want to call Peter Minot. He's not a criminal lawyer, but even if he went to Podunk U., he could go circles around Jeffie."

She did not offer to come down, and I was glad. I don't think I could have stood kindness and pity at that point. Instead, I went out the back door, so as not to wake Cindy, and strolled down to where Dave Spitz stood at his lonely outpost.

"Hi, Dave, it's getting warm. Would you like a Coke or something?"

He looked embarrassed. "No thanks, Alex. I'm okay."

I pulled out my cigarettes and offered him one. He started to reach for it, then pulled his hand back, as if he didn't want to accept anything from me.

"What was all the excitement earlier? Clues jumping from every bush?" I blew smoke casually and leaned against the other fender of his car.

"I really can't discuss that." He turned beet red. "I—ah—look, Alex, it wouldn't do either one of us any good if we were talking when Jeffie comes back. Which could be any time now. And—well—it might be a good idea if you had Pete Minot here. He's a sharp guy."

He stunned me. They were treating us—me—like a prime suspect. Cindy had been right.

"Thanks for the tip, Dave. Sara Blackstone already told me Jeffie has it in for nonlocals. I may give Peter a call."

I went briskly up the deck steps and interrupted Fargo's nap, who interrupted Cindy's.

"What's up?" She yawned.

I told her of the earlier activities and my brief conversation with Spitz.

"Damn!" She reached in my shirt pocket for her monthly cigarette. I admired and disliked her self-control. "Well, do you want me to go call Peter? Funny, he gave me his card last night. Maybe he also reads tea leaves."

"Don't call him yet. Let's see what our Jeffie pulls next. Spitz apparently expects him soon."

The sheriff arrived a little before noon, waving two warrants. One for the house and grounds, one for my car.

I suppose the search made some kind of sense as a precaution, but not much else. If Jeffie knew Mickey's head had been hit with a rock, presumably he *had* the rock. Was he expecting to find blood-stained clothing? We'd had all night to weight it down and take it up to the "bottomless" tarn. Obviously his wallet had been found intact, and apparently his face had not been disfigured in some effort to prevent identification. So he would not find a bloody hammer in the mudroom.

Surely he did not expect to find a half-written letter: "And so, Mom, we'll be home as soon as we kill Mickey." Perhaps he deduced that one of us kept a diary and had made some guilt-ridden or triumphant entry.

Johnson and Spitz came inside, two other deputies started on the car. Cindy supervised the car search, while I went upstairs to oversee Johnson and the obviously nervous Spitz. They found literally nothing in the guest room except linens and soap in a small cabinet and extra blankets in the closet.

The kids' rooms held a few games and books, some odds and ends of clothing and the ubiquitous linens. I followed them downstairs to see Cindy climbing the deck stairs. The car apparently had yielded nothing of interest. The deputies, she said, had moved on to the yard.

In the living room, Jeffie had ordered Dave to take the half-burned logs from the cold fireplace and out to the deck. Meantime he scraped around the ashes, scattering soot over himself and a large portion of the carpet. Cindy came in and immediately lost her temper.

"What the hell are you doing, you oaf! You're ruining the carpet! By God, you'll get the cleaning bill. What are you looking for? The plans for a nuclear bomb?"

"There might have been burnt clothes. It'll probably vacuum clean."

"It will require professional cleaning," Cindy was now all sweetness. "Mr. Willingham will love to hear that." Johnson looked slightly uneasy.

Spitz came in, holding his blackened hands before him like a gift.

"Go wash them in the mudroom," I ordered, "before you touch *anything!* You, too, Sheriff." He gave me a dirty look, but complied.

They returned marginally cleaner and looked around the rest of the living room. All the pillows were carefully shaken and felt, and Cindy and I exchanged a fast look. Johnson discovered a stack of household bills in a table drawer and went over them in detail.

"Mr. Willingham will be thrilled that you took such an

interest in his personal business," Cindy gushed. She was on a roll, and I didn't envy the sheriff.

"McCurry could have been blackmailing him," Johnson pointed out.

"And sent him a monthly bill which he filed along with the gas and electric companies'?"

Spitz gave the bookcase a fast once-over. Finding no secret panels, he announced he was moving on to the kitchen. I heard a drawer or two open and close, a cabinet door click shut and the squeaky oven door come open for a fast look-see. And the heartfelt kitchen search was ended. I heard his footsteps come out of the mudroom as we trailed Johnson into the master bedroom. I was last in the line of three, and Spitz crooked his finger at me in a come-here motion.

I quietly joined him in the mudroom, where he stood staring at the three guns.

"What's this armory all about?" he asked softly. "Is there ammo for them?"

"They were here when we got here. I assume they are Ken's. None of them had been fired or cleaned in a hundred years. None of them are loaded, but ammo is in that drawer. Take a look at the .22—it's more a danger to the shooter than his target."

He gently lifted the rifle from its pegs and turned it toward the window. Pulling back the bolt, he grimaced. "Jesus, what a mess."

"The shotgun is the same and so was the pistol."

"Was?"

"Yes, I cleaned and loaded it a couple of days ago, just for general safety—two women alone, a rather isolated cabin, unfamiliar territory. It has not been fired, nor would it have been without extreme provocation and immediate threat."

"You sound like a cop."

"I'm a licensed PI, my brother is the cop."

He stifled a guffaw, pulled the pistol from the holster, smelled it and looked it over carefully. Returning it to the holster, he reached as high as he could and placed it and its box of cartridges atop a bare rafter. They were out of sight from floor level, but where it had hung, there was a light spot on the wall. I looked around and took a full length apron from a wall hook—Mrs. Fouts'?—and hung it on the nail that had held the holster.

We looked at each other, smiled slightly and returned to the kitchen in time to hear Cindy yell, "You bastard!"

Dave Spitz ran for the bedroom, with Fargo and me hard on his heels. His broad shoulders blocked my view, but, looking around his arm, I glimpsed Sheriff Jeffie Johnson holding a brief, diaphanous, lace-trimmed black nightgown against his corpulent body and seemingly doing a little dance step.

"What happened?" I ducked under Dave's arm and yanked the gown from Johnson's unresisting grip.

Cindy was red with rage. She pointed to Johnson. "This dirty-minded pervert of a law officer held this gown of Frances's up to his body and did his elephantine dance with it while he asked me if it is what I wear when you and I go to bed."

"Jesus, Jeffie! What the hell were you thinking?" Dave looked mortified.

"Hey, folks, I was just kidding around. I didn't mean nothing."

"Did he touch you?" I'd kill him!

"No."

"Even so…I imagine you report to the town council?" Spitz nodded for the frozen Jeffie.

"Good." I tossed the gown back in the bureau and slammed the drawer. "I imagine they will be almost as interested as Mr. Willingham to learn you were cavorting with his wife's *lingerie* and asking their cousin what she wears to bed at night!"

"I still don't see why y'all are makin' such a fuss…"

A deputy interrupted Jeffie by marching past us and dumping three river rocks on the bed.

"Look what, I found on the back porch, Sheriff."

They were three of my four bookends-to-be. "There should be a fourth, Deputy. Why didn't you bring that one in? It's right beside the others," I explained.

"There wasn't no fourth. Just these three lined up along the edge of the back porch."

"Oh, shit," I sighed.

Jeffie laughed.

CHAPTER TWENTY-ONE

We all trailed the sheriff down to his car, where he still had the fourth rock in a plastic bag in the trunk. It seemed a rather carefree way to handle evidence in a murder investigation.

He handed me the bag and I looked thoroughly at the rock, trying not to see the caked blood and little gobs of hair caught in the rough, almost flat underside of the rock I had once thought so pretty. It was brown with an orange cast and a couple of yellowish areas I had found interesting.

"Well," I said, handing the bag back to him. "It could be mine or one very much like it."

"So you admit it is yours."

"No, Sheriff, I admit the possibility. And even if it is mine, it was kept on the back porch with three others in plain view, as your deputy can verify. Anyone on the path—or even the mountain road—could have noticed it and picked it up."

"And I can tell you," Cindy added, now demure and helpful, "you'll find Ms.Peres' fingerprints on it, probably mine and Mr. Mellon's from the next cabin up. He noticed it and asked to look at it. And, of course, if you are lucky, you may find the prints of the killer."

"Mellon was the one who found McCurry. He walked down early to the mailboxes to get his Sunday papers from his mailbox and saw the body. He's the one who called it in. He thought McCurry, maybe with some drinks in him, had fallen off the bridge. Mellon said a fellow did fall there, some years ago, and landed on his head…but he lived. Loony, but alive." Dave seemed happy to provide this information, and Jeffie not pleased to hear it.

"Perhaps McCurry would have survived if he'd been found sooner, the night was pretty cold," I put in. It was a weak effort, but any red herring in a storm, I always say.

"That doesn't explain your rock being the weapon."

I propped my foot casually onto the car's bumper and lit a cigarette, willing myself to look like a good ol' mountaineer. "Well," I drawled, "maybe it's not my rock at all. Maybe somebody saw mine and liked it and just helped themselves to it. It could be in California by now. Maybe the one Mickey landed on was just coincidentally similar to mine."

"And maybe not. Law of averages makes it mighty strange you find one unusual rock somewhere in the creek and then another one just like it turns up right where Mickey's head landed…if he did fall."

"If we hypothesize that it was my rock, it still makes no sense, Sheriff. There are probably dozens of rocks within reach of where he died. Why would I carry that one, which might be identified as possibly mine, down the hill? Why not just use one that came easily to hand?"

"Who knows? Maybe it was symbolic or something." He smirked.

"Another question for you, Sheriff. What are those little scratches on the rock? They were not there when I picked mine up last week. They look like tiny little thumbtack scratches."

"I don't know myself. They were there when we first saw it. I was hoping you could tell us what they were."

I shook my head and shrugged. "No. I've no idea. But it leads me to think that it is definitely not my rock at all. I most certainly would not have picked up one that was already marred. As I told you, we were going to use them in the house as bookends. These marks, of course, ruin it, and prove that either it was never mine, or someone had it after I did."

"Sheriff," Dave Spitz added, "Mr. and Mrs. Mellon did have guests last night. Maybe McCurry was coming up the trail as they were coming down and he made a drunken remark to one of the women and her husband objected and they fought. The husband was losing, so one of his friends picked up the rock and hit Mickey in the back of the head, just meaning to stun. And they took him down to the bridge where he was likely to be seen. We'll have to interview Mellon and his guests before we start coming to conclusions."

Johnson tightened his lips and shook his head. "Oh, we will do that, Dave, and we both know not a thing will come of it."

I believe that was the first thing I had ever heard our Jeffie say that I heartily agreed with.

"Dave." I leaned against the windowsill. "Did you say he was hit in the back of the head? I thought it was the top."

"It was the back, but almost to the top—kind of where the crown of your hair grows. Why?"

"Wouldn't that lead you to think the assailant was shorter than Mickey? The short killer would have been swinging his arm and reaching up. If he were as tall or taller than Mickey, he would have lifted his arm and brought the rock down on top of Mickey's head. Yes?"

Dave looked thoughtful, as if he were trying to visualize the attack. "I see what you mean. I'd have to check it out."

Johnson sighed. "If we're goin' to spend the day with 'what-if's' and 'ain't it possibles,' let's go sit down. These shoes are murder." He laughed at his accidental humor. I uncrossed my feet

167

and took a step toward the kitchen, when he held out his hand to stop me. "Now Ms. Peres, I bet those sneakers are comfortable. Would they maybe be Champion brand, the ones with the funny tread design?"

"They are Champions. I don't know that the tread is unusual."

"Oh, it is, it is. We've got some pictures and a cast of a shoe just like yours, even down to the size, I think, and the photos were taken right up where McCurry's body lay. I'm going to ask you to let me borrow them, ma'am. What shoes would you like Dave to get out of your suitcase in the car?" Sugar wouldn't melt in the bastard's mouth, now that things were going his way.

"And that print, if it is from my shoe, could have been made any time in the last week. Get my loafers, please, Dave." I kicked off my sneakers and left them in the middle of the floor for Jeffie to pick up, and padded into the kitchen, where Cindy had started another pot of coffee. I could have used something stronger, but not now. I needed all the wits I could muster.

For example, Johnson had said *up* near Mickey's body. And the deputies had earlier gotten all excited about something they found *up* the trail. Yet the body had presumably been found *down* near the main road. Were they confused? Were they not telling us something? Were they trying to get *us* confused? They had certainly succeeded, but I was damned if I would ask.

While Cindy poured us all coffee, Jeffie thought he'd found a gold mine with the guns in the mudroom. Dave didn't even get up, he just called. "Break that shotgun and look down the barrel...and the .22 is worse."

Johnson came back and took a chair. "It's a shame to let weapons get in that shape."

"Yes, it is." I thought to establish a bit of rapport. "It's a good shotgun, and the pump-action .22 is antique—probably a 1912 model."

"You know your guns." Jeffie looked interested. "You own any?"

"Several handguns," I smiled. "All in my safe at home. If I go skeet shooting, which is rare, I borrow my brother's shotgun."

While Jeffie was still pondering my collection, Dave informed him why I had it. "Ms. Peres is a licensed private investigator, Jeffie, and her brother is a cop."

Jeffie tried hard to look cordially interested, while I would have bet he was regretting some of his morning's actions that weren't exactly according to the Police Officer's Handbook. But I had to give him credit: he was clumsy, he was also tenacious.

"Ladies, I would like to get your fingerprints, just for elimination purposes, on those three river rocks. Our killer may have hefted them all before he made a choice, and hopefully he didn't wear gloves."

"Don't forget, your deputy handled them all," I reminded him.

"Oh, I won't forget." His smile was sour. "And neither will he." He raised his voice. "Bailey! Get the fingerprint kit out of my car and bring it in. And when you finish with the two ladies, remember to take your own."

"Take my own?" The man looked confused, and then the light dawned. "Oh, yeah. Gosh, Sheriff, I'm sorry."

"Now there you got it right. You are sorry. I guess now I'm goin' to have to try to find Sayles and Emory. I know it takes some time to cover twenty acres of property, but they been gone long enough to have a picnic and a nap. I thank you for the coffee, Miss." He was back to the Policeman's Handbook.

As he began to shuffle his obviously still hurting feet toward the back door, he was hailed through the kitchen window.

"Sheriff, can you please come out here? We don't want to bring this mess into the house." The missing officers were heard from.

"Stay right there!" Johnson bellowed, with a sideways glance at Cindy. "I'm on my way."

His curiosity put a little speed in his step, and his face held a satisfied expression. What did he think they had found? Surely not another body! A cold fire with scraps of burned clothing? I

169

hoped so: any police lab would prove in a hurry they were not Cindy's or mine.

The sheriff's minions had all followed him out. Cindy and I looked at each other, shrugged and mentally agreed we had as much—more—right in the backyard than anyone else, so out we went.

The two deputies were truly a sight to behold: they were nearly covered in mud for a base coat, sprinkled liberally with what looked like sawdust and dotted artistically with last winter's leaves. They looked as if they had posed for some surrealistic Jackson Pollack painting, and their associates were enjoying one of those particularly satisfying laughs that say. "Better you than me, buddy!"

I was enjoying a laugh along with the rest, when I spotted what one man had clutched in his arms. It was a piece of dark clothing, and I thought—feared—I knew what it was.

"What you got there, Emory, and where in the name of God did you go to find it?" Johnson was still chuckling.

Emory gave an embarrassed grin. "Went nearly all the way up the path to the edge of Blackstone Farm. We found this just off the trail under an old pine log that was literally rotting apart...as you can see." He brushed fruitlessly at his uniform jacket.

"You still ain't showed me what treasure was worth ruining a uniform for."

"Oh, sorry." The deputy held the article of clothing out at arm's length. Underneath all the forest detritus was a man's blazer, dark green except where it produced a blue glint in the sunlight flickering through the small, early tree leaves. In addition to being decorated much like the men's uniforms, it also held what I was certain was a large splotch of half-dried blood in the area of the right shoulder.

And I was almost certain where I had seen it last.

CHAPTER TWENTY-TWO

"Well, well." Once out of the house, Johnson had lit a cigarette and now took a satisfying puff. "Before it fell on hard times, I'll bet this was someone's handsome jacket, wouldn't you say so, Ms. Hart?"

"Possibly, Sheriff. It's hard to tell. But before you ask, I do not own—never have, as I recall—a green blazer. I have a green sweater, but it is a much lighter green and an entirely different weave. You'll find it in the larger Coach bag in the car."

"The Coach?"

"It's the name of the luggage, boss." Dave stifled a smile. "Want me to get it?"

"Not right now." Johnson turned to me and pointed at the grime-covered blazer. "Ms. Peres, how about you modeling this piece of finery for us?"

"I wouldn't touch it, much less put it on. But if you have

Deputy Emory hold it up by the shoulders, I can point some things out to you." I picked up a small fallen limb to use as pointer.

I moved closer to the ruined jacket and began my lecture. "You will note that the shoulders are too wide for me, and the sleeves at least three or four inches too long. The body of the jacket is way too long for me, it would reach down around my knees. And I certainly do not own a jacket with a big splotch of blood on it."

I turned to go back to the house. I was getting tired of every possible clue being manipulated to fit Cindy or me.

Remembering one last shot, I turned back again. "And the only blazer I brought with me is navy blue. It is also, like Ms. Hart's sweater, a lightweight wool, not polyester, as I believe your dark green jacket will prove to be."

Johnson fired off some order to his deputies, and they departed, having taken Cindy's and my fingerprints. I took it more or less as a necessary nuisance. But Cindy took it *very* personally. I wasn't at all sure whether she was about to collapse into heartbroken sobs or pour boiling oil out the window over the lot of them. And I'm not sure which choice I preferred.

This left the three of us, standing on the back porch staring at each other.

"I got rid of my boys so we could talk in private, and I reckon your boy don't gossip much." He reached down and patted Fargo. I was surprised to see a tail wag.

"Assuming you're not wired, Sheriff. What was it you wanted to discuss?"

"First," he admitted. "I'm tired. I ain't slept much lately. And I got a pint of the best first-run white lightnin' from a copper pot still. You ladies may not be up on the details of making our Crooked Creek Mountain Dew—but you want a copper pot, and you want that first, smooth, sweet run. It's a glorious experience I plan to share with you, if you got some ice and some Coke."

I had to laugh. I had been dying to taste some good white lightnin'; I was exhausted both mentally and physically; and I figured this might just get the sheriff and me talking sense instead of *can-you-top-this?*

"Sheriff, if you got the booze, we got the mixin's." I brought out three glasses, two cans of chilled Diet Coke, and put some ice in a bowl with tongs. Jeffie brought out an unlabeled pint bottle from his coat, shook it up and turned the bottle sideways.

"You see how them bubbles all float half above and half below the line of liquid? That means it's one hundred proof, so I'll let you mix your own." He placed the bottle in front of me.

I poured about a shot and a half of the liquor, added about four ounces of coke and three ice cubes and let it set while Cindy made hers...about half the size of mine. Jeffie settled for more booze, less Coke and some ice.

We clinked glasses, and I said, "Here's to better understanding and a fast, honest solution to this miserable case."

The other two said, "Hear, hear," and we drank.

I sipped my drink, and it went down like a dream. Then it kicked like a mule. It was Jack Daniels with attitude. I would watch my intake. Cindy took a tentative swallow and did her eyebrow trick. Jeffie had a thirsty swallow, with no obvious reaction.

"Okay," I said. "Let's talk this out. Correct me if I'm wrong. Branch sold Advantage Construction on a development for summer people and maybe some year-round people, with time-share condos and houses of various sizes all along the private road and crest of Crooked Creek Mountain, going up around the tarn. The only holdback was getting easements to run a public road or two across various private properties."

"Right," Jeffie agreed. "The problem was most farmers, most current summer people and just about all of the retirees were against it. I don't think Branch had got more than three or four releases. And Advantage was losing money by the day. So they sent McCurry up to be their closer. In all honesty, I don't think they knew what kind of man McCurry really was. He was supposed to up the ante a little bit, explain all the benefits and money it would bring into the village, and tell them how sorry they would be if they missed out on it."

"Instead they got some psycho drunk—and maybe a druggie."
Jeffie lit a cigarette and continued. "Ever' body I've talked to said
he was threatening—but not in a way you could call the cops
over. Like he might say, 'Now, Ms. Peres think how much better
for your car to have a nice paved road instead of this rutted track.'
And you still wouldn't sell your right-of-way. So next morning,
you got up to four flat tires and no clue who did it."

"I think he loved hurting animals," Cindy added. "And I'm
sure he was thrilled when someone mourned an animal they
loved, like Sara or Mrs. Lauter. I would not be surprised if he got
some kind of sexual kick out of it."

"I would not argue with you, ma'am. And the thing that
scared me bad, was I was afraid he was workin' up to people, not
animals. I know he had it in for Clay and Sara and the two of you,
and, maybe not quite so much, Peter Minot, since Minot was
workin' for Clay, you might say."

"How did you know that?" I asked.

"Mickey hung out at the Dew Drop Inn, and he had a big
mouth when he was drunk. A gal named Mildred clued me in.
She's a…well, she kinda hangs out there, too, and she don't miss
anything. She was worried he was going to hurt someone, and
she named Clay and Sara and you two, plus Peter Minot."

A chill went over me, and I took a swallow of my drink. It
didn't hurt at all. I wished Cindy hadn't heard him, even though
McCurry was no longer a threat. An unbalanced man was one
reason we were on vacation here in the first place. But she was
not down for the count. She asked him a toughie.

"Sheriff, you've been in the law business for some time. I'm
sure you know that most of us are fairly peaceable and rarely
break any laws of consequence. But I'm equally sure there are
little legal no-nos that we all commit which would let you arrest
us on some far-fetched old law. Couldn't you have done that
with Mickey? You could have safely locked him up till somebody
either sued him or Advantage got him out of town. You didn't do
that, and many bad things happened, including, actually, his own
death."

"Yes, ma'am I admit to that." He paused and poured himself and me a small dividend. I added lots of Coke and ice. Cindy just covered her glass. "Why, we've got a law on the books that I can arrest you for not attending church on Sunday. There's another that prohibits social contact with people of dubious morals, whatever that may be these days. But I didn't enforce none of them. I knew he'd be out on bail in an hour or so, and likely to be more violent than ever. Unless I could have proved something serious, I thought it was safer to just watch him...or try to."

I believed there was some truth in what the lawman said, but I still wondered if the person he most wanted to protect from Mickey's wrath wasn't himself.

"Sheriff." Cindy had had enough of this waltz. "I know you are a busy man. Is there something you wanted to ask us?"

He took a deep breath, like one finally facing something he had thus far managed to avoid.

"Not ask, ma'am: tell. First of all, I looked through Mr. Willingham's bills and canceled checks for anything which might have indicated blackmail or even an attempt to buy off McCurry once Ken heard what all he was doing. And second, I want to apologize about your cousin's nightgown. You looked so pale and sad, I thought maybe it would look silly and you'd get a laugh out of it. I'm sorry."

Cindy looked as if she couldn't make up her mind whether to lace into him or burst into tears. I thought I'd better rescue her from either choice.

"I must say, Jeffie, you did look a sight. You might keep that getup in mind for Halloween. Now what's really on your mind? What can we clarify for you?"

He gave me a serious, almost paternal look. "It's what I need to *tell* you, Ms. Peres, not *ask* you. Please let me finish; then we can talk about any disagreements you have. Okay?"

"Okay," we chorused.

"Doc Ellis says Mickey died between two and five a.m. It's hard to pin it down. The night was chilly, and he was lying partly in the creek, which was also cold. I doubt if twenty people in

Beulaland have an alibi for that time. Most of them would say they were asleep with their other half—and who's to say nay?"

He smiled and continued. "For example, your coat check from the Bromfield Inn was time-stamped for 12:03 a.m. Assuming you came straight home, you were here in no more than ten minutes, so you would probably tell me you were sound asleep between two and five."

We both nodded, although the phrase "*sound* asleep" would hardly describe our restless night.

"Now, Doc Ellis is doing an autopsy as we speak, but earlier this morning he told me something interesting. He says that many times a person with a serious head wound will remain semiconscious, or will regain consciousness. Sometimes for hours, usually for maybe half an hour or less. During this time they may carry on intelligent speech with another person, although usually they babble to themselves. Sometimes they remain where they were struck—or fell—other times they may wander or walk with a purpose, such as returning to their home. Eventually they lose consciousness again, or die. Now bear that in mind for later."

Cindy and I gave each other a look that passed for a shrug. Very interesting tidbit, but hardly anything to do with us. But our sheriff was far from finished.

"Now here's how I think your evening ended. You arrived home a little after twelve, to find McCurry waiting nearby. He attacked you, Ms. Peres, wanting to get even for the morning at the Delly, and you two fought. He was stronger than you, and when he hit you in the face, you went down. Meantime, however, Ms. Hart had spotted the river rocks and picked one up. His back was to you, ma'am, and you hit him in the head with the rock, hoping to stun him until the two of you could get in the house, or perhaps back to your car. You got up, Alex, and looked at Mickey. He was obviously much more than stunned. In fact, you thought him dead."

This would have made a helluva TV story if Cindy and I had not been starring in it. And I was having trouble staying quiet. Cindy looked mesmerized.

Jeffie took a drink and lit a cigarette. Inspired, I followed suit, as he went on with our presumed actions.

"You didn't want a body on your doorstep, and you didn't want blood on your clothes. Between Miss Cindy's probable efforts and the heavy rain, we found no blood on or near the house. We'll never know for sure if it was there or not. But we *will* know about the gray fibers all around where you dragged his body and laid it down by a tree, up where the trail turns, won't we, Alex? You even remembered to take the rock and place it near his head, like he fell on it. And we found your footprint there also, probably shielded by his body from any rain still falling, so we got a good print...good enough to see if you either have a worn place on the side of one shoe or you slipped in the mud."

"Gray? I thought you said green. The blazer they found earlier wasn't gray. Not the one I saw. And I've been up and down that trail half a dozen times in the last few days. If it's my footprint, it isn't new. What are you pulling here?"

I had sort of fallen for his gentle approach, but he was trying mousetraps again.

And Jeffie's mild avuncular attitude was fading fast.

"I'm pulling damned hen's teeth tryin' to get you two to tell me *exactly* what you did. You keep sayin' I'm wrong, but you ain't come up with anything you say is right."

"Let's try once more, then," Cindy said reasonably. "We did not kill or injure him. The last time we saw him was at the Delly the morning he threw me against the table—and Alex took lovely pictures of the bruises. Peter Minot will have a set in his mail Monday."

She picked up her drink, sniffed it and put it down. "To continue, we have already told you—McCurry was not here when we arrived home shortly after twelve. The dog ran around the yard and found no one and no odors of interest. Once in the house, Alex collared the dog and I picked up the fire tongs and we went from room to room. McCurry was not here, and from Fargo's reactions, had not been here."

"We had some brandy to calm down and went to bed. So,

Sheriff." I shrugged. "If McCurry was killed near this building, it was before we got home. Had we been here, *we* might have slept through whatever kind of fight went on, but Fargo would not. And just for the record, my gray blazer is in Provincetown. The only blazer I have here is navy blue wool. To the best of my knowledge, Cindy has no gray blazer anywhere."

"Oh, it'll turn up somewhere, I'm not worried about that. But just to finish our little play here. Alex, I think you about got back to the house, when you heard something behind you. I think Mickey had woke up—like Doc Ellis says they sometimes do—and was staggering down the trail. In his mind he might have been trying to get to his car, or might even have been coming here for help, forgettin' it was one of you who had hit him in the first place."

He lit his last cigarette and winged the crumpled pack into the wastebasket.

"You couldn't let him just go on, so you yelled for Cindy's help. And she gave you that old green coat she was wearing, which she had found, probably tossed by who knows into the mudroom. You pulled it on and supported Mickey on down the hill, hoping to get him into his car. But we saw a badly mashed shrub about halfway there and guessed he finally fell. After that, you carried him to a level spot near the road and laid him out again, like he fell. Either you put his face in the water to make sure he stayed put, or he moved and accidentally did it himself. Anyway, I'm pretty sure Doc will find he drowned. Then you went back to the first place, walked around until you found a log where you could hide your coat, then got your rock, and put it by him. Case closed."

I was almost tempted to laugh, and to cover it turned and asked Cindy to make some coffee.

"Case crazy." I told him. "Jeffie, I am in fairly good shape, but Mickey was a heavy man. Not fat, muscle. *Maybe* I could have dragged him up the trail. But he's my height and solidly built. I'm not at all sure I could do it. And I can tell you, I could not carry him from here to the back door! And then trot a half-mile up the trail to get the rock, run down again to put it near him and come *back* up the trail to the house? Next you'll have me leaping tall buildings in a single bound! And after all this, you are saying he drowned? If you got this as far as a courtroom, the jury would be rolling on the floor."

The bastard just smiled and looked smug.

I thought of another point to burst his thick balloon. "You'll have to send a bunch of stuff to your county forensics people. That will not only take time, it will prove you wrong."

"Oh." He gave me a sweet smile. "It won't take long at all, our own forensics department will have it put together in a day or so, and Doc Ellis is doing the autopsy."

"You have a forensics department?" I couldn't believe it.

"Yep. One of our girls is pretty darn good at stuff like this."

Cindy carefully handed me a mug of coffee and got back into action. "One of your *girls*? How old is she, fifteen?"

"Fif...oh, I see. Pardon me. The young woman is thirtyish. Have to have a couple of female deputies these days or we'd be in trouble. Anyhow, Gloria is fascinated by it and has read a lot on the subject." He actually looked proud.

"Oh, God," Cindy murmured. I about choked on my coffee.

"Now I'm not about to arrest you ladies today. I know the case is a little wobbly in spots. They will be cleared up shortly, however. And I am telling you: do not leave town. I mean it. You will not get a hundred miles. And I assure you, you are much more comfortable here than in our little jail. Good-day, ladies, I'll be in touch."

CHAPTER TWENTY-THREE

We sat and looked silently at each other for a few minutes. Then Cindy snapped into cleaning mode.

"Throw those terrible drinks out—they are poisonous—and put the glasses in the dishwasher. And wash those ashtrays." She, in the meantime, was scrubbing the white pine kitchen table as if she were removing the Ebola virus. I tried the vacuum in the living room, but it was far from a total success. Professionals would indeed be needed. As I finished—or gave up—she came in, plumped and straightened the sofa pillows and plopped onto it.

"Well, Mr. Moto missed a big fat clue that would have yanked the filthy rug out from under our calm night's sleep story."

"What's that?" I felt drained and groggy.

"When he came into the living room this morning, the sofa was a mess, where the three of us had tried to sleep on it, and the bed in our room was neat as a pin, where I had made it...

yesterday morning."

"So it was. I just had my mind on getting the gun out of his way."

"Yes. You know, this whole plot of Johnson's would have me thinking I was living in a sequel to *Weekend at Bernie's*, if it weren't so serious. Changing clothes, running up and down the trail dragging and carrying a body that's not a body, going back for the rock. It's *Keystone Kops* all the way."

I wasn't so sure. There was a dull ache in the back of *my* head where certain little ideas were trying to take shape. If I were absolutely sure we would not be arrested I might have simply crossed them all off. A bad, dangerous man was dead, frankly that bothered me not at all. But if I did nothing there was bound to be publicity of a type that would tie Cindy to Ken and certainly damage his political ambitions and, to a lesser extent, not do Sonny any good either. Cindy and I, of course, would have our fifteen minutes in the spotlight—and not in a flattering manner.

In all probability, we would eventually be released for lack of evidence. Of course, that was not proof of innocence. It was just that nothing criminal could be proven. Or, if it went to trial, a good defense lawyer, whom I knew Ken would provide, could probably make a fool out of the local prosecutor. On the other hand, however, juries were fickle. A good solid Baptist jury might not be too anxious to believe two interfering furriners—and lesbians to boot.

I had some serious thoughts about one piece of evidence, but had trouble letting my mind even drift in that direction. It was painful and seemed somehow unfair.

Cindy was staring at me. "You were a million miles away."

"Yeah, I guess I was."

"Anything I can do?"

"No, I think I'm just overtired."

"Gee, I wonder why?" She gave me her gamin grin. "All that running up and down the mountain lugging a body along...I never knew you had it in you. But if you are okay, I'm going to go call Ken. I don't want him to hear this in some public way."

"Good idea. I think when you're finished, I'd better call Sonny. I don't think he can do anything, but he should know what's happening and why we are not going to get home on time."

Returning to the living room, Cindy looked white and worn out. But she was smiling. "Ken is livid that we have even been on Jeffie's short list. He says don't let him back in the house, that there's a shotgun if you need it. I didn't tell him the shape it's in. And he's going to call my parents—I told him I didn't have the nerve. And he says he'll be here by noon tomorrow."

"Maybe I'll clean it for him later. It's the least I can do for all the grief we've given him. Well, let me go call big bro. I don't look forward to this."

Actually Sonny proved understanding and comforting, until he said, "You know I'll have to tell Mom." That brought the first tears I had shed over this mess, and brought fast replies and fast goodbyes from my brother who couldn't stand weeping women. "I won't alarm her, don't worry, everything will be fine, I will see you sometime tomorrow. Don't panic. So long." Click.

Sonny certainly had no legal authority in Tennessee, but God, I was glad he was coming down. Cassie would probably fly him. If she couldn't, he had sounded like he might turn to the Air National Guard. He could frequently be a know-it-all big brother—but from the time since I had been old enough to yell for help, he had never, ever let me down.

With our numbers about to grow, we made up the bed for Ken in the master bedroom, one for Sonny in the guest room and the two twins in little Frances Jr.'s frilly pink room for us. I would feel like an oversized Cinderella, but hopefully we wouldn't occupy it for long. Next we put out towels and assorted toiletries. We were glad of something to do.

When we finished, we realized the sun was low, and the deck too chilly to be comfortable. I made a fire in the fireplace while Cindy took the last *filets mignon* out of the freezer and cut up a salad for later. I set the dining table. We were being determinedly normal.

I heard steps on the deck and squared my shoulders to turn the sheriff away. But instead of a beer-belly man in a sloppy uniform, I saw a rather handsome young man in a light gray suit, a black vest and a backward collar. Probably a matter of car trouble and he needed a phone. Cells worked intermittently here, and land lines were still much in demand.

I opened the door. "Hello, Father, can we be of assistance?"

"Hello. I'm Vicar Alan Reed Hampton of St. Luke's Episcopal Church in Elizabethton...but please call me Alan, and you must be Alex."

"Ah—yes, yes, I'm Alex Peres. But how did you know?"

"From your Aunt Mae. She is concerned that you and Cindy have been beaten and thrown into some old Confederate dungeon, eating moldy corn pone and drinking water with tadpoles in it." He was trying to look serious, but his dark brown eyes danced, and his lips twitched.

I laughed aloud. "That's Aunt Mae, all right. But I only spoke with my brother about an hour ago. How did she get hold of you so soon?"

"Through the Bishop of East Tennessee. She apparently doesn't start at the bottom."

"Oh, good grief!" I stood aside. "Do come in, Alan. I hope you haven't been put to a lot of trouble. And here's Cindy Hart—Cindy meet Vicar Alan Reed Hampton. Alan has been sent from Aunt Mae, via the bishop of this area, to check on our welfare—or lack thereof."

Cindy shook her head. "That woman could penetrate the Kremlin if she set her mind to it. Bless her heart, she really is a love. We were just about to have a glass of wine. Will you join us? White or red?"

"White if it's handy, red if it isn't. But, seriously, are you two all right? Why on earth is Johnson thinking of you two as suspects?"

We told him, and when we finished he was leaned back in his chair wiping his eyes and laughing aloud. Finally he sobered.

"I hate to laugh at a man's death. Even such a one as this

McCurry. But this sounds more like a marathon than a murder! Your dragging a body up a mountainside and then having it come to life and walk partway down. Then you casually carry the corpse again *down* the mountain and go up one more time to get a rock! I run five miles a day and I tell you, I could not do all that if I had to. I cannot believe this tale will ever come to court!"

"That's what Ken says," Cindy added.

"That's also what my brother says, he's a cop back home. He and Ken will both be here tomorrow, by the way. Look, Alan, we are about to have a dividend of wine and a little dinner. Won't you join us? You've been so kind to come out here, and we really do appreciate it."

"It has been my pleasure, but I must get back for Evensong. I know you have both been going through a terrible time. This is when faith grows faint, but try not to lose it. God hasn't gone away, he's just a little dim behind the cloud of human ignorance and meanness. He is with you. Be of good cheer. I'll report to Aunt Mae later tonight." He shook hands with both of us and started out. "Let me know if I can be of help...of any variety."

"I'll walk you to your car," I offered.

"Why, thank you."

As soon as we were out of earshot from Cindy, I cleared my throat. "Ah, Alan, I need to talk to you in, uh, your professional position. Can you promise this will go no further?"

"We'll consider it a confessional, so my lips are sealed. What's troubling you? What have you gone and done?"

"It's more what I haven't done than what I have," I answered. "I know some things and am pretty sure I know some others that would wreak havoc on Jeffie's theory of how this killing went down. And to reveal part of it seems criminal in itself; remember the book *To Kill a Mockingbird?*"

"Yes, very well. Do you want to tell me what mockingbird you feel you would be killing?"

I lit a cigarette and offered him one. He looked around guiltily and then took it.

"Okay," I said. "It's like this." And I told him. When I finished, his face looked grave and pained.

"Lord, Alex, what a burden you've been carrying! I don't know much about criminal law, so remember that my advice to you will be based on some laws I do know about. Since you have not shared these facts and possibilities with Cindy, if you keep quiet about all this, she has no vote in what you do—although she is equally suspect in Johnson's mind. You place her in jeopardy, when she might not wish to be there, especially since she is suspected of delivering the fatal blow to McCurry's head. You and she would be tried, technically by your peers, but actually by people who are very different from you."

I fieldstripped my cigarette and tucked the filter in my pocket.

"I thought of that. I just figured it was so ludicrous we'd never be convicted."

"But you *would* be tried. Think what that would put you both through...not only your presumed actions against McCurry, but your personal lives as well. Any trial makes the tried look bad. Would your clients continue to trust you with their personal problems? Would Cindy's clients trust her not simply to put them in the investments that gave her the largest commission?"

We reached his car and he jabbed the cigarette in the ashtray. He sat in the driver's seat with the door open. I leaned against the door.

"Your families are already suffering," he pointed out, "But let's cast a wider net. The people you are protecting may know or guess you covered for them. This would make them feel indebted to you...for life! Although they could never thank you. And they would always wonder if someday you might tell the truth. And they would grow to hate you, because they were desperately afraid of you."

"Oh, hell, Alan!" I hit my fist on the top of the car. "I certainly don't want to risk Cindy. I love her very much. But Mickey was such a bastard, it just seemed unfair to rat on someone who was trying to keep Mickey from killing somebody even if he was an angel with kind of dirty wings...oh, you know what I mean. And the other person, I strongly believe, was honestly trying to help Mickey survive."

"You can make those feelings quite plain to the police and to the defense lawyers, Alex. This is a bit more serious than catching me at age twelve having a cigarette behind the gym and not telling the teacher. And when you take the oath on the Bible, to tell the truth, the *whole* truth and nothing but the truth...you won't have to cross your fingers." He smiled.

He reached out and took my hand. "Don't answer me, Alex. You may need to think about this, but ask yourself: Am I doing this because it is right...or because it seems noble, and I will feel good about myself? Now, I really don't mean to rush, but I am running very late. God bless you."

"Yeah. Good night."

I walked slowly back up to the cabin, boiling. Smarmy jerk throws a curve and then drives away. I wasn't being noble. I just felt probably one of them had saved my life and Cindy's, and the other had been a good Samaritan with muddled results. I'd had some childish idea we'd all laugh about it someday, but, of course, that would never happen. Alan hit that one square and hard.

In a year's time I'd bet one or the other of them would tell someone and that would open the floodgates. And if I had beat the murder charge, I'd be re-arrested for perjury. And Cindy would hate me...but I would have acted nobly.

How could I ever explain why I ratted? Then a thought hit me: I'd send them both to Alan for priestly wisdom. I was grinning as I crossed the deck.

Cindy was touching up the fire as I entered. "Well, welcome home, my dear. I was beginning to think you might have decided to make your annual appearance at church."

"I needed some advice, and I got it—in spades. I felt like a fool. Except I still feel bad, no longer being the fool. I feel guilty as hell, but I'm relieved at knowing what I should do and why I didn't. And I feel better about you."

Leaning against the mantel, she nodded sagely. "That's one of the things I love about you, Alex, you express your deepest feelings so clearly."

"I'm glad you're so calm about it all. I thought you might be pissed."

She lifted the wine bottle from the ice bucket and filled our glasses. Handing me mine, she pointed toward the sofa and said, "Sit!"

Fargo and I both moved to the couch and sat. "Now," Cindy ordered, "tell me what the hell you are talking about. I've heard people speaking Chinese that made as much sense."

I told her.

When I finished, she shook her head in wonderment. "I told you when we first met: the thing that would always cause me the biggest problem with you was your damn masochistic sense of honor! You are a good person, Alex. There is no need intermittently to nail yourself to a cross to prove it!"

"I never thought it would go to trial," I countered.

"You never thought. About me. About how things like that never stay a secret. About our families. About how much fun we'd have scrubbing floors, as that would be about the only job we could get! And where was your honor going to be when you lied in court?"

"That's about what Alan said. But I wouldn't have lied, I would just have stayed quiet."

Cindy laughed. "You couldn't stay quiet if you were gagged. Thank God for those three-name baritone Episcopal ministers!"

"For what kind of ministers?"

"Three-name. Haven't you ever noticed? Episcopal ministers all have three names. Alan Reed Hampton. Ours at home was Robert Malcolm Seale. The one in Ptown is James Winston Hockney. And they always have these lovely well-modulated baritone voices."

"Yeah, so?"

"Nothing, I just thought of it. Now, may I assume that since you have solved the McCurry Mystery, you will share it with our two relatives tomorrow, so they may tell Jeffie to buzz off?" She threw her wineglass into the fireplace with a crash.

"*Cindy!*"

"We'll buy them a new set—now that we won't have to do it by mail order through the Warden's office."

"Oh, okay." I stood, took aim and added my shards to hers. Then I pulled her onto the sofa beside me.

With Fargo still obediently sitting at one end, it was a bit crowded for what I had in mind. "Get down, Fargo."

He gave me a dirty look that clearly said, "Nag, nag, nag!"

CHAPTER TWENTY-FOUR

"Let's have breakfast at Gertrude's," Cindy suggested. "We have to get the papers anyway. And we can't just hide. God knows how long we'll be stuck here."

"Hopefully about an hour after the troops arrive. Yeah, let's go."

The rain was long gone and the sun was a bright yellow towel, rapidly drying the freshly bathed trees and meadows. It seemed impossible to have troubles on a day like this.

We picked up the papers at the Grandma and Grandpa store and waited while they went out to the car to greet Fargo. He was the spittin' image, we had been told several times, of a dog they had owned years ago. And a champion he had been!

At Gertrude's the local regulars we had come to know by sight, mostly greeted us as usual. To a few, we had become invisible. Gertrude was full of cheer. As she escorted us to a table, she advised us in a stentorian whisper, "Don't worry about nothing! They'll never find a jury in this county that would convict you!"

I gave her what felt like a sickly smile, and Cindy muttered something I didn't catch. We didn't have much left to say—to each other or anyone else. We mainly hid behind the Sunday *Times*—a day late but welcome. Fargo later received a generous doggie bag.

Shortly before one o'clock I was not surprised to see a car pull in with Ken sitting in the front passenger seat and two men— one in full State Patrol regalia—climbing out of the back. I was, however, surprised and delighted to see my brother unfolding himself from the driver's seat. How had they connected?

There were hugs and kisses all around from Ken and Sonny. We were introduced to a Dr. Thalman, a forensic specialist, who said to call him Ray. And to the State Patrol's Captain Vonley, of the criminal investigation unit, who didn't say what to call him—obviously "Captain" would suffice.

We learned that Cassie had indeed brought Sonny down, but could not stay due to a charter early Tuesday morning. She sent her love. Ken and his companions had flown in also, and the group had met at the car rental office in Elizabethton. They had stopped for an early lunch at a place Ken knew that had great ribs—which took me a moment to understand—so we needn't worry about feeding them—which was fortunate.

Ken and Sonny asked for a beer. The Captain nobly requested coffee. I took a beer. Cindy poured two coffees. We retired to the living room, where Ken looked with dismay at his carpet.

"Damn fool Jeffie! Did he really think you'd be dumb enough to burn a bunch of clothes in the house you were living in?"

"People under great stress are not always logical," Vonley pontificated. "But personally," he said with a grin. "I'd send him the cleaning bill." I liked him a little better.

"Well." Vonley set his cup on the coffee table. "Cindy, Alex, I got a tale from Ken that sounded absolutely lunatic. Please tell me what actually happened."

"Well, first, I think you should know the story you will get from the sheriff," Cindy began. "He thinks we returned from the Bromfield Inn around midnight and discovered McCurry lurking in a bush. He and Alex grappled, he hit her in the face and she went down. He was off-balance for a moment, with his back to me. I grabbed one of the river rocks we were going to take home for bookends and hit him in the back of the head to stun him. But he didn't move and I couldn't feel a pulse. So we figured I had killed him."

I lit a cigarette. Everyone looked pained but Sonny, who reached for my pack.

Ray reached for the door to the deck.

I took up the tale. "I managed to get up and dragged the presumed corpse up the trail to the creek. I laid him down near the water where it was exceptionally muddy, as if he had slipped, fallen and hit his head. I went back to the house, got the rock and placed it by his head. I then took off the gray blazer they insist I was wearing and hid it somewhere. They have not found it *yet*, Johnson says."

Taking a sip of beer, I continued. "There are numerous shrubs and some blackberry bushes along the way. Johnson says his deputies found fibers on them that will match McCurry's chino shirt and pants plus some gray ones that will match my blazer. I do own such a jacket, but it's in Massachusetts. I had just arrived back at the cabin from wherever I went to hide the blazer, when Mickey staggered down the path, muttering to himself."

"Ever helpful," Cindy said with a smile, "I ripped off a big old green coat I had found in the mudroom and had worn as I policed the area for blood or anything. I gave it to Alex to keep blood from his head wound off her clothes, and she began to support Mickey as they went *down* the path toward where the creek goes under the main road."

"I don't remember any green coat in there," Ken interrupted.

"There wasn't one in the cabin, that part was all Jeffie, I'll explain later," I answered. "Anyway partway down the trail there's a crushed bush which tells Jeffie that Mickey fell into it, and from here on, I carried the hundred-and-eighty-pound babbling corpse down the hill and placed him by the creek. Jeffie says either I put him where he would breathe some water, or he moved. Anyway, I then remembered the bloody rock with hair stuck in it, went *up* the trail, got it, came *down* the trail and put it beside him and went *up* the trail past the house. Nearly at Blackstone Farm, I shoved the green coat under a rotting log, where it was found, covered in leaves, dirt, etc—plus a splotch of blood. They also found a footprint they say matches my sneakers near the first place Mickey was laid out."

"As Jeffie then said: Case closed." Cindy gave a little bow from the sofa.

"Funny, Alex," Vonley said, "you don't look like an Olympic wrestler."

Ray laughed. "I'm not sure even one of them could have done all that. You say he weighed one-eighty, Alex?"

"Close to it. He was almost exactly my height, but square-built and very muscular. I imagine he worked out a lot."

We gravitated toward the deck. Ken went to the kitchen and came back with crackers and a slab of Stilton we had bought. We all refreshed our drinks. Swallowing a sizable bite, Vonley muttered, "Okay, ladies what really happened?"

I began. "We were at the Bromfield with two friends we had made here in town. Later I ran into Branch Redford and had a drink with him in the bar. He had had a few, but wasn't really drunk. He was upset about Mickey's actions and obviously afraid of what else he might do. Mickey was particularly, Branch told me, angry at Clay and Sara and us for putting a wrench in his works. Branch got a phone call from a woman called Mildred at the Dew Drop Inn. He had hired her to 'be nice' to Mickey, hoping that would keep him entertained overnight. I judged from the call she was refusing to go to a motel with him; he had already slapped her around and got bounced out of the Dew Drop, and she was scared of him."

I grabbed the last morsel of Stilton and talked around it.

"Branch said Mickey was a loose cannon, and he was the only man left holding a rope. He wished for Marines. He had begged Jeffie to arrest Mickey on any kind of charge and hold him till this morning, but Jeffie said he had no reason to. Then Branch squared his shoulders and said something like, 'Here goes St. George to find the dragon. Wish me luck.' Well, when St. George found the dragon, he killed him."

"That's not proof of anything!" Vonley exploded.

"I know, but it's indicative of how he saw himself: he had to save Mickey's would-be victims. Also add this—two things I finally remembered. Branch was wearing a gray blazer and, I think, gray pants. He also had on sneakers of the same brand and design as mine. I had noticed them once before. And that night, dancing with him, I noticed them again. What particularly got my attention was how small his hands and feet were—almost delicate. He's about Cindy's height, but his hands and feet are small, even for a short man. And if you find the sneakers, I think one of them will have a worn spot on the edge of the sole."

"Now there, my good Captain, you have something!" Ken sounded very relieved.

"It's enough for a search warrant, at least," Vonley admitted. "How did the actual fatal blow come about?"

"I don't know. But a good guess would be: Branch was driving up to his sister's to see that all was well. He either saw something or just stopped on impulse to see if the cabin had been entered. Mickey was here and he wasn't afraid of Branch, he held him in contempt. He would not have been leery that Branch would hurt him. Branch found opportunity to hit Mickey with the rock to stun him, so he could call the cops to arrest him for trespass. But for whatever reason, he thought he had killed him. Rather than leave him near the cabin, he dragged him up the trail to the creekside and placed the rock nearby. He probably went home, thinking Mickey was out of things for good."

"It's all possible," Sonny agreed. "How did you get that black eye, by the way?"

"Later. It's all Fargo's fault."

"The dog ate your homework, eh? Well, go ahead. How did this peripatetic corpse get down the trail?"

Cindy returned to the deck wearing a sweater and bringing one for me. As I put it on, she took up the narrative.

"The sheriff told us some story about people with head wounds suddenly regaining consciousness. They carry on conversations, sometimes walk around and sometimes even get back to their homes. I don't know if there's a word of truth in it. He says a Dr. Ellis told him about—"

Ray interrupted. "It's quite true. And I've known Butch Ellis since med school. He could have been chief surgeon at any hospital you could name, but he married a nurse who didn't like big cities any more than he did. So they opened a small clinic here. He is a fine doctor."

"I'm glad to hear it," Cindy nodded. "Because what we think happened depended on that. We think Tommy Blackstone was walking up the trail. Why he was walking in the pouring rain while his mother had a perfectly good SUV we have not guessed. Anyway, at some point he met Mickey stumbling down the trail, and we think he was probably muttering something about getting to his car. Tommy supported him, headed down to the main road where Mickey's car was found. Once again, cloth fibers were all over the place." She took one of her rare cigarettes.

I wrapped it up.

"At some point we guess Mickey passed out and fell into the brush, and Tommy carried him the rest of the way to where he was found. He obviously had spotted either the wound or the rock or both, because at some point he brought the rock down, placing it near Mickey. He may have thought Mickey had hit his head and now died...maybe he had."

"How do you know it was Tommy?" Ken asked. "I hate to see him mixed up in a killing. It will destroy Sara."

"At the Bromfield Inn earlier, he was all dressed up," I answered, "and his jacket was dark green with blue glints in it. Then a deputy found one that looks like it and seems to be about Tommy's size."

Cindy patted Ken's arm. "Don't worry about Tommy. All he did was try to help. If he hurt Mickey in any way it certainly was accidental."

"Well." Vonley grinned. "You've told a story somewhat more believable than Jeffie's, if the evidence holds up. And you have accounted for everyone but yourselves."

"Oh," I felt myself blushing...damn, always at the most inauspicious times. "Oh, our night was frightening but uneventful except for my black eye. We left the Bromfield about midnight. It had finally stopped raining but was still wet as hell when we approached the cabin. We were scared to death Mickey was around somewhere. I let Fargo out of the car. He made no fuss about anything. We explored the whole house inside and out... no Mickey."

I said nothing about the pistol. It was so old I doubted it was registered, and we had not been forced to use it, so why mention it?

Cindy grinned at Ken. "We raided your good brandy and I made coffee to go with it. Fargo whined to go out and startled me. I spun around and clocked Alex with a mug."

"So you say." Sonny teased.

"I'm sticking to my story," she fired back. "After ice packs and brandy the three of us piled on to the sofa. We tried to stay awake till daybreak, but kept dozing off until the police sirens woke Alex. We thought it was a traffic accident on the main road until Jeffie arrived on the doorstep."

"And from there it was all downhill," Vonley finished for her.

CHAPTER TWENTY-FIVE

We were stuck in Beulaland until Tuesday late afternoon. I knew it was not a long time, at all, to wrap up a murder case; and God knows everyone involved was moving at top speed. But to those two of us who were prohibited from leaving, it lasted an eon.

Vonley, who had gotten around to telling us to call him Lewis, decided to make his headquarters the cabin instead of the town jail. The jail was small and crowded, he explained, and any questions asked or information given would be all over town in an hour. And anyway, it didn't have Cindy's great coffee. Actually, I felt I was the coffee expert, but I was glad to let her accept this election.

The captain then got Jeffie on the phone, chewed him out for not reporting the murder—if it still was one—and told him to get a search warrant for Branch's quarters at Clay's house. The search warrant was to be carried out by the two female deputies—specifically looking for a gray blazer, gray pants and Champion sneakers. Two other deputies were to find and arrest Branch for assault and bring him to the cabin. Johnson was also to send Deputy Spitz—and only Spitz—to find Tommy Blackstone and *request* his presence at the cabin. He was also to offer to bring along Tommy's mother.

He had the speakerphone on in the dining room, and I could hear Jeffie sputtering and "but...but...but-ing" like a faulty outboard. Lewis simply said, "Stay where I can reach you," and hung up.

Earlier I had suggested to Vonley that Johnson not be included in Tommy's interview. "Tommy and Sara would in all probability talk to you," I told him, "and would doubtless feel reassured if Ken were present—or even me, if Ken wants to stay well clear of this mare's nest. But Jeffie has the unreciprocated hots for Sara, and neither mother nor son particularly like or trust him."

Lewis nodded thoughtfully. At least he was a good enough cop to listen!

Ray had a joyous telephone reunion with Butch Ellis and took the rental car to go to the clinic and assist with the autopsy.

Ken called Gertrude's Delly and ordered enough food to provide dinner for a regiment, plus sandwiches to have later for snacks. He also made out a list for the Bromfield bar that would have the owner smiling for several days. I offered to pick up the orders, but he insisted on doing it himself, saying that if he were in town and didn't say hello to Gertrude she would never forgive him. He did, however, sheepishly ask to borrow my car to make his rounds.

While the phone was temporarily free, I called the Bromfield Inn and got them to add up the various checks we had signed. I then wrote out my check for Ken and tucked it in the corner of his desk blotter. I wondered why we still have desk blotters, when we no longer write letters that need to be blotted? Then I wondered why I cared.

Vonley pried Cindy loose from the coffeemaker and they

walked down the trail to get some air and to see where McCurry had last been laid to his uneasy rest.

During their absence, a call came in from Jeffie. Sonny took it in the kitchen—not bothering to explain he was Detective Lieutenant Peres *from Massachusetts*, and learned that Branch had been found, very drunk, in a bar over on the state road. Did they want him at the cabin or let him sleep it off? He was really plowed.

"Why not bring him over?" Sonny answered. "*In vino veritas*, right?"

"No," Jeffie replied. "They were over on the state road, like I said...in the Hillside Restaurant and Bar...not in the Vino, wherever that is."

Sonny actually took the phone from his ear and stared at it. "Oh—uh—good! Very good. Bye," he managed to say before he burst into laughter. "Oh, boy," he said, "I can't wait to tell this one to Lewis."

Lewis came in as if on cue and laughed dutifully at Sonny's anecdote. Then he held up a plastic bag with a glove inside it. The glove had tiny sharp metal points sticking out of the palm and the bottoms of the fingers. "Either of you know what this is for?" he asked us. "Cindy spotted it beside a bush near the bottom of the trail. It looks like a medieval torture device."

Sonny shook his head. I nodded mine. It was one of those minor little inventions you wondered why you hadn't made yourself. It would never make you famous, nor particularly rich...but it came in awfully handy when you needed it.

"I don't know the proper name but you use it scaling fish. You put the fish on a wood table, or board, put on the glove and rest your hand on the fish's tail. It keeps your hand from slipping on the slippery fish so it doesn't skid off the table when you scale and gut it. Also prevents cut hands, I imagine. It could be Tommy's. I saw him using one the other afternoon."

"Ah! We'll have to ask him when we find him. Any news on that?" Vonley inquired.

"Nothing on Tommy." Sonny pulled a beer from the

refrigerator. "Branch is on his way in, as you know."

I looked at the glove again. "You know what?" I asked the air. "I'll bet that's what made the scratches on the murder weapon! For some reason Tommy must have been wearing the glove when he picked up the river rock."

Vonley looked at me seriously. "Whose job are you after? The sheriff's, mine or your brother's?" He grinned. "You probably could have your pick at this point."

"Flattery will get you many things, sir, with a few exceptions. But unfortunately, three cars are pulling into the parking area as we speak."

Dave Spitz was the first, advising us that Tommy and Sara would be along as soon as they had fed the horses. "I offered to wait," he added, "but Ms. Blackstone said they preferred to bring their own car. And I had a definite feeling I should not put any pressure on them, so I just thanked them and left."

"You done good," Lewis nodded. "They are a prominent family, and we don't believe Tommy was out to hurt anyone."

The second car held Ken and a bunch of goodies—both solid and liquid. I went down to help him carry them in.

The third, of course, held Branch and two deputies. As I went down the steps from the deck, one deputy almost lifted Branch out of the backseat. He was not his usual natty self. Unshaven, uncombed and generally grungy and bedraggled, he tried to throw himself into my arms, but the deputy held on to him.

"Oh, Alex," he cried, "I'm so glad you're here! You can tell them my heart was innocent. It was all Mickey, every bit! He was going to kill you and Cindy."

I had been feeling a combination of pity and humor, but his last sentence took me instantly back to the terror I had felt at the cabin door Saturday night. A cold sweat popped on my neck and I began to shiver.

Afraid my voice would break if I spoke, I simply waved and turned toward my car, which Ken was starting to unload. I managed to hang on to the bundles he handed me, and staggered up the steps.

Had Branch truly saved our lives, or was he now simply trying to save his own? But how did a chubby, short, out-of-shape guy like Branch manage to kill a taller, heavily muscled Mickey—with a rock, of all things—if he were not genuinely desperate? A bullet, maybe a golf club, even poison—but a rock? Up close and very personal for a nonviolent man!

Had this ineffectual little fellow indeed become St. George just long enough to slay the dragon? I knew from experience that fright, for yourself or a loved one, could sometimes bring to the surface a courage you didn't know you had. I found myself betting on Branch and hoping very hard that I was right.

Lewis was using the living room as his "office." So we set out Ken's buffet dinner in the dining room. It gave Lewis and anyone with him the illusion of privacy, although the sound of normal conversation carried into the dining room quite clearly.

Lewis had provided Branch with some food and a mug of coffee, which seemed to restore him—if not to sobriety—at least to coherence. They spoke of inconsequentials while he ate and then turned to serious interrogation.

Branch succinctly went over the Advantage plans for a mountaintop development, his difficulties in obtaining easements for even one road to reach it, McCurry's appointment as closer and his deliberate misunderstanding of how he was to approach prospects. Branch had not seen McCurry commit any of the vandalism that accompanied his arrival, but strongly suggested he was guilty. McCurry was drinking heavily and Branch was almost certain he was on steroids or some other drug.

Branch had several times asked the sheriff to arrest McCurry for disturbing the peace or some equivalent minor infraction of the law and "let him cool off" until Branch could get help from Advantage, but Johnson said he had no cause. Advantage finally recalled McCurry and Branch, when they received the letter from Clay's attorney, and Branch was trying desperately to keep McCurry under control until their ordered return to Knoxville on Monday. Branch smiled ruefully and added, "It was like telling a six-year-old to put a runaway Newfoundland on leash."

I was called in when they began to speak of Saturday night and Branch's time at the Bromfield Inn. He had known that Clay, Sara, Tommy, Cindy and I would be there where he could, for a time, keep an eye on us. We were his main worries. Clay and Sara for retaining Attorney Minot. Cindy and me for giving them the idea to get a lawyer and for giving his macho ego a bad bruise in the Delly. Tommy as a sort of hostage for Clay and Sara.

He and I had danced once, Branch said and then, since the waiters were backed up with orders, went into the bar for a drink. I blessed him silently for being gentleman enough not to mention how and how long we danced, and then I confirmed what I could of his phone call from Mildred.

I added that Branch was badly shaken to learn that instead of being with her at the Dew Drop Inn or the No-Tel Motel—I didn't know its proper name—Mickey had belted Mildred, been bounced from the Dew Drop and disappeared. Branch left the Bromfield right away to go look for him.

When asked what he had been wearing he immediately said, "Gray. Pants and blazer...gray."

"What kind of shoes?" I appended.

He stuck a foot out from under the coffee table. "These."

They were Champion sneakers, would have fit me and had a worn spot on the right sole. So much for my footprint, Jeffie, old boy!

Until now, Branch had been quite calm, but now that he had left the Bromfield in his narrative, his nerves began to show. He began to shift the dishes around on the coffee table. He pulled out cigarettes and dropped the lighter, finally recovered it and began to speak again.

"I knew he wasn't at the Dew Drop. I hoped he had gone back to his room at the No-Tel and passed out, but he wasn't there. So I tried Clay's and one of his men, toting a shotgun, told me Clay was in Kingsport for a few days and that he had not seen Mickey all evening. That left my sister and Tommy, and Cindy and Alex."

"You knew where they all were, safe at the dance," Sonny put in.

"Yes, but I didn't know for how long. I knew Sara and Tommy and his girl wouldn't stay late. Horses and a couple of cows get you up early. And I wasn't sure how good the two guards Clay had hired for their place were. I wasn't sure about the two ladies, either. I thought if they were home, maybe I'd convince them to spend the night at Clay's. I knew his men were good and had no use for Mickey."

"So you went next to Ken's?" Lewis asked.

"In a way. I *meant* to go first to Sara's and then check Ken's on the way back down. But when I got to the turnoff, Mickey's car was parked on the side of the road. That about worried me to pieces. He could be at either place. I cut my lights and went on down the road a couple of hundred yards and parked."

Branch looked longingly at my highball and I pushed it over to him, ignoring Sonny's and Lewis's scowls.

"Thanks, Alex." He sent me one of those winning smiles and I wondered for the thousandth time how we had all gotten mixed up in this. "Anyway, I walked back and started up the dirt road. I noticed lights on in the cabin, but Alex's car wasn't there, so I moved on, going to go first to the farm. Then, a movement caught my eye. It was Mickey, on the back porch of the cabin."

"Did he see you?" Lewis asked.

"He would have, so I called out and asked him what he was doing here. He said...he told me...do I have to say this here?" His hands gripped the edge of the coffee table until his knuckles whitened.

"Come on, Branch, we haven't got all night." Sonny sounded irritable.

Branch spoke very quickly. "He said he was going to show those two dykes what a real man was like and then he would kill them. I'm sorry Alex, but that's what he said."

I couldn't answer. I felt my face go white, I felt dizzy, I reached for what had been my drink and couldn't quite make it. Sonny was swearing and beating the coffee table. I was vaguely aware of his wishing he had Mickey alive right now. Then Lewis had his arm around me and was holding the communal drink to my lips. I got down a swallow and nodded. I was back among the living.

"Tell me Cindy didn't hear this," I whispered.

"No, she's in the kitchen," Sonny replied. "Are you okay?"

"I guess, but I'd like a drink of my own."

"I'll get it, Cindy won't know it's for you." He stood and headed for the kitchen.

"All right, Branch. Keep going." Lewis sounded angry.

"Uh, yeah. Well, Mickey started laughing about what a party they would have, and he dropped the screwdriver he was using to try to jimmy the door. He was bent over, feeling around in the dark for it. I thought I saw a gun stuck in his back pants pocket. If he had a gun…and if the women came home now… not even the three of us would have much of a chance against him! I looked around and saw some river rocks lined up. I didn't even think. I just grabbed one and hit him in the back of the head with it, just as he found the screwdriver and stood up. I only meant to stun him and call Jeffie…surely even he would come out now!"

Branch swished the ice around in the glass and drained the watery drink. "Mickey fell over. I took the gun and found the screwdriver where he had dropped it again, and put them in my pocket. He hadn't moved, and when I tried to wake him up, I couldn't. He didn't seem to be breathing and I couldn't feel a pulse, either, although I'm never sure what part of the neck to push."

He looked up hopefully as Sonny returned with my drink, but this time I didn't share. "It was funny." Branch shrugged and continued. "Ideas just seemed to come to me. I didn't want to leave him parked on Ken's porch with a hole in his head. I got him under the shoulders and managed to drag him up near that little footbridge across the creek. The creek was up a few inches from the runoff of the rain and the end of the bridge was under water. I laid him down like he had slipped on the wet wood or in the mud and hit his head. Remembering what he was supposed to have hit his head *on*, I went back and got the rock and put it

203

beside his head. I tossed the gun and screwdriver, along with my bloody jacket, into the creek. You can probably find them."

He put his hands over his face and squinted his eyes tightly closed, like a child denying he has swiped the cookies. "Honest! I only meant to stun him, I really *never* meant to *kill* him!"

"That's good," a voice boomed from the front door, "because you didn't."

CHAPTER TWENTY-SIX

"What do you mean?" I think everyone in the house asked that question at the same time.

Doctor Ray Thalman completed his entrance and leaned, grinning, against the fireplace. "Just what I said. Mickey McCurry was alive, if not well, when Mr. Redford left him lying by the bubbling mountain brook." Ray was obviously enjoying himself.

Lewis made a come-on gesture with his hands. "Stop teasing us, Ray, this is not the time for a joke."

"I never thought it was." He smiled. "I just thought this man you've got here might be glad to know he is not a murderer."

He pointed at Branch, who looked up at him with adoration fit to bestow on angels. Ray made a sign of sipping a drink with his hand. "I'll make the drink," Sonny volunteered. "Talk loud."

"It's been a long day," Ray explained. "Butch and I just finished the autopsy, I'll give you the short version. Time of death? Hard to guess in a guy who spent considerable time lying in cold mud, spattered with cold rain and sprayed by a cold creek. We know he was alive about midnight…so, any time between then and five a.m."

Ray nodded toward the front door. "I stood outside a few minutes and listened to Redford's confession. I can tell you it is essentially true. The rock is definitely the weapon. It's Mickey's blood and hair caught in it. The tops of his boot toes are caked in mud where he was dragged up the path, and the backs of his clothes are muddy from lying down."

"But he was alive all this time?" Sonny asked on his return.

This was the weirdest criminal interrogation I had ever witnessed or even heard of! I had thought Sonny was sometimes rather informal, but he had never served drinks and dinner while he questioned a—I guess—prisoner. Nor had the forensic specialist made his report in the presence of that prisoner and various other interested parties.

It reminded me of a situation I had stumbled upon a couple of years ago while looking for a woman who had inherited from her uncle in Ptown. The heiress and her lover had "buried" her sister in a Louisiana bayou. After turning themselves in, they were sentenced to provide a new air conditioner to the sheriff's office and put new paint on the juvenile detention quarters…and told to go and sin no more.

"He was alive all this time," Ray agreed. "The blow was somewhat of a sideswipe. I judge Branch may have been off balance already or slipped on the wet step as he wielded the rock. There was a hairline fracture, Mickey was concussed and, of course, there was an open wound which bled fairly freely. It did not, however, bleed into the brain in any large amount to cause swelling of the brain. That's what is usually fatal. It was a serious wound, he should have had immediate medical attention. But even when he was ultimately found, he probably would have been alive—and possibly able to be saved—had it not been for other factors."

"What *other* factors?" Cindy called from the dining room

where, as she so often did, was making order out of chaos.

"Well-l-l, there was a great deal of alcohol in his blood, plus signs of steroids and cocaine—can't have helped his general health or his attitude. And…and, there was a minor amount of pink froth in his lungs and mouth." The good doctor should have been on stage.

"You mean he *drowned?*" Lewis was on his feet now and looking incredulous. He glared at Branch. "How in God's name did he drown?"

Branch glared right back. "How the hell do you think I know? I certainly didn't drown him!"

"Well, neither did I!" cried a strained voice from the dining room. I think he died when he fell in the bush."

"And just who the hell are you?"

"I'm Tommy."

The Blackstones had arrived via the kitchen door.

If Ken was bewildered at this influx of loud people to his quiet mountain retreat, you'd never know it. He swept Sara and Tommy into a double embrace with a kiss for Sara.

"Well, look who's here! Two of my favorite people…and just in time for a drink and maybe a little snack from the buffet table. What will you have?"

Sara was obviously no stranger to the cabin. "Ken, I think I am a prime candidate for a snifter of that lovely brandy you hide in the highboy. We've had dinner, thanks."

As the older pair walked into the dining room, I turned to Tommy. At my invitation he looked in the refrigerator and chose a Mountain Dew…I thought it apt. He looked toward his mother, as if he would join her and Ken, but there was something I wanted to know from him before we got all bogged down on who was alive and when.

"Say, Tommy, what on earth were you doing running around soaking wet in a rainstorm Saturday night? You trying to catch pneumonia so we'll all come and bring you cookies?" I smiled, casually, I hoped.

He grinned back. "It was some rain wasn't it? You see, when

we left the Bromfield Inn, Mom dropped Cissy and me off at her folks' house. We had some coffee and cake, and talked awhile. Then Cissy was going to run me home in her dad's car. But when we got just above your—*Ken's* place and the road wasn't gravel anymore, it was just awful.

"I knew Mom would have been okay in the Hummer, but I was afraid Cissy's little Hyundai would never make it through all the mud and might even skid off into the creek. So I had her pull into your parking area. We sat in the car for a while...uh, you know. After a bit, she went home and I started walking."

He laughed and took a swig of his soda. "Usually it's an easy little hike, but that night man, it was wet! The mud was really deep and I was super glad Cissy hadn't tried to drive in it."

Well, that took care of my question.

Deputy Spitz slid into a seat at the kitchen table and patted a chair near him. "Hiya, Tommy, have a seat."

I took one, too. Why not? This was definitely a communal affair.

"Now, Tommy," Dave asked quietly, "when did you first run into Mickey McCurry? On Saturday night after you started walking home."

"Not sure, Dave, maybe twelve or after. He was up where the trail and the creek take a left bend. He was kind of trying to get up, resting on one knee and hangin' on to a tree. When he saw me, he asked me to help him up and get him back to his car. He was talking funny, like he was drunk, and I didn't want to make him mad, especially when he said Jake had sold him bad hooch and he had a mother of a headache. He might have really got mean, you know?"

"You bet. So what did you do?" I prompted.

"I didn't know what to do. I wanted to get home—I knew Mom would be getting worried and might even come looking. And, then too, I didn't think Mickey oughta drive. But he started muttering and kind of growling and I was scared not to help him. I got his arm around my shoulder and pulled him up and noticed blood. Then I saw his head and it made me kind of sick. I thought maybe when we got to his car he would let me drive him to the clinic…he looked awful bad, Dave."

"I'll bet he did. But he managed to walk—with your help?"

Dave smiled and nodded toward Cindy, who had put mugs of coffee in front of us. I patted the one remaining chair and she sank tiredly into it. I wanted her out of here and far away as soon as we could possibly manage it. She'd been playing kitchen maid long enough.

Tommy continued. "Yeah. He took a step or two and tripped on a rock. We both looked down and saw this bloody river rock. Mickey started cussin' and saying somebody hit him with it and he'd get them yet, and somethin' about somebody named Mildred and I don't know what all. I just wanted him down that hill and in his car. In the hospital, really, so I could leave him and not feel guilty."

Why anyone would feel guilty leaving Mickey any place at any time in any shape was beyond me. I'd have left him dangling over the Grand Canyon on a clothesline without a murmur.

Tommy finished his soda, flipped the can into the garbage and took a deep breath.

"We made it almost to the foot of the trail. At least the rain had quit, although everything was still dripping. All of a sudden Mickey groaned and kind of collapsed. He pulled me off balance, and the two of us fell into this soaking wet shrub. He wouldn't answer me and I couldn't get him to sit up. I felt his neck like they do on TV and didn't feel anything. I sat for a minute. I figured he was maybe dead, and I didn't want to touch him. But I couldn't leave him sprawled in that bush. He was heavy but I managed to get him over my shoulder and carried him on down to the little clearing and laid him down. At least it had been downhill! I put his head near the creek in case he woke up and was thirsty—Lord knows I was—but I did not drown him! Why would I after I had gone to all that trouble?"

"Right you are, Tommy, why would you, indeed? I'm sure you had simply—and very bravely—just tried to help him." Ken agreed. He and Sara had been standing in the dining room doorway, watching Tommy and listening carefully to his every word.

"Satisfied?" Sara asked Dave. "You have a Good Samaritan here, not a killer."

"We were pretty sure of that all along, ma'am," Dave replied. "Just two quick questions, Tommy and we're finished. What did you do with the rock you tripped over?"

"Oh, I wasn't sure what to do. But I finally decided: if somebody *had* hit him with it, the police should see it. And then I thought, but they shouldn't see my fingerprints on it, since I didn't do it. So I went back up the trail, took my scaling glove out and carried the rock back to where he was."

"I see," Dave looked serious. "What were you doing with a scaling glove at a dance, Tommy. We found it alongside the trail, near Mickey's body."

"If the rain had stopped earlier, Cissy and I were going to try a little night fishing to see if we could nab a couple of catfish for her old man. He likes 'em, who knows why? I had the glove in my jacket pocket and my knife folded up in my pants pocket. I guess the glove fell out when I thought I put it back." For the first time, he looked guilty as he looked at his mother.

"Where *is* that jacket, Tommy, come to think of it?" Sara was aiming stern irritated-mother looks at her son.

"Well, uh, well, it had a couple of tears from when we fell in the bush, and it had some blood on the shoulder and it was awful muddy and wet—you could wring it out. So I...I didn't know what to do with it, and I hid it under an old rotten pine on the way home. I'm sorry, Mom."

She sighed and then flashed a radiant smile and rumpled his hair. "I suppose if a blazer is the only casualty this family suffers from this chaos we should thank our blessings. I take it Tommy is clear?"

"Absolutely." Dave grinned. "Go in peace. Tommy, you are a good man." Tommy blushed a vivid red.

Sara turned to Ken. "If there is anything we can do for Branch, please let us know. He's family, and I've always had a soft spot for him. And thank you, my dear, for your generosity and support and especially the brandy...it works wonders, doesn't it?" She gave me a sly wink, and I matched Tommy's color scheme.

By the time I thought of a reply, they had gone.

Apparently things were calming down in the living room. There was a low murmur of voices, but no more yelling. Sonny came in the kitchen bearing a mug and asking where the tea was kept. "My stomach is revolting at the thought of coffee."

I pointed at a cabinet. He studied the selection kept there. "Can you have English Breakfast tea at eight p.m.?"

"Yes. And you can tell us how Mickey drowned while you make it." I reached over and turned the burner on under the teakettle.

"He didn't." Sonny gave his shark grin. "He had a heart attack."

"Oh, sure," I said. "And then he up and died of an infected toenail."

"Honest." He put a teabag and two sugars in his mug and stood by the stove. "Ray said Mickey had a very minor bit of pink foam in one lung and in his throat. Not nearly enough to indicate drowning. Just that he probably inhaled a little water and then coughed it up."

"So he was still alive when Tommy laid him by the creek," Cindy remarked.

"Who was that Russian guy they couldn't kill?" She mused.

"Never mind Russians. When did Mickey have a heart attack?" I was lost.

"It was Rasputin. Neither Doc is absolutely sure, but they imagine it was when he collapsed into the bush. He lived some minutes after that. At some point he moved a little and got his face in the water, but reflexively coughed up the water he had inhaled. Then he died. Finally."

"Did the head wound cause it?" I asked.

"Not directly." The kettle whistled and Sonny poured his tea. "He was dragged, carried and walked all over the place with a serious wound; he was laid in cold mud and had to be bone chilled; he was soaking wet; he was full of booze and drugs—not a real good guarantee for longevity."

"So now where does this leave Branch?" Cindy looked hopeful as she made herself tea.

"Your hero is now charged with assault and battery. In my opinion that will last about five minutes after he gets a lawyer. There is no direct proof the wound caused the heart attack. At the very least, Branch stopped Mickey from illegal trespass into a house where two women were staying...never mind all the other plans he had." Sonny stopped short, he hadn't meant to get into details with Cindy.

I covered for him. "Yes, he had said something to Branch about trashing the house so Ken would think we left it that way."

Sonny quickly resumed his tale. "I would bet Branch will walk. With the way this town feels about Mickey, they may give him a medal. Ken is going into town with them in a minute and post bail for him and bring him back here to spend the night, since Clay's away."

"Where will he sleep?" It seemed to me we were running out of beds.

"There are two beds in the room I'm using. I guess we'll be roomies for a night. Unless... I've been thinking. How tired are you two?"

My first thought had been to answer, "Exhausted," but then I realized where his question was leading. I changed my answer to, "I'm tired, but jumpy, not sleepy."

Cindy just said, "Dead."

"Okay." He grinned. "Then you get the first shift in the backseat with Fargo."

Hearing his name, Fargo crawled out from under the table and cocked his head. Were we going somewhere? It looked as if we might.

"Are you crazy?" Cindy couldn't fathom what the Peres kids were suggesting.

"Look," Sonny explained, "I really need to get back, and I can't believe you aren't ready to leave, too. Nothing is holding us here. I'll take the first driving shift. Alex can take the second after a nap, and if you feel like it, you can take the third. By this time tomorrow...or earlier...we'll be home!"

Cindy straightened. "Now that you mention it, I'm brimming with energy. Alex, let's get those bags back in the car."

"Wait." I held up a hand. "Let's say goodbye to Branch and Ken in case we leave before they get back."

We caught them at the front door and explained our plans. Ken, too, would be leaving early tomorrow morning, along with Ray. Lewis might need to stay longer. So everyone understood Sonny's need to get going. They politely didn't mention that Cindy and I might be eager to get the hell out of Dodge City.

Branch was tearfully grateful of our support and insisted that next year we come again and stay with him and Clay. I wondered if Clay was aware that Branch had become a permanent fixture. We thanked Branch for "solving our problem" and assured him we would be available if he needed us "at a later time." We thanked Ken for his "gracious hospitality," declared how we had "enjoyed the natural beauties" of the area and were "charmed by many of the townspeople we had met." Having been right up there with the politicians at saying everything while saying nothing, we both kissed both men on the cheek as they left.

And I whispered, "Hang tough, Saint George!" to Branch.

While Sonny loaded suitcases in the trunk, Cindy and I cleared the dining room table and jammed food into the refrigerator. We stacked seemingly endless plates, cups and glasses in the sink, Cindy remarking that Mrs. Fouts would have a field day. I said it would simply confirm her opinion of Yankee women and men in general.

I took the cookies and fruit and put them in the bag with Fargo's remaining food and treats. We took our light jackets from the hall closet and went out the kitchen door, leaving Lewis, Ray and Dave huddled over the coffee table filling out the endless reports that accompany this kind of event.

We stopped in Beulaland's one late-night store and bought six-packs of caffeine-packed sodas. As Sonny pulled rapidly away, I cautioned him to slow down till we were out of town. "You don't want a speeding ticket at this point," I warned.

At that moment from behind the town gasoline station came a flicker of lights and the universal horn greeting: *Shave and a haircut.* Sonny answered with: *Two-bits.*

We had received and acknowledged our final salute from Beulaland.

CHAPTER TWENTY-SEVEN

The first half of the drive home was very different from our drive down to Beulaland. The road seemed very black, and our headlights felt as if they encapsulated us even more from any life or scenery that might be near. We saw some semis, a few cars and a surprising number of RVs.

We rarely could make out the person driving or any passengers, and I wondered giddily if the vehicles drove themselves up and down the road just to give the few real people the illusion of company through an otherwise empty land.

There were, of course, the oases. Bright lights, vehicles pulled evenly into marked slots. Surprisingly clean restrooms, typical diner menus with almost every dish known to man included, and waitresses of all ages—but neat and usually friendly.

We stopped every three to four hours, mainly to give Fargo a run, occasionally to get fuel and usually to eat something. And that something became different for each of us as the hours on the road expanded. At one point a waitress placed a hamburger and fries in front of Sonny, presented Cindy with a fruit salad and gave me a generous stack of pancakes with bacon.

I was driving when I noticed the headlights didn't seem to have as long a range as they had on my last shift. I worried that something was wrong with the alternator but hated to waken Sonny—I tried fruitlessly to remember how long it had been since he had slept through a night in his own bed. But the lights grew dimmer yet. Where was an oasis when you needed one?

I looked from side to side—and suddenly realized the "problem." All night, whenever I had driven, I had stared ahead along the beams of light, not looking toward the blank black sides. Now, I could *see* things alongside the car. It was early *daylight!* I was thrilled. I tried to think of a poem about the dawn and could not.

But I felt that I must share this wonderful event with my companions, so I quoted the only reference to the sun I could remember.

I cried, "'Tis morning and Juliet is the sun!'" I threw my right arm out as I spoke and my fingers clipped Cindy on the side of her head.

"Jesus Christ! Alex, pull over. You've finally lost it."

Sonny sat up in the back. "What's going on? What's wrong?"

"Alex is quoting Shakespeare, complete with artistic gestures." She rubbed her temple.

"Are we still on the road?"

"Yes."

"Then leave her the fuck alone. You got something against Shakespeare?" He sank back down, Fargo his pillow.

At last, in mid-afternoon, we crossed the Sagamore Bridge over the Cape Cod Canal and began, what seemed to me, the longest leg of our journey…the seventy miles between the bridge and the dunes of Provincetown. I had lived in Ptown all my life and never realized there were so many towns to pass.

Long after I had given up, we reached the Orleans traffic circle, which spit us out into Eastham. That left only Wellfleet, Truro and...*home!* Sonny was driving at the time, and a few hundred yards down the road, he pulled over near a wooded area.

"Sorry, ladies, gotta go."

"God, Sonny, we are only about twenty minutes out! Can't you wait?"

"Nope." He opened his door, and Fargo squeezed into the front to go with him. They seemed to be gone a considerable time, and returned with Sonny explaining that Fargo had to sniff a dozen trees before finding the right one.

All journeys must end, as ours finally did when Sonny nosed the spattered, road-filmed car into the driveway.

The back door to the house opened and erupted people. Mom and Aunt Mae ran to Cindy and me. Trish kissed the bearded Sonny with no apparent problem. Lainey and Cassie, Peter and Wolf, Walter and Billy, Ellen, and Choate Ellis all hung back for a few minutes and then joined the hugfest. And I realized why Sonny had had to "go." He had phoned Mom to tell her where on the highway we were, and she had done the rest.

Peter and Wolf had of course come armed with champagne. Peter lifted his glass in a toast: "Welcome to your gorgeous, newly extended home!"

Cindy and I looked at each other and broke into a run toward the back of the house. There was our unpainted, unfurnished Master Suite in all its glory. The bathroom of my dreams, complete with *bidet*. When had Cindy found time to call Orrick's from Beulaland? I had forgotten all about it. I gave her a hug and kiss, and we turned to the sliding doors leading to our small, private deck. Beyond it was a petite trickling fountain and the beginnings of a flower bed. Mom and Aunt Mae had been busy.

"Was it worth all the trouble?" Mom asked from the doorway.

Cindy laughed. "My dear Jeanne, compared to our restful bucolic vacation, it was all a very minor irritation. But you and Aunt Mae have been busy. I never imagined we'd come home to a working fountain and live plants."

Her look became dreamy, and she turned in a slow circle. I knew she was decorating. Choosing just the right paint, carpet, draperies, furniture. She could see the completed Master Suite—oh, all right, the name kind of fit—where I could not. But Cindy had a marvelous eye for color. It would be perfect when she finished. Go for it, sweetheart.

"Excuse me for interrupting, girls." We would never be quite adult to Aunt Mae. "Your guests know you are tired and don't wish to prolong their welcome, but they—and I, I must admit—are dying to learn what on earth went on down there. And how on earth you survived it."

I managed not to sigh, put my arm around her shoulder and smiled. "Why sho' nuff, honey chile, it will be our pleasure."

Fortified with champagne, we gave the briefest possible account of our time in Beulaland. They were horrified, saddened, amused...much as we had been when it was going on. Only we had also been good and scared, which was difficult to put across in the safety of our living room, surrounded by relatives and friends.

Even their comments sounded familiar to ones we had made.

"How can anyone hurt or kill an innocent animal?"

"That poor old lady—so scared she got chest pains!"

"Bastard was sure hard to kill. Reminds one of that Russian fella...his name just slips my mind."

"Rasputin," Sonny supplied. "Haven't I had this conversation before, or am I just groggy?"

"That Sheriff Jeffie ought to be on TV." There was general laughter at this comment.

"He may soon have time to look in to that possibility," Sonny added. "The State Police captain intimated that our Jeffie may presently receive several suggestions that he resign to 'spend more time with his family' if he has one, or 'to pursue other endeavors' if he doesn't."

Everyone was laughing, but I was not especially amused,

"What's the matter, dear?" Mom asked. "You seem very solemn."

"I just have wondered sometimes if we weren't simply a couple of busybodies. We didn't live there or own property there, or expect to. We really knew no one, except very casually. That planned 'development' had no real effect on us. Perhaps we should just have kept quiet. Jeffie aside, they are bright folks down there. They would have worked it out in their own time and way. I am not entirely certain we didn't just make matters worse. Maybe Rasputin the Second didn't really have to die."

"Listen, Sis." Sonny poked a finger at my chest. "McCurry was on the fast track to disaster. If it hadn't been you and Cindy, it would have been someone else who just happened to say the wrong thing when Mickey had ingested the right amount of alcohol and drugs. Maybe he would have killed that Mildred woman, maybe Sara, or that outspoken Dermott guy or Branch himself. But it would have happened. Trust me."

Choate Ellis nodded. "I'm sure Sonny is right. He's experienced in such matters. And I know it resulted in a terrifying experience for the two of you. But perhaps you will feel slightly better about your intervention if you remember the words of the Parliamentarian Edmund Burke: 'The only necessity for evil to win is for good men to do nothing.' Of course." He smiled. "Nowadays that means women, too."

And that about said it all.

CHAPTER TWENTY-EIGHT

Peace. It's wonderful!

And we had had a whole eleven days of it. From the Wednesday afternoon when we got home, and for the entire weekend, we simply reveled in being *home*. Not to mention alive and well.

We finally got back to sleeping normally and eating normally and doing normal little things. Like housecleaning, getting the car washed and waxed, putting away heavy winter clothing, spading up the garden, housecleaning, planting radishes and sugar peas and housecleaning. I will leave it to you to figure out who did what.

The pets were also glad to be home. Fargo was assiduous in his patrols of the yard and announcements of visitors. We had one small problem with him. The minute we turned the fountain on, he was delighted with his new wading pool. We were still working on convincing him that taking a drink from it was fine, splashing in it was not. I had the feeling it might be a lifetime project.

Wells, too, was some concern. She was still a little nervous at having been left—even with her favorite aunt—and spent a bit too much time alternately under the bed grumbling to herself or demanding to be petted. But the vet assured us those extremes would wear off.

When Monday came, we both went back to work. I reclaimed my clients from Harvey Weinberg and took him to lunch. I visited the art galleries that handle my photos and got some good, some fair orders—enough to keep me busy for a while signing, numbering, matting and framing.

Cindy played some catch-up at the bank, but was generally pleased with the way her department had functioned. Since we hadn't managed to get souvenirs for anyone, she did the lunch bit also, and everyone seemed happy.

I was especially pleased—relieved might be a better word—at Cindy's manner since our return. When Sonny informed her that retired officer Edgar Fountain would be back in place as her lookout when she started work Monday, she accepted the fact almost casually.

"I suppose it's wise," she admitted. "But somehow I don't feel threatened." She laughed. "Perhaps after our Beulaland adventure a simple stalker is just a minor passing annoyance."

Sonny was a little more serious. "Well, he could have been a transient and has now moved on. He could have given up on you and is now busy adoring someone else, or he could have been waiting impatiently for your return. Let's give the good Edgar one more week."

"All right, whatever you think is best. But, Sonnny, there's one part of this I was too frightened and upset to tell you about earlier. And that whole situation at Beulaland didn't help."

She told him of her experience with the men—particularly the supervisor—working on the broken water main.

"I hope this hasn't caused you to waste a lot of time and taxpayer money. I was just too rattled even to bring it up. Alex didn't know, either," she added, "until shortly before we came home."

Sonny just shrugged. "It could well have caused you to think you were being followed, and you actually may have been...by him or someone else. Edgar and I will get a look at this guy if they're still dawdling along with those repairs. At least we'll know who we're looking for."

Later in the week we received a bouquet that would have been quite at home in the winner's circle of the Kentucky Derby. The enormous card hoped we would visit Beulaland again soon and was signed by all the people we had met and several we couldn't recall. Even Jeffie had managed to get his signature included.

We kept the card, divided the bouquet into quarters and took it to the clinic to be given to those who might be lacking in that sector.

We thought about the card for a few minutes and decided it was too soon to say whether we couldn't wait for next spring to go back...or whether it was the last place we would ever set foot.

When I returned from the usual errands Friday morning the phone answering machine was flashing peremptory blinks that indicated three calls had come in.

For some reason, even not knowing what they were, I was not inclined to listen to them. I had a feeling I wasn't going to want to know. I put away the groceries that needed the freezer or refrigerator. I let Fargo out—the fountain was not running, although it was still the first area he headed for.

I went in the bedroom to check on Wells. Although the Orrick crew was long gone and she knew Fargo and I were now at home, she was still in hiding. I crawled under the bed to give her a pet and coax her to come out. Suddenly I heard the dim distant chirp of my cell phone.

I lay there a moment wondering where it could be, and then remembered the T-shirt I had worn briefly yesterday. It was in the pocket. To answer or not to answer? Three calls on the tape, at least one call on the cell. Somebody really wanted me.

Reluctantly, I rolled out from under the bed and over to my bureau. See, I knew right where the little phone was!

"Hello."

"Where the hell have you been? We've been looking all over for you half of the morning."

"And it's nice to hear *your* voice this lovely day! Stop yelling, Sonny, there's no law saying I have to report to the police before I do the weekly shopping. What do you want?" I sat up and leaned against the bed.

"I want you to get Cindy and bring her over here to ID the so-called stalkers, and I figured she would be more comfortable if you were with her."

"That's very thoughtful. Of course I will. What do you mean *so-called* stalkers—and stalkers, plural? Did Edgar catch them?"

"Not exactly. He and Larry Wismer were both involved. They are at the clinic getting patched up…nothing serious. Old Mrs. Wismer is on her way here, so get a damn move on."

"What has she got to do with this?" His sweet little ol' granny? How could she be involved?

"She may have to post bail for Larry, and he's a minor so she has to be here anyway. Just *move it!*" He hung up.

I moved it. I called Cindy and told her Edgar had caught the stalker—I made it singular. I did not say Edgar was injured, I didn't mention Larry at all. I told her Sonny needed her "for identification" purposes, and that I would pick her up in the bank parking lot in fifteen minutes. I saw no reason to have her as befuddled as I was.

I read once that Einstein on one occasion gave a flip description of his theory of relativity: *Five minutes seems only a second when you are dancing with a lovely woman; it is an hour when you are sitting on a hot radiator.*

Well, I was with the lovely woman, but the ten-minute drive was feeling like an hour. Cindy was one long question, from the minute I picked her up. How did Edgar identify and arrest the stalker? How would she know him? She had never really seen him in action. Was he a local she would recognize? Did I—Alex— know him? Did Sonny think he was dangerous?

I muttered vague answers, since I had no concrete ones. After an eternity, we reached the police station and I practically ran inside, leaving Cindy to play catch-up. I couldn't face another question.

Sonny met us at the door with some questions of his own before he took us into the conference room—a transparent euphemism for interrogation room.

"Cindy," he asked at once, "do you remember where they had Commercial Street dug up for days, looking for and finally fixing that water main leak?"

"Uh, yes, sure." She looked bewildered.

"And you did have more than one occasion to be in that area while it was being worked on?"

"Oh, probably a number of times. I have lunch down that way fairly often. I remember going to the drugstore once…and maybe to Lena's Little Boutique to pick up some stockings. Why?"

"Do you remember how many workers there were and what any of them may have said to you?"

She leaned against the wall and stared at the ceiling for a minute.

Finally, she nodded. "As I told you the other day, there were anywhere from two to four young guys and an older man. The older guy was not in coveralls. He had on a blue shirt and pants, like maybe he was some sort of boss. He looked cleaner, too. Some of the young guys said stuff like, 'Hey, honey, got time to go for a beer?' and 'Meet me after work and wear that tight skirt you had on yesterday.' And one said I looked tired and did I want him to tuck me in. Oh, yes, one of them said I had a nice ass. You know, typical male macho stuff. I simply ignored it all—I didn't even bother to tell them to go to hell."

"What about the older man, what did he say?" Sonny watched her sharply.

"Nothing at first. Then one day s-something really nasty, as

224

I told you the other day...I just ignored it, tried to forget it." She was pale and obviously frightened.

"Honey, you really should have told me. Exactly what did he do?" I asked.

"I didn't quite hear every word, but I got the gist of it. It scared me, but I thought if I told you, you'd confront him and get hurt. And I wasn't even sure of exactly what he looked like. Oh, God, I've handled this whole thing wrong!"

I could see tears about to roll and gave her a kiss on the cheek.

"No, you haven't. We'll straighten it out."

Sonny took her arm gently. "Let's go in...so we can get out fast." He smiled down at her.

I followed them down the hall. Cindy looked back at me. I shrugged. She knew as much as I did.

In the conference room sat three young men in grubby coveralls bearing the logo of the Water Department and looking scared. There was also an older man with graying hair and looking somewhat like Edgar Fountain. I found myself wondering if they could be brothers. Then I noticed he wore a blue workman's uniform with an ID tag on his shirt pocket: R.J. Travis. Well, maybe they were cousins.

Sonny motioned for us to sit, while he remained standing and cleared his throat as he turned on the tape recorder. He gave the names of everyone present and finally got to specifics.

"Cynthia Hart, do you recognize these four men, and from what encounter?"

Cindy looked puzzled for a moment, and then hit her stride. "Yes, I do. They were working on the water main leak on Commercial Street about two weeks ago." Then she again went down the list of their comments to her.

Sonny indicated Mr. Travis. "Did this man make any similar comments?"

"Yes. Later. Something about a van and a hot potato...and... uh, having sex. I didn't hear it all clearly."

"Ah!" Sonny sounded triumphant. "But someone else did

225

hear it clearly!"

He turned to Travis. "You see, Mr. Travis, although Ms. Hart was almost out of earshot, a young man happened to be standing in front of the drugstore, where he was to meet a friend. *He* clearly heard you say..." Sonny looked down at a three-by-five card with writing on it. "You said, 'Tuck her *in*? I may just toss her into the van and fuck her up. Us older guys know how to treat a hot potato.' You did say that, didn't you?"

"I don't recall saying that," Travis mumbled.

"Uh-huh." Sonny gave the men his shark's grin. "All four of you are guilty of making lewd solicitations in public. You also may well have infringed on this young lady's civil rights: any woman is entitled to walk down the street without being subject to such remarks as you made."

Cindy's eyebrows had done their moving toward the top of her forehead act. I wondered if Sonny was making up laws as he went along, although his accusations did sound logical. But he wasn't finished.

"But you, Mr. Travis, are also guilty of threatening kidnap and rape."

Cindy turned pale again; obviously just this phrase frightened her badly. It frightened me.

Travis banged the table with his palm. "I didn't say no such thing! I may have said she was good-looking or something. Whoever says I was going to rape her is crazy."

"Sure." Sonny looked at him pityingly. "Well, maybe these young oafs will remember what you said if the prosecutor drops their charge to a misdemeanor." The three oafs began grinning and winking at each other. They would remember Travis threatened to shoot the president if it would get them off lighter.

Sonny frowned portentously and made a note on the card before him. I saw that it read: Pick up chicken and squash for Mom.

"Well, I'm not holding any of you until we evaluate Mr. Wismer's statement, but don't plan any trips. You may go...for now."

They cleared the room with three-alarm speed. As soon as they were in the hall, I turned to my brother. "Larry Wismer? Is that kid everywhere? Isn't he that young stock market whiz hanging around Cindy all the time? What's this with Wismer being a witness?"

"That's what I want to know," said a woman's well-modulated voice from the doorway.

Larry's dear old granny had arrived: tall, slender, attractive and late fifties max.

She wore navy slacks and an undeniably blue shirt with white collar and cuffs. Her only real sign of age was her white wavy hair, partially covered by a jaunty panama hat that matched her shirt.

Sonny was on his feet, introducing himself, Cindy and me, helping Mrs. Wismer into a chair, thanking her for being so prompt and straightening his tie all at the same time.

"Did Larry actually hear such a terrible threat? Why didn't he tell me? And where is he, by the way? Not in your custody for some reason, surely."

Sonny took a deep breath and began. "The four men were working on a water leak on Commercial Street when Cindy Hart crossed the street. One of them made a rather harmless come-on comment to her. She ignored him. Your grandson was outside the drugstore, waiting for a friend. He heard both this remark and the more serious one made by the older man, a supervisor named Travis, which comment I believe you overheard from the hallway. Yes?"

"Yes." Mrs. Wismer nodded. "Sickening. I wish Larry had told me. I would have called the Town Manager at once. Believe me, he would have had that Travis man fired in a heartbeat."

I felt an automatic liking of the lady, but I couldn't let Travis's threat be foisted off on to the dubious efforts of the town council.

"I'm afraid it is a little more serious than that, Mrs. Wismer. That kind of threat is not only a crime and possibly a hate crime, it has caused Cindy a great deal of on-going fear and stress."

"I suppose you are right, and I'm terribly sorry about what Cindy has gone through. I must admit, however, I'm not happy with Larry being involved with the police." She cocked her head at Sonny. "And I ask again: where is he?"

At that moment the intercom buzzed. Sonny picked it up, listened and said, "Thanks, Nacho. Send them in." He turned to Mrs. Wismer. "He's here."

The hall door opened, and Larry and Edgar came in. Mrs. Wismer gasped and Cindy did her eyebrow thing again. Sonny leaned over to me, stifling a giggle—we both have an unfortunate tendency to giggle at inopportune times—and he wasn't helping me much right now.

He whispered, "They look like two guys from that painting of the three Revolutionary War soldiers, all bandaged up and marching along with a drum and fife and flag."

They did indeed. Larry had a splint taped to his nose, which also looked to be packed with cotton, and a thick Ace bandage around his right thumb and hand. Edgar Fountain had a blossoming black eye and was walking very strangely and delicately.

"My God, my poor baby! What on earth happened to you?"

Obviously embarrassed, Larry tried to speak nonchalantly, no easy task when you're talking with half a bale of cotton in your nose.

"I'm okay, Gran. It's just a busted node and a sprained thub. Bud the doc gave me a pain pill and I feel funny—like I did thad time I drank the cookin' sherry." He sat down abruptly. "And I'm real sorry Offider Fountain thad I hit your eye and kicked you id the…id the lower stomach."

"Larry! You had a fight with a policeman? You're lucky he didn't kill you!"

"I'd like to," Edgar muttered. Mrs. Wismer stiffened and glared. She took a deep breath, ready for a verbal artillery blast, but Sonny beat her to it.

"All right, everybody quiet please so we can wrap this up and let our wounded heroes go home."

He shuffled some papers and continued. "Larry, you were in front of the drugstore, waiting for a buddy, and you heard what Travis said, right?"

"Yes."

"And you got a very good look at him, didn't you?"

"Un-huh. I walked over toward him to tell him he should neber speak to a lady lide that, especially Mid Hart. Bud I chickened oud; there were too many ob them."

"A smart move. Your next smart move would have been to tell the police what had happened. But it was spring break, you had several days to do what you wished, so you decided to handle it yourself."

Larry dropped his head. I hoped he didn't start the nose bleed again.

Sonny winked at me and continued. "Now, Larry, we know you have—shall we say—a warm feeling for Ms. Hart, so you began to follow her to make sure nothing bad happened to her."

I closed my eyes and took a deep breath. Of course…Larry.

Cindy whispered, "Oh, my God, why didn't I see it?"

Mrs. Wismer's feelings were more audible. "Oh, Larry, what the hell were you thinking? You asinine young pup! Having a crush on an older woman is one thing, turning into the Avenger is another! I could just shake you! Look at all the trouble you've caused and now your lovely nose will never look the same!" She burst into tears.

Larry followed suit. And this was not good for packed noses. I reached down the table, patted his hand and put my oar in the water.

"Now, Larry, listen to me. You weren't the only one to make a mistake. Cindy was frightened and should have told me or Sonny, but she was afraid one of us might be hurt. So she walked around figuring this Travis might appear any minute, toss her in a van and molest her."

I paused to light a cigarette, ignored my dear brother's meaningful glance and did not hand it to him. So he took up my commentary instead.

"Cindy had not gotten a good look at Travis, so any man over forty frightened her. You didn't fall into that category, Larry, so even if she noticed your following her, her radar classified you as *friend*, and it never occurred to her that you were her 'stalker.'"

I casually moved my cigarette pack out of Sonny's reach, smiled and picked up on what I had been saying.

"Your note on her car was not one of your brighter moves, but in the long run, it was good. It upset Cindy to the point that she told Sonny and me of her 'stalker,' and Sonny set things in motion to find him. That has been done. By the time it comes to trial, you will be able to speak English again. Your heart is as big as New Jersey, Larry Wismer, and it was in the right place all the way, even if the rest of you wasn't."

"Hear, hear," cheered Cindy and Sonny. Mrs. Wismer managed a smile. Edgar Fountain let out something between a moan and a growl.

"Yes, Edgar, I understand your displeasure." Sonny gave him a sympathetic head shake. "If I have it correctly you were in your car in the bank parking lot, not realizing Cindy was busy and working through lunch. Larry-On-Patrol mistook you for Travis, pulled you out of your car and popped you one in the eye, while yelling for someone to call nine-one-one."

I took pity and handed Sonny the lighter and cigarettes. He lit one, took a puff and went on.

"Deputy Fountain, you tried to cuff Larry, but he somehow twisted away and you grabbed at him, spraining his thumb, the pain causing him to kick out at you and cause you considerable smarting in the, as he said, lower stomach. Fortunately, two security guards then ran out of the bank and separated you. Now I know you both have a beef here. And you could each hire a lawyer and keep him or her in fine old brandy for the next five years, until you settle anything."

He took a drag. "My ardent recommendation is that you both forget it. Larry, I hope you've learned a lesson. Edgar, you know pain sometimes goes with the job…just send us your bill."

Sonny's fingers did a little tap dance on the intercom, and

within seconds Nacho and Hatcher came in briskly. Sonny gave them their directives. "Hatcher, please help Larry to his grandmother's car—he's a little woozy. Then drive Officer Fountain home in his car. Nacho, follow Hatcher and bring him back. Thanks. Now, Mrs. Wismer, let me walk you to your car. You know, that hat is perfect with that outfit."

She looked up at him and grinned. "Charmer!"

CHAPTER TWENTY-NINE

Cindy and I stood looking at each other for a moment, perhaps feeling like schoolkids no one had told that class was over and they could leave the room. Finally we laughed and skipped out, arms around each other's waists and singing that we were off to see some wizard.

Reaching my car, we agreed that lunch was in order and the Wharf Rat was the place. It didn't take us long to get there.

A weekday meant it wasn't overcrowded this early in the year. I was glad to note that Harmon and The Blues Boys were not in session. I wasn't up to another chapter of Cassie and her Three Musketeers...or to some other wild drug plot he thought he had uncovered.

I was surprised to see who *was* there. My mother and Aunt Mae were having lunch. With other customers still fairly thin on the ground, they had made themselves comfortable at a table for four and waved us over.

"Darlings! What a nice surprise. I hope you can join us?"

Of course we could, and as we sat, a waiter appeared asking if we'd care for a drink. Cindy ordered a double scotch and soda; I opted for a double bourbon old fashioned and did a credible imitation of Cindy's eyebrow trick, and Aunt Mae gave us her best myopic stare. Then they both looked at their watches and took a meaningful sip from their iced tea glasses.

"It's been a hectic morning," I offered as our excuse.

"It's been a hectic spring," Cindy underscored.

"What on earth happened to warrant double drinks barely after noon? I assume this is not an everyday occurrence," Aunt Mae asked, her mouth a prim, disapproving little pout.

I remembered what my mom had told me about Aunt Mae and Uncle Frank when they were first married—that they were definitely members in good standing of the wild party set. I was in no mood for her rare holier than thou act, and came very close to telling her so.

Fortunately, the waiter came with the drinks and asked for our food order. Cindy grabbed a menu. I ordered my favorite, a pastrami on rye with french fries and a half-sour pickle.

Cindy handed the menu back to the waiter and said, "Just double that." She was really in a recuperative mood to pass up her usual healthy salad for my kind of lunch. I was delighted.

When he left, I looked at Cindy and said, "You start."

She sipped her drink and began to tell them the tale of the stalker. She was unaware I had told them a portion of it before we went on vacation, and they—fortunately for me—were shrewd enough not to let on. Now, at least, it was presumably history. As we told them of the various events, including this morning's wrap-up, they registered, sympathy, outrage and—at the end—amusement.

Happily our food arrived then, and we could eat while we mumbled answers to their questions.

Even Cindy had one for me. "Are they going to hang the SOB?"

"No," I replied, "and I doubt he'll even walk the plank. Probably he'll technically get maybe six months in jail, but actually he'll get probation and a bunch of community service hours."

"What about the three young men?" Mom inquired.

"Probably just some community service. Frankly, I'm not sure they even broke any laws, unless Ptown has some weird antiquated ones on the books—which wouldn't surprise me."

"I'm glad." Cindy finished her highball and waved her glass at the waiter. Obviously the drink was a mellowing influence. "They weren't really bad. They just haven't figured out yet that an approach like that gets you absolutely nowhere with anyone you really want to date anyway."

She shook her finger at me for some reason. "But that Travis! I stared at him the whole time this morning and he never would look at me even once! He never even said he was sorry. And I say hang 'im!"

"Cindy dear, would you care for some coffee and dessert?" Aunt Mae inquired. I managed not to laugh at the look Cindy gave her.

At the same time Mom asked me, "Is this Travis a danger?"

"I think not," I replied. "I don't think he really intended Cindy to hear him. I think he is simply a crude man, trying to impress his young workers with the idea that he's a macho man of the world who knows how to handle uppity broads and make them like it...that he is still a better 'man' than they will ever be. His police record is clean except for parking tickets, Nacho told me, and his work record is all quite normal. He was scared to death this morning." I chortled, "if he owns a van himself, it's on the market by now. I think he's all talk."

Mom nodded. "I hope you're right. I know Loretta Wismer... lovely lady. I must call her and see how Larry is, poor boy. She adores him—he's really all she has—but I give her credit, she hasn't spoiled him. Well." She checked her watch. "We must be going..."

"Whither bound?"

"Oh, nothing exciting. Barbara Kincaid is still on a walker with that broken fibula. So we are running her errands and doing some shopping for her...probably all wrong, but she'll be too nice to mention it."

I smiled. "Still another star in your crowns."

"We'll take all we can get, right, Mae?" She gave us each a pat on the head and they left.

And shortly, so did we. After I dropped Cindy, munching on a mint, back at the bank, I circled around and started out toward the airport. I had spoken with Cassie on the phone since we got home, but hadn't seen her. I thought, if she was there and not busy, a small visit would be nice...I could find out if there was anything new with the Pittsburgh pirates.

As I turned onto the airport road, I glanced back at the town. Green spots were showing here and there, trees had lost their bare look, even the houses looked brighter and some rooftops seemed actually to sparkle in the sun. There was no season here I didn't love, although if winter were the tiniest bit shorter, I wouldn't complain. Even so, it was home, and I was glad to be here.

Walking into the large hangar where Cassie parked her beloved plane, I thought I was seeing double. I turned my head this way and that in confusion. Two twin-engine Beechcraft planes sat side-by-side, both painted blue and white, both with their noses in the air as if they were above it all, even on the ground.

Cassie appeared from her tiny office in the corner.

"Yes, madam, having a problem with double vision?"

"Don't be silly. The one on the right is painted a slightly darker blue and kind of an off-white."

"Truth to tell, it's just dirty." She laughed.

"I see. And have you learned to fly two at a time?"

"Alex," she said, her tone now serious. "I have recently had—I think—two pieces of absolutely fantastic good luck. Even the timing is just about perfect. I can still hardly believe it is all true."

Not yet even knowing what it was, I was already happy for her; if anyone deserved good fortune it was Cassie. She was one of the most generous and caring people I had ever known.

"Explain, woman!" I commanded.

"Come on into the office where we can sit." She began talking as we walked across the now less empty hangar.

"There's a fellow from Vermont who flies in here every month or so on business.

"He told me about this plane for sale cheap at his home airport."

She took a seat behind the small desk. I carefully removed a bunch of charts from the other chair and put them on the floor before I sat.

"I flew up to have a look at it. It seems it was privately owned by a fella who just flew it weekends and maybe holidays and vacations. Why he thought he needed this much airplane just to circle the neighborhood, I'll never know. He had bought it new, and the logbook showed less than six hundred hours. The farthest he ever flew was occasionally down to the casino in Connecticut and sometimes over to Buffalo to visit an ailing parent."

"Just got to be too much for his budget?" I asked.

"Well, yes and no." She took a pack of cigarettes from her desk drawer. "Don't tell Lainey. I'm supposed to keep them in the car, so I have to walk all the way out to the lot to get one."

She offered me one and I took it, figuring somebody else's didn't count against the five I try to allow myself daily.

"The man had some bad luck," Cassie continued. "He blew a tire on landing and ground-looped off the runway onto the grassy area. Consequently, he had a collapsed undercarriage, a bent propeller and maybe shaft and a slightly damaged wingtip. That accounted for the low price."

"So what was wrong with the plane?"

"I just told you!" She looked at me in amazement.

"No, you told me that *he* had a collapsed undercarriage…"

"Oh, shut up!" She grinned. "Anyway, I thought of buying it right then and having it trucked down here. It really was a bargain basement price. But I finally decided it wasn't worth buying when I didn't even have a pilot for it and would have to pay someone to repair it—it was way beyond my capabilities—so, very reluctantly I told him no thanks."

"From time to time you've mentioned several people who wanted to fly for you using just the one plane," I recalled. "Giving you a little time off in the busy season until you could afford a second plane. Aren't any of them still around?"

She nodded. "Oh, yes, but they all seemed just a little off to me. One man told me he was forty-five, but I happen to know he has a son who's a co-pilot with United. At fifteen, maybe? Another fellow is a bit heavy on the booze. Another one was rough with the plane…you know how I feel about that, Alex. There was a woman I thought would be okay, but I heard her husband was dead against it, so that could have been trouble. All of them had just a little something that made me a tad untrusting."

"Gotcha. But the plane is here."

"Yep. While you were away chasing bears around the mountains and drinking mountain dew, a new woman walked into my life."

She laughed at my expression and explained, "Not that kind of woman." She pointed at the new plane. "*That* kind of woman."

"Jeesh! Don't do that to me."

"Sorry. One day this woman just walked into the hangar, looked around and said, 'How do you feel about a relief pilot and mechanic with twenty years experience?' At first I thought it was a joke."

She laughed and continued. "Her name is Rhoda Bannister and she just finished a twenty-year stint with the Air Force. She wasn't a pilot, she was a mechanic. However, she'd bootlegged several hundred hours in propeller-driven planes including ones like mine. We took it for a spin and you'd think she had been born in one! She got her commercial license the day she got out of the military, I think."

"Sounds perfect, Cassie. How did she end up here?"

"Her lover—also a twenty year Air Force non-com—

something in communications—is an artist, always wanted to do seascapes as she sat in Colorado and Texas looking at mountains and deserts. So here they are, with pensions, but wanting something extra in the way of money and activity. So Rhoda and I went up to Vermont and looked at the plane and I bought it on the spot—well, me and Choate Ellis and my dad. Had it trucked down, and Rho will start working on it Monday. If she can get it ready for the summer, she'll be flying almost every day, great for both of us!"

I was delighted for her. In the busy summer months, Cassie was stretched so thin you could about see through her. Sometimes she had to turn down potential customers, which, of course, is never good…all too often they don't bother with you again. This would relieve a lot of pressure.

"Bright idea time," I said as I doused my cigarette. "If you and Lainey aren't busy, why don't we see if Rho and whatsername are free for dinner at that new Italian place. And the Poly-Cotton Club opens tonight—we could see what they've got going to start the season."

"Good thinking, actually a good idea to see them in a social setting. I'll check with them and Lainey and call you." We stood and started back to the main door.

"By the way," I asked, "what do you hear from your peripatetic Pittsburgh pirates?"

"Finally, *finally*, it's all locked up. One week from today at approximately two o'clock we will turn in to a fish market and depart for Findlay, Pennsylvania."

"Oh, good. You got paid? You got a place to stay? Someone will be standing on the landing strip with a candle when you get there?"

"Yes, Mother. Half the fee in advance, half when we get there—before we unload. New floodlights on the strip. And I am staying with a Mrs. Somebody at her nearby B&B…her husband is a deacon in the local church. Can I go now, Mums? I have to pee."

"I guess so, but don't say *pee*, dear, it's too, too gross. Say you

238

have to *use the facilities*."

She aimed a kick at my backside and we parted.

Everyone's calendar was clear for the evening, so Lainey and Cassie picked us up and we headed for the new restaurant in the East End. Rho Bannister and her lover Janie Allen were there ahead of us, their apartment only a couple of blocks from the restaurant. They stood to greet us, and I noted they were both blond and both, as Harmon would say, square-rigged. Standing side by side, they reminded me of bookends. But they were also pleasant, intelligent women and the evening promised well.

So did the new restaurant. The menu included numerous northern Italian selections, so we were not limited to food smothered in thick acidic red sauce, which was what some of our local restaurants termed *Italian*. And the service was quite good for people not yet used to working together. They even had arias from various operas playing in the background.

During dinner, I had another one of my bright ideas.

"Say, Cassie, are you planning on taking Rho along as co-pilot on your Pennsylvania run?"

Privately, I was almost certain she was not, but I would feel much better if she did. Lainey gave me a grateful look, and I intuited that she had already made this suggestion and been turned down.

Cassie shook her head and swallowed a bite of food. "No. The men are trying to keep the price down, for one thing, and a second pilot would run up the bill. And the trip isn't all that long. Anyway, one of them—Frank—is a pilot and can relieve me for a while if I need to *use the facilities*." She gave me a sweet smile.

I returned the smile. "I just thought it would make a good orientation flight for Rho. You could explain that to your passengers, not charge them for her time, and pay for her B&B if they squawk about that."

Lainey gave my hand a squeeze under the table. "See, Cassie, I told you Alex would agree with me! And I will feel so much better."

Cassie grumbled, "I don't know which of you is more of a wuss. But all right. Rho, it really would be a freebie on your part. The price I finally quoted them doesn't give me any money to pay you, but you can function as first pilot and log the hours as such. Want to do that? It's quite okay if you don't."

Before Rho could answer, Janie spoke up. She was obviously on the ball.

"I seem to sense a certain tension around this flight. Would you say there is anything unusual about it?"

Cassie laughed. "Only that we are carrying a load of fresh seafood to a cookout for about four hundred people and unless we have nose clips, we better not get stranded en route."

Cindy looked at me, as did Lainey, but I said nothing. Rho and Janie were new to town and would never understand that Harmon's phantom drug dealers were everywhere from the Baptist church pulpit to the mansion of the wealthiest family in town. It was Cassie's business.

Rho finally got her answer out. "Suits me fine, just pray for a good brisk tailwind."

I managed not to take a deep breath, which was more than Lainey and Cindy could claim. But I was as happy as they that Cassie would have her own companion on the flight.

We moved on to the Poly-Cotton Club, and our evening went rapidly downhill. The entertainment consisted of two hip-hop guys who plucked frenetically at their guitars and screamed threats to parents, cops and bitches and, I think, the audience and possibly each other. They were too overmiked to be sure.

At the end of the set our table and most of the others were all waving for checks.

Otherwise, it had been a successful evening. It seemed to me that Rho and Janie made a good addition to Ptown.

At home, I let the pets into the yard to use whatever facilities they could sniff out to their satisfaction. By the time we got back in, Cindy was already in bed.

"Tired?" I asked.

"Not really." She grinned. "Why?"

"I thought you n' me might do a li'l hip-hop aroun' duh bed."

"We might do a waltz, or a salsa or even a do-si-do—but don't ever suggest hip-hop to me again. Got that?"

"Yes, ma'am." I undressed and got into bed, counting softly: "*One*-two-three. *One*-two-three…"

CHAPTER THIRTY

I had been around art galleries on the Cape all my life and had come to two conclusions about them. Men who owned or managed them tended to dress up for work, perhaps to underscore that these premises were indeed dedicated to works of *art*. Women who owned or managed them were inclined to dress down, perhaps not wishing to compete with their wares for attention and appreciation.

When I called upon them with my photos, I just tried to be clean and neat and hope the pictures would speak for themselves. Usually it worked. This morning it would not have mattered had I been garbed in ragged shorts and a T-shirt smeared with muddy paw prints or a gold lamé gown with split skirt and deep décolletage.

I had already called upon one of my galleries in Wellfleet and restocked the most popular prints. They had also taken four new photos they liked and made a note to call me the beginning of June to see what refills they needed.

At my second gallery I received doubly upsetting news. Unknown to me over the winter one of the owners had developed a terminal illness. The partners had sold the gallery and returned to their native Texas to spend their last months together and near his family. The new owners imparted this news in the same sepulchral but somehow disapproving tones they used to tell me that they would no longer handle my photos. Now that they owned the place, they explained, they would handle only *true art*.

They turned businesslike immediately. She handed me an inventory list and a check for the six pictures they had just happened to sell in the off-season before they could get them off the wall. He gave me a carton holding the remainder. I staggered out the door, which neither of them offered to hold, and made my way down the sidewalk toward where I was parked. I felt saddened for the two previous owners. I decided my opinion that the two new owners bore a strong resemblance to members of the Addams family might be just a little overstated.

I would have staggered right past my friends Billy and Walter, had Walter not literally taken the heavy carton from my arms. They were both teachers and I wondered what they were doing wandering around the Wellfleet shops on a Monday. The school had to be closed for two days with some dire electrical problem, they explained, and they were just enjoying the good weather.

We walked on toward my car, with me delivering my screed in the whiny voice even I hate. They offered condolences on all counts and I shut up.

As Walter placed the carton of photos in my trunk, Billy snapped his fingers and hit me lightly on the shoulder. "Boy, are we brain-dead or what, Walter?"

Walter and I both stared, assuming some explanation would follow.

"There's that new gallery in Orleans...the wife of one of our teachers just opened it. We know them pretty well, and they're good people. Let's take a run down there now. You've got plenty of samples to show her and even enough to leave some if she wants them. It won't take long."

We piled into my car, and I was more excited than I tried to show. I had never been able to place anything in Orleans. The introduction would help and it would be a real triumph for me if we could carry it off.

We did. Marian Prescott kept twelve shots with backups to hang in a good area.

"With people getting so interested in 'green' and protecting wildlife, this is a natural," she said. "Stay in touch." You bet I would!

We started back to my car and I repaid them slightly by warning against the Poly-Cotton Club's current show. They were grateful for the information and pleased that Cassie had found another pilot.

"Two planes now!" Walter exclaimed. "She'll be putting Delta out of business."

"If she lives long enough." I told them of Harmon's latest drug imaginings and they got a real kick out of that. It was how we had met. Harmon had mistaken Walter for a murderous drug dealer victimizing elderly ladies.

"Well." Billy laughed. "At least he is consistent."

I dropped them at their car and went home, still sad about my ex-customer's illness, but simultaneously elated by my new connection in Orleans.

And the week held still more welcome news for us. Wednesday evening Sonny and Trish stopped by on their way to a movie. Sonny had good news, or at least I thought it was.

"The young Lotharios and Stalker Travis pled out," he announced. "So neither Cindy nor the Wismer boy will have to go through the stress of a trial. Now ain't that great?"

I saw Cindy close her eyes and take a deep breath. I wondered if she was sending up a prayer of thanks or simply trying not to cry with relief. Possibly both.

"What did they plead guilty to?" I asked.

"All four pleaded guilty to using graphically suggestive and salacious language in public."

I laughed. "Oh, come on, Sonny, you just made that up—that can't be a law this day and age."

"It can and is." He took a cigarette from my pack, and I didn't even glare. "Back in 1871 the daughter of one of the bank executives attended a girlfriend's afternoon tea. Afterward she walks over to the bank and waits for her father to come out so they can stroll home together."

He finally got the cigarette lit and continued. "She is standing on the sidewalk, leaning on her parasol. A young man mistakes her for a prostitute. He asks her, in apparently explicit words, to let him purchase what he assumes she was selling. The girl beats the man about the head with her umbrella and then goes screaming into the bank, police are duly summoned, and the law went onto the books, where it has dozed ever since."

"How did you ever know about it?" Sonny occasionally surprised me to the core.

"Oh, partly old records—they can be fascinating, you know. And old newspapers and copies of personal journals the library has hung on to. And sometimes things the old geezers tell you about."

"Has that law ever been used again?" He had me interested now.

"The latest account I have found was nineteen forty-two, when a drunken Coast Guardsman made essentially the same mistake with a Selectman's young wife."

"This is all fascinating," Cindy added, "but what happened to our four men?"

"Ah, yes. Well the three young guys got six month's probation, forty hours community service and—what doubtless hurt them the most—one week's house arrest."

"And that bastard, Travis?"

"The judge gave him two year's probation, eighty hours community service and one month's house arrest. And unofficial word has it, he will keep his job of twelve years, but with a temporary demotion and a transfer up-Cape."

"Oh, Sonny! That's *nothing!*" Cindy sounded furious.

"Cindy, it's not as light as it may sound," Sonny explained. "Two whole years of knowing the cops are breathing down your neck gets nerve-racking. Community service is not raking leaves in the park on a lovely autumn day: it's cleaning the municipal restrooms, picking up trash from the sidewalks and gutters. It's working the garbage trucks on nice hot days and mopping floors at town hall. And house arrest, I'm told, is no fun at all after the first couple of days. It's not so much that your house is unpleasant, it's knowing that you absolutely *cannot* leave it."

"And Travis may get rather lonesome there," Trish added with a wicked grin. "This is off the record, but Mrs. Travis was in our office to see Attorney Frost the other day. Of course, I have no idea as to their conversation," she said with a simper, "But I believe it is public knowledge, since it was uttered in the reception room, that she is now visiting her mother in Lynn while she 'does some thinking.'"

Even Cindy laughed at that. "I imagine Mrs. Travis now has the excuse she has been looking for the last twenty years."

"Sonny, look at the time, we've got to run. The movie might actually start on schedule." Trish got to her feet.

They left, carrying our thanks out the door with them, and we returned to the living room. Cindy turned to me on the couch.

"Sonny is quite the local historian, isn't he." Cindy commented.

"He actually does have an intellect," I agreed. "He's just afraid someone may notice it."

"Strange," she mused, "that's usually a female trait."

"In Sonny's case, I'm pretty sure it is that he feels—perhaps with good reason—that people do not like having cops around who are too bright."

"What do you think of this judge's sentencing? Not the young guys, they'll probably learn a lesson that will hopefully mean something to them. But Travis?"

"Darling, I know Travis put you through hell and upset a

number of other people as well. But I think the prosecutor was wise to accept his plea, and the judge was wise in his sentence. Travis is not, in fact, a criminal, he's a dirty middle-aged man. I really do not think he is dangerous, but loss of job and pension plus a year in a prison might make him so."

She thought that over. "I suppose."

"And, m'dear, a trial is no fun, even for the innocent victim. The defense lawyer would make you out an hysterical woman with a thing going on the side with underage Larry Wismer when you got bored having a thing going with me."

"Alex!" Then she began to laugh. "You're probably right. Okay, okay. I surrender."

I thought that was a fine idea, and leaned over to kiss her.

CHAPTER THIRTY-ONE

I had forgotten earlier this morning to give Cindy the three checks I needed to deposit. It was Friday and I didn't want them sitting around until Monday. I had learned the hard way not to hold checks from art galleries overlong. Sometimes their cash flow was problematic. It didn't really matter, I could stop in the bank on the way home from the firing range where I had a high noon appointment.

In order to protect my PI license to carry and my eligibility to be deputized to the Provincetown Police force, I had to spend an hour, twice a year on a firing range. I always forgot the time and had to wangle an appointment whenever they could fit me in—like eight a.m. or four thirty p.m. or noon. Always times I would prefer to be somewhere else. Ah, well...it was my own fault.

Right now it was not quite ten o'clock and Fargo was staring intently at me, trying—I was fairly certain—to implant a thought in my mind. "Beach, Alex, *beach*. Please, please, please!"

Already there was a sign up in the parking lot, saying "No Dogs on Beach." In a week or so there would be enough tourists to limit our beach runs to very early mornings. Today—the few people we would encounter would just have to share.

It was the only Ptown law I ever deliberately broke. I knew that, being Sonny's sister and a sometime fellow cop, I would not be hassled by any patrolling officer unless I did something really bad. But I did not want to take advantage of being "family," I did not want to embarrass Sonny, and I genuinely thought most laws were logical and good. But when it came to Fargo and tourists and the beach...screw 'em.

When we got to the beach, there were a few cumulus clouds lurking in the distance over the ocean. They would sail majestically in-shore later in the day, but they meant no harm, simply positioning themselves to form the palette for a delicate pink and orange sunset.

Fargo busted up a meeting of loudly protesting gulls. As they flapped over the low surf, he plowed through it, apparently happy in the frigid water. He came out shaking himself and rolled sensuously in the sun-warmed sand.

I got what should be a wonderful shot of a small girlchild stretching out one hand in a gesture of tentative friendship to Fargo, while he bowed to her, forelegs outstretched and hindquarters raised in the universal invitation to play. It looked as if she were knighting him.

What could go wrong on a day like that?

Not much. My session at the firing range actually went well. I tried some headshots and surprisingly made most of them. My other shots were nearly all in the kill range, even with moving targets coming or going in different directions at different speeds.

I had just reloaded my trusty Glock 9mm when the owner/instructor called, "Time's up, Alex. And—sorry, but I've got another appointment, and he's here. You done good, kid. Here's

249

your certification, see you in six."

I thanked him, and rather than hold up his waiting client still more by taking time to unload the weapon, I merely made sure it was on safe and shoved it in the rear pocket of my jeans.

Driving back to Ptown, I found myself in the beginnings of the weekend traffic and got off onto the old road in Truro, hoping to miss a few of the early-bird tourists. Just after crossing into Ptown I caught sight of Rho Bannister getting into her car. I pulled in behind her, walked up and stuck my head into the passenger's window.

"All set for the maiden flight of Lobster Airlines?"

"You bet!" She smiled. "I just had to come home and change clothes, I spent the morning putting the old wheel and undercarriage back on, even found a leaky old tire to go with it. And I was filthy."

"You're going to use the old parts?" That didn't sound like Cassie.

"Lord, no!" Rho laughed. "They wouldn't last a hundred feet at takeoff speed…not that you could *get* to that speed with one engine. No, this just lets us push it out of the hangar and work in a better light. More room and better air, too. We're still waiting for the parts to start the real work."

"Makes sense." I backed out of the window. "Give Cassie a hug, and safe trip to both of you."

She gave me a snappy salute and pulled away.

As I started to follow her, I remembered the checks locked in the glove compartment. The bank, Alex, don't forget the bank. I took the next left turn.

CHAPTER THIRTY-TWO

The bank parking lot was crowded early on this Friday afternoon. I had to park in the back and walk around to the big front doors. Inside, people were obviously cashing and/or depositing paychecks, taking out cash for the weekend, paying off loans, whatever. All of the free-form marble stands seemed in use, but toward the back I spotted one where a solitary woman was writing diligently in a small ledger, and figured I could fit beside her.

When I approached, she smiled and waved her hand, indicating stacks of various coins and a few dollar bills.

"Sorry to take up so much room."

"No problem." I smiled back. "I just have to endorse a couple of checks."

"I'm a Girl Scout leader, but I think the bookkeeping for a Fortune five hundred Company is probably simpler." She sighed.

I started to reply courteously when I noticed Cindy come out of some back office, looking down at a clipboard and making what appeared to be check marks.

Then I noticed three men crossing the area leading to the vault. Two of the men carried pistols that looked like .44 caliber to me, and the fat one carried something that looked like an Uzi.

The vault at Fisherman's Bank had a history of being open during business hours. Centuries ago it had proved the bank was solvent; now it was tradition. There was a locked brass grille to keep out the curious or the souvenir-takers, and that was it.

It was not as foolish as it sounds. There was only one highway and a choice of two bridges off the Cape. Should robbers have come in a boat, there was a Coast Guard station with cutter and helicopter at the end of the beach.

Unfortunately, I felt, there were no fighter planes at our little airport—for I was now certain this was how the three men I watched would leave the Cape…in Cassie's plane, quite possibly over her dead body.

But right now Cindy was my worry. She wasn't watching where she was walking, and she was on a collision course with one of the men headed for the vault. I quietly slid my own pistol out of my pocket.

The woman next to me looked down at my hand and screamed, "A gun! Help, someone, she's got a gun!"

"Shut up," I hissed and automatically ducked. I pulled her down with me just as Fatso let fly with the Uzi. Chips of marble pinged and twanged all over the place but the sturdy marble table held, and as far as I knew, neither of us was hurt.

But the woman was still screaming for help. I gave her a kick in the butt. "Close your effing mouth, you idiot! I'm a cop." I stretched it a little. "And you're gonna get us killed. One more shriek and I'll shoot you myself." Maybe I was just the slightest bit nervous.

But she did shut up and lay moaning softly to herself. It was an improvement.

I peeked around the corner. Oh, dear God! Cindy had walked right into one robber's arms as he started to shoot the lock off the vault gate. He had her left arm twisted painfully up against her shoulder as he fired three shots into the lock. On the fourth shot it flew apart and the gate swung open.

The man yanked Cindy inside with him, stuffed his pistol in his belt and started pulling at the large canvas bags with one arm.

"Come on, guys, get in here! I need some help."

Fatso fired off a blast from the automatic for effect and then screamed, "Down, everybody down or you're dead." As he ran for the vault I couldn't see anyone who wasn't already down. I didn't know if any were hurt or not.

I looked cautiously around, trying to spot the security men. I saw one of them on the floor. Hurt? Playing doggo? And I saw the third robber backing slowly toward the vault, gun in hand.

He called softly, "Now don't panic, folks. Just lie quiet. We don't want to hurt anybody. Just be cool and we'll be outa here." He sounded like the "nice guy" on my tape at home, and I was slightly encouraged.

Suddenly an aging security guard appeared from somewhere, walking slowly toward Nice Guy. His hands were held out, palms up, to show he was unarmed.

"All right, son, we don't want to hurt anyone either, so just give me your gun and tell your friends to put theirs down and you can go. Nobody will hurt you."

"Shut up, Dad, and lay down. You're buggin' me."

"Now, son, just give me your weapon." God, what was wrong with him? This wasn't a kid misbehaving at the prom!

Nice Guy gave it to him, all right—high in the chest. I saw his white shirt turn red in front, and he went down.

Somebody screamed and Fatso treated us all to another spray of lead.

The guy I had decided was Frank bellowed, "Get in here! *Now! We don't have all weekend!*"

They got, and I took a moment to look out the large front

window. As I had thought there would be, a car was parked in front of the doors, a man sitting in it. The passenger's front door and both back doors were open, along with the trunk. They were ready to roll. Would they take Cindy with them?

Probably. I imagined their plans had been to grab a female hostage at random on the way out, just in case. Cindy had just offered up herself a little early. Now she was a chip in a poker game I couldn't see the good guys winning. But I had to think of something. I could not let them leave here with Cindy. If they did, her chances were small. No way was I going to let that happen!

The cops would be here shortly. With Fatso Arnold Schwarzenegger, enjoying his Uzi, bullets would fly and you can bet Frank would have Cindy in front of him.

Think, Peres!

They were moving out of the vault. First, Nice Guy carried out two big bags. Fatso managed one and, of course, his trusty weapon. Frank had let go of Cindy's arm but had his pistol firmly against her back. He carried a large bag, somewhat clumsily in one hand, as they started across to the exit.

I could shoot him as he passed, but that had two drawbacks: even if I hit him fatally, he might shoot Cindy before he fell, or my bullet conceivably could pass through his body and into hers. I had to get his attention away from her. Stand up and yell? Offer to swap Ms. Scout Leader for Cindy? Then I had my bright idea.

I stood up and fired six evenly placed shots across the top of the enormous plate glass window that covered almost the entire front of the bank. It came down in a swooshing, crackling sheet as graceful as a theatre curtain. Small pieces of glass covered the floor.

I screamed, "Cindy run, turn left!" I meant her to turn left outside the doors. The getaway car was parked to the right of the front doors. I was parked to the left. As the glass fell, Frank looked up at our window-fall, and his gun drifted off to the right. Cindy was already skittering across the glass. She slipped and went down on one knee but was up like a bird. She flung open one of the big doors as if it weighed a pound and was outside and turning left.

Then I fired again. Frank dropped his gun and grabbed his wrist. He lost his balance and fell. Had I really shot his gun out of his hand? I had been aiming for the middle of his back. Surely I wasn't that shaky! I ran after Cindy, slowing as I passed Frank to kick his gun away. He was getting up as I went through the door.

I caught up with her at my car, we jumped in. I finally got the key into the ignition and we were away, the getaway car ahead of us and turning onto the street. I thought I heard sirens, but didn't want to wait. There was Cassie, you see. And Rho.

As I raced a couple of blocks down Bradford and then turned to get over to Route Six, I said, "I think my cell phone is in the compartment. Call Cassie."

"Number?" she asked. I told her and she dialed. "Cassie, Cindy. Hold a minute."

She turned to me. "Tell her what?"

"Her seafood charter just robbed the bank and shot it up and are headed for the airport. They are very, very dangerous. They will be there in six or seven minutes. Run or hide. Do not—repeat not—let them find you."

She quoted me just about verbatim and hung up. Noticing she was shivering, I turned on the heater. I was sweating. "Now call Nacho, give her the scoop and ask for backup. I've only got six shots left." She made the call, put the phone back and pulled out a packet of tissues I keep in the compartment.

It was then I noticed her pants leg was bloody. "Darling, you're hurt!" She was busy trying to staunch the blood and not having much luck. "Are you shot?"

"No. Just a cut from the glass. I'm okay. Thanks to you, angel, although I doubt Choate Ellis will be calling you angel when he sees his prized window." We both laughed and she leaned her head against my shoulder for a moment and I felt wonderful.

As we turned into the airport I saw the big gray Chrysler stopped near the plane, already out on the ramp, motors idling.

Frank and the getaway driver were visible in the cockpit. Nice Guy tossed the last bag into the cabin, climbed aboard, helped Fatso up the short ladder and closed the door. There was no sign of Cassie or Rho. Hopefully they had gotten away.

The men began to taxi toward the end of the runway to make their takeoff run into the wind. The only hope of stopping them would be to take my car out into the middle of the runway and block their takeoff. And I was not about to get us shot or sent airborne in a fireball.

"Well, it looks like they're getting away. I didn't see Cassie or Rho in the plane, did you?" Cindy asked.

"No. I hope they're far away."

The plane turned toward us and began to accelerate. It seemed slightly off kilter to me, and the engines sounded unsynchronized. I started to laugh. Then I saw a piece of metal drop down from the wheel well and scrape along the runway. I began to laugh hard.

Cindy took my hand and gave me a concerned look. "Alex?"

"It's okay, honey, I haven't freaked. They've got the wrong plane! Somehow Rho and Cassie got the propeller put back on and these idiots took the plane that can't fly! Just look at that right wheel."

As if on command, the right wheel crumpled, the right wing dropped several inches and the plane veered to the right, crossways on the runway. That move took care of the right propeller. It flew off, continued to turn in the air for a few yards and settled gently in the grass beside the runway.

The plane stopped just in time for four police cars to scream around us and surround it. The officers jumped out, crouching behind the doors. I hoped Nacho had remembered to mention the Uzi.

Sonny was immediately on the bullhorn. "Turn off your engines and throw your weapons out the door. Then come out slowly and lie down on the ground. I've got a SWAT team here and I'd love for them to get some practice."

There was a moment when it seemed nothing was going to

happen. Then the remaining propeller slowed and stopped, and there was silence. Then the plane door opened and the ladder went down. The getaway driver appeared in the door and tossed out the Uzi plus three pistols. He came down the ladder and lay down. Nice Guy came out next. At the bottom of the ladder he raised his hands and called "I've got to help this guy, he's hurt. Give me a minute."

Everyone tensed, but nothing happened except that Fatso half fell down the steps and had trouble getting down on the ground. I wondered what was wrong. Frank was the last man out, still cradling his hand.

Sonny looked at him curiously. "Which security man got you in the gun hand? That takes some shooting."

"Neither," Frank answered. "One of them spent the whole time lying curled up like a scared kid. The older one said we oughta surrender to him before someone got hurt and Earl shot him—dead, I guess." He pointed at Nice Guy.

Yeah, I nodded, he looked like an Earl.

"So who got you?"

"The woman over there." He pointed at me. "I dropped my gun, and she and the other one ran away." He indicated Cindy.

Sonny looked at me, turned beet red and hissed, "How many damn times have I told you not to try a fancy shot when it matters? What if you had missed? He could have shot back. You could have hit a bystander. You could be *dead*. How would I have told Mom?"

"Shut up!" I hissed back. "You're babbling. If you must know, I was aiming for the middle of his back. And you needn't tell that to the world!"

"Jesus Christ, Alex…" Before we could add to this enlightening conversation, Rho and Cassie burst out the side door of the hangar and came running toward us, Cassie calling, "Thank God you're here! Is everyone all right?"

"Pretty much so," I answered. Hugs went around. And I finally got to ask, "How on earth did you rig it so they got the wrong plane?"

She and Rho both laughed. "The wheel was already on, like I told you," Rho explained. "Between the two of us we managed to put the old propeller back on the engine—it wasn't even fastened. I can't believe it lasted as long as it did."

Cassie added, "We pushed the plane out onto the tarmac, and left the keys in it. We closed and locked the hangar. It seemed probable they'd be in a hurry and not look at details...just start her up and run for it. And that's what they did. Then we locked ourselves in the office, and peeked through the blinds."

Sonny shook his head admiringly. "Sometimes I wonder where women get their ideas. Men would still be shooting it out. Hatcher! Come and drive our two wounded heroes down to the clinic."

"I'm not hurt," I announced. But I was, I realized, shivering in the warm sun. And for the first time, I noticed my left sleeve was bloody. Now what the hell was that?

"Take them in her car," Sonny ordered. "Then call for a pick-up at her house."

CHAPTER THIRTY-THREE

So once again I sat in Dr. Gloetzner's office at the end of a totally draining day. Only this time Cindy was with me. The cut on her knee looked nasty and had taken two stitches, and she still looked a little pale. Any sympathy I had felt for Frank's shattered hand had disappeared.

My "wound" was truly minor. A small piece of flying marble had lodged in my forearm. Gloetzner pulled it out with one painful yank, squirted something on it that stung and slapped a large Band-Aid into place. And that was it.

"How's the security fellow?" I asked. "Did he make it?"

"Mr. Penny is critical, but stable."

"I've never understood what that meant," Cindy said.

"In Mr. Penny's case it means he is out of surgery, not yet any better, but shows no sign of getting worse. With luck, he will recover."

"What about the fat guy?"

"He got a sizable sliver of glass in his left buttock. We had to knock him out to go after it."

"I'd have been glad to knock him out for you. Could I do it now?" I was feeling lightheaded.

"Thank you, no. If needed, we will call you."

He swung one leg over the corner of his desk and said, "Now, ladies, I would speak seriously with you. On the matter of stress. It has come to my attention you have had a rough time of late. First a stalker."

Thank you, Loose Lips Lainey.

"Then according to your Aunt Mae, you visited Cindy's cousin, I believe, in Tennessee and were in considerable danger, plus in trouble with their local police."

Thank you Babbling Brook Mae.

"And now, the events of today." He continued. "These things add up. They not only affect your emotional balance, they begin to put a strain on your physical health.

"So." He reached back on his desk. "I have written you each a limited prescription for mild tranquilizers. They won't make you a zombie, they just take the edge off. And if you would like to see a counselor—our man is pretty good, or there are several others you may wish to consider."

He handed us the scrips. "And perhaps most important of all, I recommend you get away for a truly restful vacation. Not New York or Atlantic City—Vermont or Maine perhaps."

I managed not to hit him. Cindy dredged up a smile and her social voice.

"Doctor, thank you so much for your kind concern. We will certainly fill your prescriptions and consider some psychiatric advice. As for vacation, I am convinced that Vermont would have an earthquake that would blow off the end of the Richter scale, and Maine would manage a tsunami with a sixty-foot tidal surge. The gods have forbidden us a vacation this year."

"What we need," I explained, "is our beautiful, calm everyday life—Cindy dealing with idiot clients, while I try to explain to an irate tourist that their B&B is not responsible for their getting drunk and falling into the goldfish pond. We need Wells to get in a boxing match with the neighbor's tomcat and Fargo to eat my sugar peas off the vines before we can pick 'em. We need to go to the cottage for a restful weekend and spend it helping Aunt Mae rearrange her herb garden and put up new shelves in the shop. And we look forward to a few good fights over decorating a new room on the house. This what we need."

He smiled. "It may well be. Well, we are here if you need us."

"We know that." This time Cindy's smile was genuine. "And it's a great backstop."

"Do you want to stop and fill the prescriptions?" Cindy asked.

"If you do, sure."

"I don't think so. I think a scotch and watching the sun set over the pond would do it for me."

"Especially," I added, "if the furballs are with us."

Cindy nodded, so we stopped by the house just long enough to collect the little darlings and moved on to the cottage. The sunset was duly lovely. The little darlings had their usual tiff over the miniature soccer ball that Fargo liked to drop in the pond so Wells couldn't play with it. We ordered lots of Chinese food that we all four liked and ate all of it.

We talked about a color scheme for the new bedroom.

We discussed what sort of thank-you gift we should send to Ken and Frances. We decided on the game of *Clue* to add to their small stack of rainy day board games. And a bunch of specialty breads from a very good bakery downtown, plus some fancy bottles of various "waters."

Satisfed with our creativity, we retired for the night.

We went back to the house Sunday evening so that Cindy could check her wardrobe for the week ahead. And so that I could make a list of things I needed to do in the coming week, a list Cindy was happy to assist me with.

Late Monday afternoon Harmon arrived to mow the lawn,

saying I shouldn't do it with an injured arm. How he knew it was even slightly damaged, I would never know—Provincetown's jungle drums never missed a beat. I usually did the lawn, and could have easily done it today, but I didn't want to hurt his feelings.

And truth to tell, I was rather glad to let him do it. I had spent the morning at Peter and the Wolf's B&B dealing with an obnoxious guest who had been sitting on the porch banister, lost his balance and fell into an azalea bush. They had been happy to apply a soothing ointment to his several scratches, but thought that covered their responsibility.

He, on the other hand, wanted a doctor to check out his back plus punitive damages for his "emotional trauma." He planned to sue. I pointed out to him that there had been four empty chairs on the porch, when he chose to sit on the railing. I added that he had been drinking. If he sued and lost, I added, he would be out enough money to have spent his vacation on the Riviera. He finally agreed.

While Harmon mowed I put in some radish seeds and planted the frail little lettuce plants he had brought as a gift. I knew they were a lot tougher than they looked, but I still felt I should tuck them in with a light blanket. As he finished up the yard, I gave the seeds and plants a gentle drink. I shivered slightly under the now cloudy sky and suggested we go into the kitchen for a beer. He agreed happily.

Just as we sat down, the phone rang. It was my mother.

"Hi, Mom, how are you?"

"Fine. It's you two that have my concern. Is Cindy really all right? And what about you?"

"Absolutely fine, both of us. I got some radishes and lettuce planted while Harmon kindly mowed the grass."

"How nice of him!"

"Nice indeed." I winked at Harmon, who blushed. "What's up?"

"Next Saturday and Sunday afternoon is the church jumble sale. I wondered if you and Cindy would be up to manning a booth?"

I cringed, but then, Mom did a lot of favors in a lot of places, and rarely asked for one in return.

"Sure! Wouldn't miss it. Anything but clothing. Some of it smells of mothballs and it makes me sneeze. But anything else would be fine."

"Thank you, darling. I knew I could count on you. I must run—more calls to make. I love you both."

I said we loved her, too, to a silent phone.

Harmon and I moved to a second beer and talked of garden things. I heard a car door close and assumed it was Cindy, but it was Sonny who came through the kitchen door.

"Hi, you two. How goes it? Mind if I have a beer?"

"It goes fine," I answered. "Help yourself."

He joined us at the table. "Cindy not here?" he asked.

I looked at the clock. "She's running a little late. She should be here any minute. Can I help with something?"

He sipped his beer. "Well, maybe…"

Before I learned how I might be of service to my brother, a car door slammed and Cindy caromed through the back door, kicking off her shoes as she came. She fell heavily into the fourth chair and picked up my bottle of beer. She took a healthy swig directly from the bottle, and reached for my cigarettes. Sonny and Harmon sat wide-eyed and shocked.

But I knew the symptoms. "Bad day at the bank?"

"Well, I ask you, how am I supposed to run a department and maintain customer trust in us when the accounting people have a combined IQ about as high as the speed limit?"

"What happened?" I prompted.

"We have a customer named William Lawrence. Coincidentally, we have a customer named Lawrence Williams. In their infinite wisdom, accounting decided we had accidentally opened two accounts for one man, so they combined them. William Lawrence got a statement showing him with about double the money he really has, while Lawrence Williams got no statement at all—he doesn't exist."

"But you fixed it." I guessed.

"Oh, sure, but what a mess! I'm going to change clothes. Could I have a beer all my own and in a glass? I'm going to change clothes...oh, I told you that. Excuse me, gentlemen. Hello, darling." She left me with a kiss on the cheek. Typical bad-day explosion—short and snappy and all gone.

"Whew." Sonny exhaled. "I'm glad I'm not a bookkeeper at Fisherman's."

"Aren't we all. What was it you started to ask?"

"Oh, yeah," he replied. "Next week is Trish's birthday. I thought Cindy might suggest something I could get her. I'm no good with presents."

That was certainly true. When I moved into this house several years back and had to learn a little simple cooking, he had given me a black organdy apron perfect for a French maid in a house of ill repute.

Harmon spoke up. "You know, Sonny, I ran into Trish the other day and I noticed her with one of them big apache cases all the lawyers carry around. One of the handles was almost worn through—bound to break soon. How about a new one for her?"

"Perfect!" Sonny beamed. "A monogrammed attaché case. Harmon, you're a genius!"

"Well, I don't know about that." He smiled, almost demurely. "But there is something I wanted to tell you. There was this cruiser I noticed tied up at one of the docks in the bay...expensive-looking twenty-eight footer. There seemed to be just one fella aboard and he was going over some kind of list—marking some things out and adding other things. Now, Sonny I was just thinking..."

"Yes, Harmon?" Sonny sounded weary.

I wasn't. Life was back to normal and it was just fine.

Publications from
Bella Books, Inc.
The best in contemporary lesbian fiction

P.O. Box 10543, Tallahassee, FL 32302
Phone: 800-729-4992
www.bellabooks.com

WARMING TREND by Karin Kallmaker. Everybody was convinced she had committed a shocking academic theft, so Anidyr Bycall ran a long, long way. Going back to her beloved Alaskan home, and the coldness in Eve Cambra's eyes isn't going to be easy. $14.95

WRONG TURNS by Jackie Calhoun. Callie Callahan's latest wrong turn turns out well. She meets Vicki Brownwell. Sparks would fly if only Meg Klein would leave them alone! $14.95

SMALL PACKAGES by KG MacGregor. With Lily away from home, Anna Kaklis is alone with her worst nightmare: a toddler. Book Three of the Shaken Series. $14.95

FAMILY AFFAIR by Saxon Bennett. An oops at the gynecologist has Chase Banter finally trying to grow up. She has nine whole months to pull it off. $14.95

DELUSIONAL by Terri Breneman. In her search for a killer, Toni Barston discovers that sometimes everything is exactly the way it seems, and then it gets worse. $14.95

COMFORTABLE DISTANCE by Kenna White. Summer on Puget Sound ought to be relaxing for Dana Robbins, but Dr. Jamie Hughes is far too close for comfort. $14.95

ROOT OF PASSION by Ann Roberts. Grace Owens knows a fake when she sees it, and the potion her best friend promises will fix her love life is a fake. But what if she wishes it weren't? $14.95

KEILE'S CHANCE by Dillon Watson. A routine day in the park turns into the chance of a lifetime, if Keile Griffen can find the courage to risk it all for a pair of big brown eyes. $14.95

SEA LEGS by KG MacGregor. Kelly is happy to help Natalie make Didi jealous, sure, it's all pretend. Maybe. Even the captain doesn't know where this comic cruse will end. $14.95

TOASTED by Josie Gordon. Mayhem erupts when a culinary road show stops in tiny Middelburg, and for some reason everyone thinks Lonnie Squires ought to fix it. Follow-up to Lammy mystery winner *Whacked*. $14.95

NO RULES OF ENGAGEMENT by Tracey Richardson. A war zone attraction is of no use to Major Logan Sharp. She can't wait for Jillian Knight to go back to the other side of the world. $14.95

A SMALL SACRIFICE by Ellen Hart. A harmless reunion of friends is anything but, and Cordelia Thorn calls friend Jane Lawless with a desperate plea for help. Lammy winner for Best Mystery. Number 5 in this award-winning series. $14.95

FAINT PRAISE by Ellen Hart. When a famous TV personality leaps to his death, Jane Lawless agrees to help a friend with inquiries, drawing the attention of a ruthless killer. Number 6 in this award-winning series. $14.95

STEPPING STONE by Karin Kallmaker. Selena Ryan's heart was shredded by an actress, and she swears she will never, ever be involved with one again. $14.95